Dear Reader,

I really can't express how flattered I am and also how grateful I am to Harlequin Books for releasing this collection of my published works. It came as a great surprise. I never think of myself as writing books that are collectible. In fact, there are days when I forget that writing is work at all. What I do for a living is so much fun that it never seems like a job. And since I reside in a small community, and my daily life is confined to such mundane things as feeding the wild birds and looking after my herb patch in the backyard, I feel rather unconnected from what many would think of as a glamorous profession.

But when I read my email, or when I get letters from readers, or when I go on signing trips to bookstores to meet all of you, I feel truly blessed. Over the past thirty years I have made lasting friendships with many of you. And quite frankly, most of you are like part of my family. You can't imagine how much you enrich my life. Thank you so much.

I also need to extend thanks to my family (my husband, James, son, Blayne, daughter-in-law, Christina, and granddaughter, Selena Marie), to my best friend, Ann, to my readers, booksellers and the wonderful people at Harlequin Books—from my editor of many years, Tara, to all the other fine and talented people who make up our publishing house. Thanks to all of you for making this job and my private life so worth living.

Thank you for this tribute, Harlequin, and for putting up with me for thirty long years! Love to all of you.

Diana Palmer

DIANA PALMER

The prolific author of more than a hundred books, Diana Palmer got her start as a newspaper reporter. A multi–*New York Times* bestselling author and one of the top ten romance writers in America, she has a gift for telling the most sensual tales with charm and humor. Diana lives with her family in Cornelia, Georgia.

Visit her website at www.DianaPalmer.com.

THE Essential COLLECTION

DIANA

New York Times and USA TODAY Bestselling Author

PALMER

NOELLE

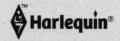

TORONTO NEW YORK LONDON
AMSTERDAM PARIS SYDNEY HAMBURG
STOCKHOLM ATHENS TOKYO MILAN MADRID
PRAGUE WARSAW BUDAPEST AUCKLAND

In memory of Ryan Patton Hendricks, whose light still shines brightly in the hearts of all those who loved him.

Recycling programs
for this product may
not exist in your area.

ISBN-13: 978-0-373-36386-5

NOELLE

Prologue

The street was wide and dusty—and because it was late in the afternoon, there was a lot of activity in the small town of Terrell, New Mexico Territory. Most of the buggies and wagons had stopped, however, to watch the developing confrontation in front of the adobe courthouse, where the circuit judge had just ruled against a group of small ranchers.

"You sold us out!" a raging-mad cowboy yelled at a tall, distinguished man in a dark, vested business suit. "You helped that land-hungry British son of Satan kick us off our land! What will we do come winter when we don't have a place to live or food for our kids? Where will we go, now that you've taken our land away? It isn't even as if Hughes needs it. By God, he owns half the county already!"

Jared Dunn, the tall, elegant man he was facing, watched him without blinking, without moving. His pale blue eyes were narrow and intent—dangerous—but the cowboy was too far away to see them.

"It was a fair trial," the man said in a cultured accent, with just a trace of a drawl. "You had attorneys."

"Not like you, Mr. New York City big-shot lawyer!" the man said, his expression turning ugly. He was wearing a side-arm. Many people did in 1902, although not in towns, most of which had regulations against firearms. But this little place was much as it had been in the late 1880s and the law was just getting a toehold here. This was still a territory, not a state.

The angry cowboy had come heeled, and Jared Dunn had anticipated he would. The sheriff of this town was a mild little man who was elected for his sunny personality, not his toughness, so he could expect no help from that quarter. In fact, the sheriff had conveniently vanished when the cowboy started yelling threats across the street.

The cowboy's hand dropped lower, hovering over his gun butt.

"Don't do it," Jared warned, his voice deep and clear and ringing.

"Why? Are you afraid of guns, Mr. Big Shot?" the cowboy demanded, with a faint sneer. "Don't you city boys know how to shoot?"

Slowly Jared unbuttoned his tailored jacket, and, without taking his eyes from his adversary, smoothed the jacket back…past a worn leather holster slung low across his lean hips. It contained a Colt .45 revolver with an equally worn black handle.

The way the revolver was worn would have been enough to warn most men. But even the smooth action of the hand sweeping back the jacket spoke for him. He stood very quietly, his posture elegant, deceptively relaxed, his eyes focused only on the cowboy.

"Ed, give it up," one of the cowboy's friends demanded. "You can't shoot lawyers, more's the pity. We'll find some other land, and this time we'll make sure the seller has legitimate deeds."

"It's my land. Deeds be damned! And I'm not getting off it because some rich man paid a city lawyer to take it away from me!" He began to crouch; his hand made a claw over the gun butt at his waist. "You draw or you die, fellow."

"Just like old times," Jared murmured to himself. His blue eyes narrowed, steady and unblinking, and he smiled coldly.

"Draw!" the cowboy yelled.

But Jared didn't move. He simply stood there.

"Coward!"

Still Jared stood his ground, waiting. He'd learned that it wasn't the man who was fastest who won this sort of fight—it was the man who took his time and placed his shot.

Suddenly the cowboy dug for his revolver. He managed to get it out, and he even got off a shot, but not before Jared's bullet had smashed a bone in his gun arm. The concussion jerked his fingers and set off his pistol as he fell, crying out, to the dusty street.

The wild bullet hit Jared's leg just above the kneecap, but he didn't fall or cry out. His gaze unwavering from his adversary, he went slowly toward the cowboy's prostrate, groaning form and stood over him, the smoking pistol still held level in his lean hand. His eyes, to the spectators, were frightening in their unblinking blue glitter.

"Are you finished, or do you want to try again?" he asked, without a breath of sympathy. His index finger was still on the trigger, the pistol aimed at the downed man. It was evident to everyone that if the cowboy had reached for the pistol lying near his uninjured side, Jared would have sent a second bullet right into the man without hesitation.

The white-faced cowboy looked up at death in a business

suit. "Say," he managed in a rough whisper, "don't I know you?"

"I doubt it."

The cowboy shuddered at the force of the pain. "But I do," he insisted. "I saw you…in Dodge. I was in Dodge City, back in the…early 80s. There was a Texas gunman. Killed another gunman… Never saw his hand move, never even saw it coming, like just now…" He was barely conscious as loss of blood weakened him, while around him people were rushing in search of a doctor for the wounded men.

A dark-eyed man carrying a medical bag pushed his way through the crowd. He looked from Dunn's bleeding leg to the red-splattered arm of the cowboy on the ground.

"It's 1902," he informed Dunn. "We're supposed to be civilized now. Put that damned thing away!"

Dunn reholstered the gun with a smooth spin that wasn't lost on the physician, but he didn't back down.

"Shattered his gun arm, didn't you?" He examined the cowboy and nodded to two of his companions. "Get him to my office." He turned and looked pointedly at the lawyer's bleeding leg, around which he was calmly tying a white handkerchief that quickly turned red. "You can come along, too. I thought you were a lawyer."

"I am."

"Not the way you handle that gun. Can you walk?"

"I'm only shot, not killed," Jared said curtly. His blue eyes met the other man's, still cold from the confrontation. "I've been shot before."

"A lawyer should expect to be."

"Ah. An anarchist, I presume."

The doctor was motioning to the cowboy's friends, somewhat subdued now, to bring him along. "No, I'm not an anarchist," the doctor replied. "But I don't believe a handful of men should own the world."

"Believe it or not, neither do I." Jared walked on his own, even when a sympathetic bystander offered him a hand. He looked neither right nor left, following the doctor and the victim into the office. It amused him when the man's friends quickly withdrew into the waiting room with nervous glances in his direction. Over the years, that reaction had become familiar.

When he'd left Texas to practice law in New York ten years ago, he'd thought that the days of cold steel and hot lead were over forever. But most of his cases took him West. And the frontier might be closed these days, but there were plenty of men around who grew up in wild times and still thought a gun was the way to settle a dispute.

He knew shootings even occurred in such civilized places as Fort Worth, because he read about them in the local paper his grandmother sent to him in New York. There was an ordinance against weapons there, in Fort Worth, but apparently few people obeyed it, despite the city's large police force. Here in Terrell, the sheriff wanted to be reelected, so he didn't encourage unpopular gun-control ordinances. Such a lawman wouldn't have been tolerated back in Texas.

Jared sat down heavily in a chair while the doctor worked on the wounded cowboy, with some assistance from a younger man who worked with him.

His mind was on the case, not his wound. He'd learned in his wild young days to ignore pain. He was thirty-six now, and the lesson had stood him in good stead.

He'd been tricked into thinking that the landowner was the victim in this town. It was only at the end of the case that he'd realized how untrue that was. His loyalty was to his client, and he'd researched the deeds well enough to know that the small ranchers had no real claim on the land at all. That didn't make him feel any better when the judge ruled that they must be evicted from homesteads where they'd planted crops and had cattle grazing for five years before the absentee rancher even knew they were on the place.

But there was no such thing as squatters' rights under the law. The fact that they'd been sold the land by an unscrupulous speculator, without legal counsel, was beside the point. The seller had long since skipped and couldn't be found.

"I said, let's have a look at that leg," the doctor repeated testily.

He looked up blankly and realized that he and the doctor were alone in the room, the assistant having helped the other wounded man, now bandaged, out into the embrace of his friends.

Jared climbed onto the table and watched as the doctor cut his pant leg to give him access to the wound. He examined it carefully, applying antiseptic before he probed it with a long instrument. He found the bullet and began to withdraw it. He glanced up to see if he was hurting his patient and found the man's steely blue eyes as calm as if he'd been reading a newspaper.

"Tough character, aren't you?" the doctor murmured when he'd withdrawn the bullet and tossed it into a metal pan.

"I grew up in wild times," Jared said quietly.

"So did I." He applied more antiseptic and began to bandage the wound. "You've got some damage there. No bones broken, but a few torn ligaments at the least. Try to stay off it as much as possible and have your own doctor take a look when you get home. I don't think there will be any permanent damage, but you'll have a hard time walking for a few weeks. Leave that bandage on until your own doctor sees the leg. You'll have some fever. Have your doctor check it for infection when you get back to New York. Gangrene is still a very real possibility."

"I'll keep an eye on it."

"Sorry about your trousers."

Jared shrugged. "Fortunes of war." His eyes fixed on the doctor's face. "I'll take care of both bills—for myself and the man I wounded. For two bits, I'd call out Hughes and make a clean sweep of this. He lied to me. I thought the trespassing had been recent."

The doctor's eyebrows went up. "You didn't know that those men had homesteaded the land for five years?"

"Not until today."

He whistled through his teeth.

Jared got to his feet and reached for his wallet. He peeled off several large bills and handed them to the doctor. "If you have any contact with the man I shot, tell him that he's got a good case against the man who sold him the land. Anybody can be found. I know an ex-Pinkerton man who lives in Chicago—Matt Davis, by name." He took a pencil and pad from his pocket, scribbled a name and an address. "He's a good man, and he's a sucker for a just cause. I've worked with him frequently over the past ten years."

The doctor fingered the slip of paper. "Ed Barkley will be grateful. He's not a bad man, but he lived on the border for years before he married and tried to settle down. Sank every penny he had into that land, and now he's lost everything." He shrugged and smiled faintly. "In the old days, there would have been quick justice, right or wrong. Civilization is hard work."

Jared's eyebrow quirked. "Tell me about it."

He left the doctor's office and started toward his hotel. He hadn't taken off the gun belt.

The sheriff came toward him, clearing his throat. "I believe we should discuss this gunplay…"

Jared, in pain and furious that the official hadn't even tried to do his duty, swept the jacket back again with cold, insolent challenge.

"By all means, let's discuss it," he invited curtly.

The sheriff, unlike Ed Barkley, knew what the angle of that holster and the worn butt meant. He cleared his throat again and smiled nervously.

"Self-defense, of course," he muttered. "Sad thing, these bad-tempered men… Fair trial. You, uh, leaving town?"

"Yes." Jared gave the man a cold glare. "Someone could have been killed out here today. You were elected to protect these townspeople, and you ran like a yellow dog. I've been in places in Texas where they'd have shot you down in the street for what you did today."

"I was otherwise occupied at the time! And what do you know about being a lawman, a city feller like you?" the man asked.

Jared's thin mouth tugged up at the corner, but his eyes were blazing. "More than you'll have time to learn."

He whipped the jacket back over his pistol and kept walking, the limp more pronounced with every step he took. But even with that impairment, he looked threatening.

He went to his hotel, packed and checked out, and caught the next train east to St. Louis, where he could make connections to return to New York. People were still watching when the train pulled out of town. Imagine, a real gunfight right there in the street, two boys were remarking excitedly, and they'd seen it!

Chapter One

"**D**amn!"

The expletive resounded through the elegant law office. Alistair Brooks, the senior partner of the firm of Brooks and Dunn, looked up from the brief he was painstakingly writing by hand at his oak rolltop desk. "What?" he asked.

Jared Dunn threw down the letter he'd received from his grandmother in Fort Worth, Texas, with a flourish of his long, darkly tanned hand. "Damn," he repeated under his breath, and sat brooding, his reading glasses perched on his straight, elegant nose—over eyes that could run the blue spectrum from sky blue all the way to gunmetal gray.

"A case?" Brooks asked absently.

"A letter from home," Jared replied heavily. He sat back in his chair with his long legs crossed, a faint grimace accompanying the action. He favored the right leg a little, because the damage done by the bullet in Terrell was fresh enough to be painful. He'd been carefully checked by his own doctor, the wound rebandaged with directions to leave it alone until it healed. The fever had gone down in the few days he'd been back in New York, and if he felt pain or weakness from the wound, it didn't show in the steely lines of his lean face.

"From Texas?" Brooks echoed.

"From Texas." He couldn't quite call it home, although it felt that way sometimes. He turned his swivel chair to face his partner across the elegant wood floor of the oak-furnished office, the long, narrow windows letting in light through sheer curtains. "I've been thinking about a move, Alistair. If I leave, Parkins would enjoy taking my place in the firm. He has a good background in criminal law, and he's been in practice long enough to have gained an admirable reputation in legal circles."

Brooks put down his ink pen with a heavy sigh. "It's that land case in New Mexico Territory that's depressed you," he began.

"It's more than that," Jared replied. "I'm tired." He ran a slender hand over his wavy black hair. There were threads of pure silver in it now, at his temples. He knew that new lines had been carved into his face by the pressures of his profession. "I'm tired of working on the wrong side of justice."

Brooks's eyebrows arched disapprovingly.

Jared shook his head. "Don't misunderstand me. I love the practice of law. But I've just dispossessed families that should have had some sort of right to land they'd worked for five years and I feel sick about it. I seem to spend more time working for money than I do working for justice. I don't like it. Cases that satisfied me when I was younger and more ambitious only make me uncomfortable now. I'm disillusioned with my life."

"This sounds as if you're working up to dissolving our partnership," Brooks began.

Jared nodded. "That's just what I'm doing. It's been a good

ten years since I began practicing law. I appreciate the boost that you gave my career, and the opportunity to practice in New York City. But I'm restless."

Brooks's dark eyes narrowed. "Would this sudden decision have more to do with that letter you've just read than the case in New Mexico Territory?" he asked shrewdly.

One corner of Jared's thin mouth pulled down. "In fact, it does. My grandmother has taken in a penniless cousin of my stepbrother Andrew's."

"The family lives in Fort Worth, and you support them," Brooks recalled.

Jared nodded. "My grandmother is my late mother's only living relative. She's important to me. Andrew…" He laughed coldly. "Andrew is family, however much I may disapprove of him."

"He's very young yet."

"Serving in the Philippines during the war gave him an exaggerated view of his own importance," Jared remarked. "He struts and postures to impress the ladies. And he spends money as if it were water," he added irritably. "He's been buying hats for the new houseguest, out of my grandmother's housekeeping money. I have a feeling that it was Andrew's idea to take her in."

"And you don't approve."

"I'd like to know whom I'm supporting," Jared replied. "And perhaps I need to become reacquainted with my own roots. I haven't lived in Texas for a long time, but I think I'm homesick for it, Alistair."

"You? Unthinkable."

"It began when I took that case in Beaumont, representing the Culhanes in the oil-field suit." His blue eyes grew thoughtful. "I'd forgotten how it felt to be among Texans. They were West Texans, of course, from El Paso. I spent a little time on the border as a young man. My mother lived in

Fort Worth with my stepfather until they died, and my grand-mother and Andrew live there now. Although I'm partial to West Texas—"

"—Texas is Texas."

Jared smiled. "Exactly."

Alistair Brooks smoothed the polished wood of his chair. "If you must leave, then I'll certainly consider Ned Parkins to replace you. Not that you can be replaced." He smiled faintly. "I've known very few truly colorful personalities over the years."

"I might be a great deal less colorful if people were more civilized in courtroom trials," Jared replied.

"All the same, New York judges find your mystique fasci-nating. That often gives us an edge."

"You'll find another, I have no doubt. You're an excellent attorney."

"As you are. Well, make your plans and let me know when you want to go," Alistair said sadly. "I'll try to make your path as easy as I can."

"You've been a good friend as well as a good partner," Jared remarked. "I'll miss the practice."

He remembered those words as he sat in the passenger car of a westbound train a week later. He watched the prairie go slowly by, listened to the rhythmic puffing of the steam engine, watched the smoke and cinders flying past the windows as the click-clack of the metal wheels sang like a serenade.

"What a very barren land," a woman with a British accent remarked to her seat companion.

"Yes, ma'am. But it won't always be. Why, there'll be great cities out here in a few years, just like back East."

"I say, are there red Indians in these parts?"

"All the Indians are on reservations these days," the man said. "Good thing, too, because the Kiowa and Comanche used to raid settlements hereabouts back in the sixties and seventies, and some people got killed in bad, bad ways. And there wasn't only Indians. There were trail drives and cow towns like Dodge City and Ellsworth…"

The man's voice droned on unheard as Jared's thoughts went back to the 1880s. It had been a momentous time in the West. It had seen the Earp-Clanton brawl played out to national headlines in Tombstone, Arizona, in the fall of '81. It had seen the last reprisal skirmishes in the Great Plains and Arizona, following the Custer debacle in Montana in '76. It had seen the death of freedom for the Indian tribes of the West and Geronimo's bid for independence—and subsequent capture by General Crook in Arizona. The last of the great cattle drives had played out with the devastating winter of '86, which cost cattlemen over half their herds and all but destroyed ranching.

Simultaneously in 1890 came the frightful massacre of Indian women and children at Wounded Knee and the closing of the frontier. The old cow towns were gone. Gunfighters and frontier sheriffs, feathered war parties intent on scalping and the endless cavalry chase of Indians in search of old ways, all were vanished off the face of the earth.

Civilization was good, Jared reminded himself. Progress was being made to make life simpler, easier, healthier for a new generation of Americans. Social programs for city beautification and welfare relief, children's rights and women's rights and succor for the downtrodden were gaining strength in even the smallest towns. People were trying to make life better for themselves, and that was better than the lawless old days.

But a wildness deep inside the man in the business suit quivered with memories of the smell of gunsmoke, the thick blackness of it stinging his eyes as he faced an adversary and watched townspeople scatter. He'd only been a boy then, in his late teens, fatherless, spoiling for a fight to prove that he was as good as any son of married parents. It certainly hadn't been his poor mother's fault that she was assaulted one dark evening in Dodge City, Kansas, by a man whose face she never saw. She had, after all, done the right thing—she'd kept her child and raised him and loved him, even through a second marriage to a Fort Worth businessman that saddled Jared with a stepbrother he never liked. His mother had died trying to save him from the wild life he was leading.

On her deathbed, as he visited her in Fort Worth—before she followed her beloved husband to the grave with the same cholera that had done him in—she'd gripped Jared's hand tight in her small one and begged him to go back East to school. There was a little money, she said, just enough that she'd earned sewing and selling eggs. It would get him into school, and perhaps he could work for the rest of his tuition. He must promise her this, she begged, so that she would have the hope of his own salvation. For the road he was traveling would surely carry him to eternal damnation.

After the funeral, he'd taken her last words to heart. He'd left his young stepbrother, Andrew, in the care of their grieving grandmother and headed East.

He had a keen, analytical mind. He'd managed a scholarship with it, and graduated with honors from Harvard Law School. Then a college friend had helped him find work with a prominent law firm, that of Alistair Brooks, senior and junior. His particular interest had been criminal law, and he'd practiced it with great success over the past ten years, since his graduation from college. But along with his success had come problems, most of them with Andrew at the root. The boy had run wild in his teens; it had been left to his poor grandmother to cope. Jared had helped get him into the army just before the Spanish-American War broke out. Andrew had gone to the Philippines and discovered something he was good

at—exaggeration. He made himself out to be a war hero and
lived the part. He had a swagger and an arrogance that kept
Jared in New York. He rarely went home because Andrew irritated him so. He rued the day his mother had married Daniel
Paige and added his young son, Andrew, to the family.

Andrew had no idea of Jared's past. Grandmother Dunn
never spoke of it, or of Jared's parentage. That was a life long
ago, in Kansas, and had no bearing on the life Jared had made
for himself. For all anyone in Fort Worth knew, Jared was
a practicing attorney from New York City who did nothing
more dangerous than lifting a pen to documents. He'd been
quite fortunate that his infrequent contretemps with angry
antagonists over points of law hadn't made their way into
the local paper; Jared tended to intimidate curious reporters,
and most of his adversaries weren't anxious to admit to their
idiocy in pulling a gun on him. There had only been a handful of incidents, quickly forgotten, since he'd put up his gun
in the '80s. He was still a dead shot, and he practiced enough
with the weapon to retain an edge when he needed one. But
he hadn't killed anyone in recent years.

His eyes narrowed as he thought about that wild, early
life, and how reckless and thoughtless he'd been. His mother
must have worried about his restlessness, the dark side of
him that had grown to such proportions before her death. She
had no idea who his father was, and she must have wondered
about him. Jared had wondered, too, but there was no one in
Dodge City who resembled him enough to cast any light on
his lineage. Perhaps his father had been a drunken cowboy in
town on a trail drive, or a soldier home from the war. It didn't
really matter, anyway, he told himself. Except that he'd like
to have known.

He looked out the window at the bland expanse of grass-
land. News of this woman who'd been taken into his family
disturbed him. He paid the bills for his grandmother, and,

necessarily, Andrew. It would have been politic to ask if he minded another mouth to feed before they dumped this woman in his lap. He knew nothing about her, and he wondered if they did. It had apparently been Andrew's idea to send for her; she was actually a distant cousin of his, which made her no relation at all to Jared.

He remembered so well the wording in his grandmother's letter:

> …Andrew feels that she would be so much better off with us than in Galveston, especially since it holds such terrifying memories for her. She would not go back there for all the world, but it appears that her uncle is insisting that she accompany him now that the city is rebuilt and he has work there again. While it has been a year and a half since the tragedy, the poor girl still has a terror of living so close to the sea again. I fear her uncle's insistence has brought back nightmarish memories for her…

He wondered about the remark, about why she should be afraid of going to Galveston. There had been a devastating flood there in September of 1900. Had she been one of the survivors? He recalled that some five thousand souls had died that morning—in only a few minutes' time—as the ocean swallowed up the little town. And didn't he remember that his grandmother had written of Andrew visiting the Texas coast only recently? Connections began forming in his mind. He was willing to bet that this so-called cousin of Andrew's was little more than a new girlfriend upon whom he was fixated. If that was the case, Jared had no intention of supporting her while his stepbrother courted her. She could be sent packing, and the sooner the better.

As the train plodded across the vast plains, he pictured the woman in his mind. Knowing Andrew, she would be pretty and experienced and good at getting her way. She would probably have a heart like a lump of coal and eyes that could count a wad of money from a distance. The more he thought about her the angrier he grew. His grandmother must be getting senile to even allow such a thing. That feisty little woman, who'd moved in with his stepbrother after he left for New York, had never been known for foolish behavior. Andrew must have pulled the wool over her eyes. He wouldn't pull it over Jared's.

The train pulled into the station late that night. He got off at the platform with only his valise and made arrangements to have his trunk delivered to his home the next morning. Although it was late, he was still able to find a free carriage to hire to take him around to the sprawling Victorian home, on a main street, where his grandmother and Andrew now lived.

He felt his age when he disembarked at the door, valise in hand. He hadn't wired them to expect him. Sometimes, he'd reasoned, surprises were better.

He walked with a pronounced limp after the exercise his wounded leg had been forced to endure on the long passage from New York. His dark, wavy hair was covered by a bowler hat, tilted at a rakish angle. His vested navy blue suit was impeccable, if a little dusty, as were his hand-tooled black leather boots. He looked the very image of a city gentleman as he walked up the flower-bordered path to the porch.

Although it was dark, he could see that the elegant house was in good repair. Light poured in welcome from its long, tall windows, spilling onto the gray porch where a swing and settee and some rocking chairs with cushions sat. He had never lived in this house, but he'd visited it on occasion since he'd bought it for his grandmother to live in. He approved of the neat cushions on the chairs and the swing, with their wide ruffles in white eyelet. They gave the house a subdued elegance that went well with the exquisite gingerbread wood-work all around the eaves of the house.

He paused to open the screen door and use the brass door knocker, in the shape of a lion's head. The noise provoked voices from inside.

"Ella, could you answer the front door please? Ella! Oh, bother! Where is Mrs. Pate?"

"Never mind, Mrs. Dunn. I'll see who's there."

"Not you, Noelle. It is not fitting…"

The admonition in his grandmother's soft voice trailed off as her instructions were apparently ignored. He got a glimpse of thick auburn hair in an upswept hairdo before the door opened and a lovely, oval face with thick-lashed green eyes looked up at him inquiringly.

His blue eyes narrowed so that even their color wasn't re-vealed under the brim of his hat. His gaze swept over the woman, who was wearing a simple white blouse with a high, lacy neck and a dark skirt that reached to her ankles.

"What do you want?" she asked in a voice that, while pleas-ant, reeked of South Texas backcountry and contained a bel-ligerence that immediately raised the hair at Jared's nape.

He removed his hat out of inborn courtesy, leaning heav-ily on the cane. "I would like to see Mrs. Dunn," he said coolly.

"It's much too late for visitors," she informed him. "You'll have to come calling another time."

He lifted an eyebrow. "My, aren't you arrogant for a ser-vant, madam," he said, with biting sarcasm.

She flushed. "I'm no servant. I'm a member of the fam-ily."

"Like hell you are!" he returned abruptly. His eyes were glittery now, steady, unblinking—dangerous.

She was taken aback by those eyes, as well as the curse, which was at such variance with the deep, soft tone of his voice. No gentleman used such language in a lady's presence!

"Sir, whoever you are—" she began haughtily.

"Andrew should have made you aware of my identity," he continued coldly. "Especially since I pay the bills here. Where's my grandmother?"

Belatedly she realized to whom she was speaking. Andrew had mentioned his stepbrother, of course. He hadn't mentioned that the man was Satan in a business suit. He was very good-looking, despite those gray hairs at his temples, but he was tall and intimidating, and his eyes were like blue steel...in a face about that yielding.

"You didn't present your card," she said, defending herself as she quickly opened the door for him.

"I hardly felt the need in my own house," he returned irritably. His leg hurt and he was worn out.

She saw the cane then and noticed the taut lines around his thin mouth. "Oh...you're crippled," she blurted out.

Both eyebrows went up. "The delicacy of your observation leaves me speechless," he said, with biting sarcasm.

She did blush then, partially from bad temper. He was tall, and she had to look a long way up to see his face. She didn't like him at all, she decided, and she'd been foolish to feel sorry for him. Probably he'd gotten that bad leg kicking lame dogs...

"Mrs. Dunn is in the drawing room," she said, and slammed the door.

"My valise is still outside," he pointed out.

"Well, it can let itself in," she informed him, and swept past him toward the drawing room.

He followed her, momentarily bereft of speech. For an indigent relative, the woman took a lot upon herself.

"Jared!" the little woman on the sofa exclaimed brightly,

diverting him, and held her face up to be kissed. "My dear, what an excellent surprise! Are you passing through, or have you come to stay for a while?"

He looked at the auburn-haired woman across from him as he spoke to his grandmother. "Oh, I've come home," he said, watching the expression change in the younger woman's green eyes. "I decided that I needed a change of scene."

"Well, I'm delighted to have you," Mrs. Dunn said. "And I'm sure Andrew will be. He's away for the week, on business, you know. He does sales work for a local brickmaking concern. He's been in Galveston lately to take orders. That's where he found our lovely Noelle."

He glanced at the young woman. She was younger than he'd thought at first—probably not yet out of her teens.

"This is my grandson Jared, Noelle. And Jared, this is Andrew's young cousin, Noelle Brown."

Jared looked at her without speaking. "How did he chance to discover the relationship?" he asked finally.

"A mutual acquaintance pointed it out," Noelle said. She clasped her hands together tightly at her waist.

"An observant one, no doubt, as you certainly share no surface traits with my stepbrother, who is blond and dark-eyed."

"His mother was auburn-haired," Mrs. Dunn pointed out, "and his mother's people were Browns from Galveston. Naturally when he made mention of it, an acquaintance there told him of Noelle's existence, and her sad plight."

"I see."

"Dear boy, what has happened to you?" she asked, nodding toward the cane.

He leaned on the cane a little heavily. "A slight accident."

"Only that?" Noelle asked sweetly. "What a relief to know that you weren't slammed in the leg with a fence post, sir."

He cocked his head and stared at her pointedly. "You're very plainspoken, Miss Brown."

"I've had to be," she replied. "I had four brothers, sir—none of whom ever made allowances for my lack of muscle."

"Don't expect me to make allowances for your youth," he countered in a dangerously soft tone.

Her eyes went to the gray hair at his temples. "You may also expect that I'll make none for your age."

One dark eyebrow lifted. "My age?"

"Well, you're quite old."

He had to choke back a retort. Probably to a girl in her teens, he did seem elderly. He ignored her latest sally and turned back to his grandmother. "How have you been?" he asked, and his tone changed so drastically that Noelle was surprised.

Mrs. Dunn smiled warmly at him. "Quite well, my boy, for a lady of my years. And you look prosperous, as well."

"New York has been good to me."

She looked at the leg. "Not altogether, apparently."

He smiled. "This happened in New Mexico Territory. An accident."

"Surely you weren't thrown from a horse," she began, such an accident being the first sort to occur to her.

Noelle looked at him as if she expected that a man in such an expensive suit, an attorney, moreover, who lived in a huge eastern city, wouldn't know which end of a horse to get on.

"Horses are dangerous," Jared replied, deliberately evasive. He was enjoying their young houseguest's evident opinion of him. He could almost see the words in her green eyes: milksop; dude; layabout; dandy...

Her eyes met his and she cleared her throat, as if she'd spoken the words aloud. "Would you care for some refreshment, Mr., uh, Mr. Dunn?"

"Coffee would be welcome. I find travel by train so

exhausting," he said, with a mock yawn, deliberately assuming the facade of a tame city man.

Noelle turned quickly and left the room before she burst out laughing. If that was Andrew's formidable stepbrother, she was in no immediate danger of being thrown out. Although, just at first, there had been something in those steely eyes, in the set of his head, in his stance, that had made her very uneasy. Probably she was being fanciful, she thought, and continued on to the kitchen.

"Now," Mrs. Dunn said, when Noelle had closed the door and her footsteps could be heard going down the hall, "what happened?"

"I had a disagreement with an armed cowboy in a small community called Terrell," he said, sitting down across from her. "My shot broke his arm, but a wild bullet got me in the leg. It still pains me a bit, but in a few weeks, I'll be as good as new. So will he, fortunately," he added grimly. "Maybe he'll be more careful about who he pulls a gun on from now on."

"Gunfights, in such a civilized age," his grandmother said coolly. "For heaven's sake, this is just what Edith wanted to avoid! It's why she begged you to go East to school in the first place."

"I have avoided it—mostly," he said, dropping the cane idly by his side. "There are still uncivilized places…and men who reach for a gun before they look for a man with a badge. In court cases, tempers run hot."

"That's probably why you chose law as a profession," Mrs. Dunn said curtly. "It's a dangerous job."

He smiled. "So it is, from time to time. I'm going to open an office here in Fort Worth. New York has lost its appeal for me."

Her blue eyes, so like his own, softened. "Are you, truly,

Jared? It would be such a joy to have you home all the time."

"I've missed you, too," he confessed.

She bit her lower lip. "No one knows about your past here," she said gently. "I've never told anyone, least of all Andrew. But these scrapes you get into… What if any of your adversaries turn up in town?"

He chuckled. "What if they do? Gunplay is a thing of the past, except in saloons and during robberies. I'm hardly likely to find myself a target for young gunmen, except in dime novels," he added dryly.

"Don't remind me," she muttered, recalling that he'd been featured in one with a lurid cover and six guns in both his hands—ridiculous, since he'd only ever worn one gun, even in his young and wild days.

"I'm a respectable attorney."

"You're a hard case," Mrs. Dunn said shortly. "And neither of us is as respectable as we want people to think we are. Why, I was working in a saloon in Dodge when your mama had you. And now I belong to the Women's Benevolent Society and the Temperance Union and the Ladies' Sewing Circle and the prayer group. However would people look at me if they knew my real past?"

"The same as they look at you now, except with more fascination, you naughty woman," he murmured dryly.

She laughed. "I hardly think so." She shook her head. "Oh, Jared, how hard are the lessons we learn in youth. And all our indiscretions follow us like shadows into old age."

He searched her tired, lined face with compassion. Her life had been a much harder one than his own, although he carried scars, too. Despite the fact that he'd never killed without reason, the violence of the past occasionally woke him in lurid detail, and he had to get up and pace the floor to subdue the nightmares.

"You have your own demons," she said, recognizing the fleeting pain in his eyes.

"Don't we all have them?" He sighed heavily. "What about our redheaded houseguest?" he added. "Tell me about her."

"She's very kind," she said. "She can cook if she's ever needed in the kitchen, and she doesn't mind hard work."

"That isn't what I asked."

She grimaced. "She's sweet on Andrew, and vice versa. He was attracted to her at once. When he found out her circumstances, he insisted that she come here. Her family died in the flood that hit Galveston in the fall of 1900, and she's been living in Victoria with an elderly uncle. But he has the offer of a good job in Galveston and she was terrified to go back there. Perhaps the uncle wanted to be rid of her. So Andrew invited her to come and live with us." She tucked a fold of her dress into place. "He knew you wouldn't like it, but he said that he did contribute to the household accounts and he'd be responsible for her keep."

"He contributes ten dollars a month," Jared remarked. "The rest he spends on new boots and fine livery for his carriage."

"Yes, I know. But his father was good to Edith."

"And to you. I remember. Andrew is the cross we must bear for his father's kindness."

"That was unkind and uncharitable."

"I'm not a kind man," he reminded her, and for an instant, the old, wild look was in his eyes.

"I might agree if I didn't know you so well. You're kind to the people you love."

"There were only ever two—you and my mother."

She smiled gently. "You might find a woman who could love you and marry one day, Jared. You should have a family of your own. I won't live forever."

"Andrew will," he muttered darkly. "And I expect to find myself responsible for him until I die."

"Cynicism does not suit you."

"I find that it sits heavily on me of late," he returned, tapping the boot on the foot he'd crossed over his knee. "When I started practicing law, I wanted to be on the side of justice. But lately, more and more, I find myself on the side of money. I'm tired of helping the rich disinherit the poor. Ambition has paled for me in recent months. Now, I want to do some good."

"I'm sure you already have. But you will find worthy people here in need of representation."

"Yes. I think I will." He narrowed one eye. "Is Andrew serious about Noelle?"

She grimaced. "Who can tell? Andrew is fickle. He was trying to court Amanda Doyle for a brief time… You remember her father, Jared—he has a big house in town and three daughters. He fought in the cavalry in the Indian Wars."

"Yes," he said as an impression of a dignified old man flashed before his eyes. Like himself, Doyle had grown up in wild times, but his daughters had been protected from everything unpleasant and his wife was a socialite.

"But Miss Doyle would have nothing to do with Andrew," his grandmother continued. "It was about that time that he went to Galveston and found Noelle."

"And devastated her with his swagger, no doubt," Jared murmured dryly.

"Dear boy, he does cut a dashing figure with his exaggerated war record and his blond good looks and his arrogance."

"And his youth," Jared added, chuckling. "Your houseguest seems to class me with the aged and infirm."

"She knows nothing about you," she reminded him. "And you seem to be encouraging her mistaken impression of your character."

"Let it lie," he said. "She seems to be no more than a bad-tempered child, but if she came here expecting someone to support her for the rest of her life, she's going to be badly disappointed."

His grandmother flushed. "I never thought of the imposition it would mean to you, bringing her here," she said, embarrassed.

He held up a hand. "You were coerced," he said simply. "I know Andrew, remember. But we know nothing of this girl. She could be anybody."

"Andrew said that her uncle was well-known, and the family was a respectable one," she told him.

He didn't want to know anything about the girl. She irritated him too much already.

"And it occurred to me that Andrew might have brought her here because he was considering marriage," his grandmother added.

He didn't like that. He laughed coldly. "Andrew isn't ready to settle down," he added deliberately, more for his own benefit than hers. He leaned back and rubbed gingerly at his sore leg.

"Do you intend asking her to leave?" Mrs. Dunn asked slowly.

"I might," he replied. "It depends on what I learn about her. Let's say that she's here on suffrage until I make a decision." He smiled at her. "I'd like to hear more about these new organizations springing up in Fort Worth, the ones you've been writing me about. What exactly is the Civic Betterment Project?"

Chapter Two

It rained on Jared's first morning at home. He walked to the window of the dining room while he waited for the family housekeeper, Mrs. Ella Pate, to get breakfast on the table. Mrs. Pate did all the cooking and washing for the family. The elegant house was well kept and had all the most modern conveniences, including a very nice big bathroom with sound plumbing.

The tangles of pink roses on the bush outside the window were in glorious bloom, but they didn't impress the man on the other side of the windowpane. He saw neither the silver droplets of rain sliding down the glass nor the roses. His eyes were on the past, which being in Fort Worth had brought back most painfully to his mind.

This house wasn't the one that Jared's mother had lived in with his stepfather; it was newer. But even if the house was different from the one his mother had died in, being with his grandmother had kindled painful memories of his late mother and the past. He hadn't expected that.

"Aren't the roses nice, Mr. Jared?" Mrs. Pate asked pleasantly. "Old Henry keeps the bushes in order for us, although Miss Brown likes to putter around out there—in men's overalls—when he isn't looking. She has the touch with vegetables, not to mention flowers."

Mrs. Pate's starchy comment about Noelle's choice of clothing amused him. He could imagine how straitlaced Fort Worth would take to a young woman in men's clothing working in full view of the street. He wondered what else she had the touch for, but he didn't say a word. She came from poverty, and he still wasn't certain if her reasons for being here didn't have something to do with improving her own situation.

His grandmother came through the dining room doorway with Noelle just behind her.

"Good morning, Jared. Did you sleep well?" she asked brightly.

"Well enough." He glanced at Noelle, who was helping his grandmother into the chair. Very solicitous, he thought, and wondered at once if she was putting on a show just for him.

"Thank you, dear," Mrs. Dunn said. "Breakfast looks delicious, Ella."

"I hope it tastes just as good," Mrs. Pate said, with a grin.

"Let me have your cup, Jared, and I'll fill it for you," Mrs. Dunn offered.

He slid it over to her. His eyes met Noelle's above the pot. She wasn't looking at him. She was looking out the window at the rain and seemed lost in thought.

"Where are your thoughts, Miss Brown?" he asked.

She jerked her head around self-consciously. "I was wondering if Andrew would be home today." She bit off any further explanation, angry because he made her feel like a schoolgirl.

"He said that he hoped to be back this evening," Mrs. Dunn remarked. "He'll be glad to see you, Jared."

"Do you think so?" He creamed his coffee, leaving out sugar. "He wasn't here when I passed through last year at Christmas." That had irritated him, too—that his grandmother would have been alone at the holidays except for his impromptu visit.

"He was visiting some friends in Kansas City." Mrs. Dunn refrained from mentioning that one of them was female. "Andrew's job takes him away quite a lot."

He sipped his coffee and then took the platters as his grandmother passed them to him, filling his plate with eggs, sausages, tomatoes and biscuits. There was a mold of fresh butter on the pretty rose pattern of the scallop-edged English bone-china saucer. Mrs. Pate bought fresh butter every week for the family. There was also a variety of preserves, jams and jellies that Mrs. Pate and Jared's grandmother had made last summer and fall. He was especially fond of the creamy peach preserves and took two spoonfuls of it from the elegant silver dish.

"It won't be long until we'll have fresh vegetables," Mrs. Dunn remarked. "The kitchen garden is growing nicely."

"Indeed it is," Noelle remarked absently. "I've covered the young tomato plants against the chill, to make sure they aren't hurt by any unexpected frost."

"Henry asked me why there was so little weeding to be done," Mrs. Dunn remarked.

Noelle cleared her throat. She had to bite her tongue to keep from mentioning how heavily old Henry was hitting his whiskey bottle lately. She had found out accidentally, and she didn't want to give Jared a worse opinion of her by running down his gardener. The family seemed to dote on the man.

Noelle didn't. She found his halfhearted gardening irritating. "I had some free time…"

"Mrs. Hardy down the block noticed you working in the garden in those overalls and mentioned it to me. It seems that her sense of proper ladylike behavior was ruffled."

Noelle's green eyes flashed. "I'm a countrywoman, Mrs. Dunn," she murmured. "I've done everything from milking cows to scouring floors, and it's hardly appropriate to wear a long dress in muddy ground."

"Yes, but you must be more discreet here," the older woman said worriedly. "Henry was employed to do the gardening, you know."

Jared had to fight down laughter. His grandmother had been one of the world's worst at taking jobs away from servants when she'd moved to Fort Worth with her daughter and that young woman's new husband. It had taken her some time to learn the ways of polite society. He presumed she was hoping to spare Noelle some of the painful lessons she'd had to learn.

"I promise that I'll try, Mrs. Dunn," Noelle said respectfully, thinking all the while that she wasn't giving up her gardening—or her overalls—no matter what.

Her tone was even, but she was mutinous. Jared knew it as he glanced at her, although he didn't understand how he knew it.

"It's for your own good that I say these things," Mrs. Dunn assured her gently. "I don't want you to have to learn the hard way. Wagging tongues and gossip can be very damaging indeed."

Noelle sipped her coffee. "I'm not used to living in such a grand manner," she commented.

"Grand manner?" Jared said sarcastically.

"A house with servants is grand to me, Mr. Dunn," she returned, stung by his tone. Her complexion was just the least bit pale. She took her napkin from beneath her utensils belatedly, having noticed that everyone else had a spotless white linen napkin on their lap, not on the table. She spread it over her skirt and then peered at Mrs. Dunn's hand to see how she held her silver fork.

Watching her, Jared was amused. She was willing to learn proper manners, but too proud to ask anyone to teach her.

"What did your father do for a living, Noelle?" he asked abruptly.

She finished a bite of eggs before she answered. "He was a carpenter."

"As your uncle is, I understand." He looked straight at her. "Why don't you want to go back to Galveston?" he asked unexpectedly. "Are you afraid of water, Miss Brown? I understand that it was over a year and a half ago that the flood came, and the city fathers are constructing a seawall to prevent overwhelming tides in the future."

Galveston. The sea. The flood. Her family... She had thought that the nightmarish memories were behind her for good. But her uncle had insisted that they return to Galveston, where they could live with his half brother and he could do some odd jobs to earn money as the rebuilding of the city continued. Noelle had been very upset at the thought of living in the city where her eyes had been filled with such horrible scenes of death...her family's death. It made her uneasy to remember, and going back would mean having to face that horror every day of her life, every time she went to shop or to church.

There had never been anyone to whom she could describe what she'd seen. Even Andrew, whom she found attractive, quickly changed the subject when she wanted to discuss it— almost as if he were squeamish, a war hero who couldn't talk about a disaster. She had needed to talk about it. She still did.

Despite the amount of time that had passed, she could see the faces of her parents, distorted…

"Miss Brown?" Jared persisted. "It couldn't be the flood that disturbs you, after so long a time. Do you have some hidden reason for not wanting to return to Galveston? Are you in trouble of some kind?"

Mrs. Dunn started to speak, but a quick wave of Jared's hand stopped her. His intent pale blue eyes bit into Noelle's as mercilessly as if he'd been in a courtroom. "Answer me," he said evenly. "What do you have to hide? What is it about Galveston that made you fling yourself on the mercy of a distant relative rather than return there?"

She glared at Jared. "You make me sound like a criminal," she said accusingly.

He leaned back in his chair and watched her with cold, calculating eyes. "Not at all. I just want to know why you're content to live on my charity, rather than keeping house for your elderly uncle who, presumably, is going to suffer without your support."

She felt her face heat with bad temper. She gripped the napkin tight in her lap and fought an urge to throw a glass of water over him. Why, the smug, sanctimonious reprobate! Who did he think he was?

She got to her feet, almost shaking with temper. "My uncle has a brother in Galveston who is married and has six daughters. I assure you, he won't suffer from lack of attention. And if my presence here is so offensive to you, if you feel that I do nothing to earn my keep, then I'm quite content to leave!"

Tears stung her eyes. Jared's accusations seemed to suffocate her as much as the nightmarish memories of Galveston. She flung the napkin on the table and lifted her skirts as she ran for the back porch.

It had been a long time since she'd cried. But Jared had infuriated her and cost her the control over her emotions that she prided herself on. She wept brokenly, so that it left her shaking, with tears running down her cheeks. She gripped the porch railing hard, trying to sniff back the wetness that threatened to escape her nose, feeling the rain mist in her face, hearing the *ping* of the droplets on the tin roof while she drowned in her own misery. She'd burned her bridges. She would have no place to go! Well, she wouldn't go back to Galveston, even so. They couldn't force her to—

"Here."

She started as a lean, darkly tanned hand passed her an immaculate white linen handkerchief. She held it to her mouth and then her cheeks and eyes. "Thank you," she said gruffly.

"My grandmother told me that you lost your entire family in the flood. I didn't know that. And I didn't realize that you were still so affected by it."

She peeked up at him over the handkerchief and found an odd compassion in his eyes, replacing his earlier mockery. "Neither did I," she confessed.

He knew about bad memories. He had enough of his own. "I've never been to Galveston," he continued conversationally, "but I spoke with several people who were there just days after the flood. You saw your parents, afterward, didn't you?" he added, because it was the only thing that made sense of her strong reaction to any discussion of the flood.

She nodded and tried to turn away.

He took her firmly by the upper arms and turned her back to face him. His narrow, insistent blue eyes bored into hers, so close that they filled the world, so intense that they made it impossible for her to move.

"Don't hold it inside. Tell me," he said firmly. "Tell me everything you remember."

She was compelled to answer, needed to answer. The memories tumbled helplessly out of her mouth, and she couldn't stop them. It was such a relief to speak of it, at last, to someone who would listen.

"They didn't look human," she whispered. She dabbed at her nose, wincing at the memory. "They were piled up, row upon row upon row of bodies, some so horrible…" She swallowed. "I felt so guilty, you see. I was in Victoria with Uncle. If I had been at home, I would have died with them. We went to town on Saturday, every Saturday, to shop. They would have been in town when it happened," she told him, "my parents and my four brothers. It was midmorning and the flood came unexpectedly. They said a wall of water covered the entire city, drowning everyone in its path. They wouldn't have known what happened…or so I was told. Over five thousand people died there in a space of minutes. Minutes!" She stopped to hold the cloth out in the rain, wetting it. Then she patted her face with the cool cloth and paused to choke down the nausea. "They were laid out on the street, and not together. At least they were found…in time… So that they could still be…identified." Tears were hot in her eyes as she remembered the sight of her beloved family like that. She pressed the handkerchief to her mouth.

He frowned slightly as he studied her drawn, tearstained face. He'd seen death so often in his younger days that it didn't really disturb him very much. His mother had slipped from life very peacefully, holding his hand. But Galveston had been a nightmare of corpses, they said, more than men saw even during wartime. He could only imagine how it would have been for a sensitive young woman to see her entire family lying dead on the street. Drowning victims of that sort were a nightmarish sight. It would have been even worse a few days later, as people had to be forced to gather the decomposing corpses…

He stuck his hands in his pockets and jingled his loose change as he watched her cope with her outpouring of emotion.

He sensed that it was unusual for her to give in to tears, especially in front of strangers. He didn't touch her. Some part of him wanted to, but he wouldn't have appreciated a stranger's attempt at comfort and he didn't think she would, either.

She got herself back in control at last and wiped the traces of moisture from her eyes. They were red now, like her straight nose and her cheeks. "My uncle's insistence on returning to Galveston resurrected all the memories. I thought that I'd put it behind me, but I was never able to talk about it. I thought Andrew would be the one person who could let me pour it all out, since he was in the war…but he wouldn't listen to me. He actually seemed to go pale when I mentioned it. Of course, I must have imagined that."

He knew that she hadn't. Andrew had never seen raw death, Jared was certain of it, and the young man had a squeamish stomach. "Go on," he coaxed.

The sound of the rain grew insistent on the roof. She sighed. "So there was no one else to tell. You accused me of running from something. You were right. I would rather die than go back to live in that city, with the memories of all the faces, the pitiful faces." She stopped. "I'm sorry," she said huskily.

"No, I'm sorry," he replied at once. "I made some cruel remarks. My only excuse is that I didn't know your entire family had died in the flood."

The apology was unexpected. She lifted her eyes to his and searched them. "My uncle was down with his back when the flood came. I had gone up to Victoria to keep house and wait on him several weeks before the flood came. I would have gone home the following Monday. I felt so guilty that I hadn't been with my family when they died."

"That was God's decision, surely?" he replied solemnly.

"You mean, that He spared me for a reason?"

He nodded.

She considered that silently. Her grief had made all her

memories painful. He had forced her to face them, to face divine purposes, as well. "Thank you for listening to me. Most people don't like to hear of such horror." She managed a faint smile for him. "And city men as a rule have no stomach at all for unpleasantness." She frowned as she searched his eyes shyly. "It…did not disturb you too much, what I said?"

He had to stifle laughter. "No," he said simply.

The twinkle in his eyes puzzled her. "I'm glad. Thank you for listening."

"Life goes on," he reminded her. "We do what we must."

"Have you lost someone you loved?" she asked curiously.

His face closed up. "Most people have."

He wouldn't talk about himself. She hadn't really expected it to be otherwise. He seemed very reticent, and he was an attorney, which meant that he had to be intelligent, as well. She blew her nose on the cloth and gave in to the exhaustion that followed her outburst. "You've been kind," she said reluctantly. She grimaced. "I'm…sorry that I was antagonistic. It was being told that I was living on charity—"

"Oh, hell," he said irritably. "I didn't mean it."

She glanced at him. "You shouldn't curse."

He laughed. "It's my house," he pointed out. "I can curse if I like."

She started to argue, but thought better of it.

"My grandmother says that you do more than enough to earn your keep. Stay as long as you like. I must confess that I shouldn't enjoy living in Galveston, even though I didn't lose anyone in the flood."

"Andrew was afraid that you wouldn't want me here. He told me that you would probably make me leave. I suppose I was anticipating it when you arrived. It made me hostile toward you."

He cocked an eyebrow. "My stepbrother knows very little

about me," he pointed out. "He was a boy when I left home, and my visits have been infrequent."

"Andrew was good to me, although I realize that he brought me here without your permission. When he learned about my circumstances, he insisted," she said, and her green eyes softened. "He's quite dashing and very brave, and he impressed my uncle greatly." She looked nervously at him. "He said that I could be a great help to your grandmother as a companion, to earn my keep. I have done my best to ease her path, and I've been helping Andrew with his correspondence and paperwork in the evenings. I can use a typewriter and a Dictaphone. Andrew taught me how."

He was getting an interesting picture of his stepbrother's benevolence. It wasn't flattering to Andrew. Apparently Noelle was working for him as an unpaid secretary, in addition to running his grandmother's errands. No doubt she was earning her keep, but it was Jared, not Andrew, who was paying the bills.

He frowned as the dampness on the porch began to make his leg ache. His hand was gripping the cane hard, and he grimaced as he used it to prop his sore leg.

"I'm sorry for the remarks I made about your handicap," she added unexpectedly, nodding toward his injured appendage.

He lifted an eyebrow. "I'm not touchy about it," he said.

"How did it happen?" she asked, without thinking.

"Would you believe that a horse threw me?" he drawled. It wasn't the truth, but he wasn't ready to impart that to anyone in the household just yet.

"Yes, of course," she said. "The cane makes you look distinguished," she added helpfully.

"Distinguished, or ancient?" he taunted.

"Mummies are ancient, not people," she argued.

His lips turned up briefly. "Comforting, Miss Brown. Very comforting."

An awkward silence fell over them while the rain increased its rhythmic pounding on the tin roof. "I must go and see if Mrs. Dunn needs anything. Thank you again," she said sincerely.

"I had no intention of throwing you out on one day's acquaintance," he said before she left. "Andrew misjudged me. I'd do almost anything for my grandmother's comfort. Any service you do her will please me."

She smiled. "Thank you, then." She continued on her way, ruffled but a little more at ease with him.

Later, when she told Mrs. Dunn about the unexpected compassion from Jared Dunn, the older woman was visibly surprised.

"Jared is a hard man," Mrs. Dunn said. "He hasn't had an easy life, and there's a shell around him that no one in recent years has been able to breach. He cares for me, in his fashion, but he doesn't like most people. He can be dangerous, and he makes a formidable adversary, especially in a court of law."

"I hope that he never becomes mine," Noelle said, with feeling.

Mrs. Dunn smiled at the very thought. "That's hardly likely, my dear."

Andrew arrived back at the house that evening, in a hired carriage with a driver to bring in his two bags and trunk. Noelle's face lit up like a Christmas candle when she saw him, and she almost jumped out of her chair when he walked into the living room. But it was Mrs. Dunn, not Noelle, that he went to first. Noelle's face fell. Jared, watching, found her adoration of his stepbrother oddly irritating.

"Grandmother, how wonderful to see you!" Andrew enthused as he embraced her. "I've been to Galveston and Victoria and even to Houston. I brought you a Paris hat—green velvet and feathers and fur. You'll love it! And Noelle, I found a pretty little pearl pin for you—" He stopped as Jared moved into the lamplight. "Jared! Why…how nice to see you."

"And you, Andrew," Jared said, with a cool smile. "You look well."

Indeed he did, in his fashionable suit and tie and hand-tooled lace-up shoes and bowler hat. Andrew was as tall as Jared, but a little less streamlined. He had a curling blond mustache that matched his shock of blond hair, with even features and dark eyes that twinkled. He was the epitome of a dashing ex-soldier, and women loved him. Noelle was no exception. Her face was flushed and eyes were bright with excitement as she greeted him.

"It's lovely to have you back again, Andrew," Noelle said breathlessly.

"It's nice to be back." He chuckled, reaching down to grasp her small hand and kiss it lazily. Her flush delighted him.

Jared could only imagine how he measured up against the younger man, with his gimpy leg and his lined face. But he wasn't jealous of Andrew, who had the nature of a friendly puppy coupled with the shrewd craftiness of a coyote. He did know never to turn his back on the younger man, or trust him very far. Those were lessons that Noelle very obviously hadn't learned yet. She looked like a ripe little peach hanging over a hungry boy's head, and that continental bit of hand-kissing had flustered her visibly.

"How long are you staying, Jared?" Andrew asked, moving away from Noelle.

"For a long time. I'm moving my law practice down here from New York," Jared replied, smiling at the shocked response. "This is my house, Andrew," he added pointedly—in a tone that brooked no protests.

"Yes, of course it is. And you're always welcome here," Andrew said quickly. He laughed. The sound was nervous and too high. "I shall have to look to my laurels with such a famous trial lawyer around, drawing the attention of the ladies!"

Jared leaned heavily on the cane. "I have no interest in such attention, I assure you," he said coldly, and his eyes flashed. "My prime interest is the practice of law."

"I say, Jared, what happened to your leg?" he asked suddenly when his stepbrother moved forward and sank down into a wing chair by the empty fireplace.

"An accident," Jared said firmly.

"I'm sorry. Will it heal?"

"Andrew, what a thoughtless question," Mrs. Dunn chided. "Do sit down, dear boy, and tell us about your trip."

"Oh, yes, do!" Noelle enthused.

He dropped elegantly to the sofa beside Mrs. Dunn and patted her hand affectionately. "I had a successful tour," he said. "I met with some representatives of our sister company in Houston and I sold tons of bricks to businesses in Victoria. Perhaps soon there will be a market in Galveston. Progress on the seawall is moving along quite rapidly. Once finished, it certainly should forestall any further invasions of the sea. Forgive me, Noelle," he added quickly.

She nodded and smiled. "It's all right, Andrew," she said in a husky, soft tone. And surprisingly, it was. Talking her grief out to Jared had made it bearable.

Andrew smiled his relief and plunged into the subject of the new construction, with the two women giving him their full attention. Jared just sat and listened. Andrew was smug and far too arrogant, but that didn't seem to bother Noelle, who hung on his every word as if he were dispensing holy law. It made him irritable, and after a short time, he excused himself and went to bed.

"How long has he been here?" Andrew asked Mrs. Dunn when Jared was safely upstairs.

"For two days," she replied. "He was tired of life in the big city and wanted to come home. He's feeling his age, I think."

"The poor old thing," Noelle said, with genuine sympathy. "It must have been very difficult for him to get around in a big city like New York with such a handicap. Perhaps he will find a quieter life here."

"I hope that he doesn't interfere too much with our own lives," Andrew muttered.

"You're ungrateful, my boy," Mrs. Dunn told him bluntly. "Jared paid for this house and everything in it, lest you forget."

"I'm grateful for his gifts," Andrew returned. "But he's hardly a welcome addition to our household. I remember his earlier visits. He was always glowering, watching, somber. He's a cold and intimidating presence."

"He's an attorney," Mrs. Dunn replied. "It wouldn't benefit him to be frivolous, Andrew."

"Yes, well, when he establishes his practice, perhaps he won't be around so much and things can go on as before." He looked pointedly at Noelle and smiled warmly. "Because I have hardly had time to get to know my cousin Noelle. Now that I am excused from further travels out of town for a while, we can spend some time together."

Noelle's heart leapt into her throat and she beamed at him. "That would be lovely, Andrew."

He leaned back in his chair and crossed his legs, covertly drinking in the fullness of her figure, the pretty lines of her face. She wasn't the sort of woman he would marry, because she was much too countrified and simple for his taste, and she had no social background to speak of. But she would make a sweet little mistress. There was the minor complication of his stepbrother, but Jared would present no real problem. He

was confident that he could seduce Noelle without difficulty.
Afterward, well, he'd worry about that when the time came.

The soft mewling at the back door caught Noelle's attention even above the rumble of thunder and the patter of hard
rain when she was cleaning out the pantry a few days later.
She wiped her hands on her white ruffled apron, grimacing
at the smudges she left there, and went down the long, wide
hall to the back door.

Outside there was a tiny marmalade kitten with big blue
eyes. She picked it up and laughed as it curled under her chin
and began to purr.

As she started back down the hall, Andrew passed her on
his way to the study. He paused, scowling. "Noelle, put that
filthy thing out. We can't have a cat in here. They're nasty."

She gaped at him. "But it's a kitten. And it's pouring
outside."

"I don't care. I won't have a cat in the house. I hate cats. I
can't stand the sight of them." He kept walking.

She glared at his back. "Well, you don't have to look at it,
do you?" she asked under her breath.

She dried it on a soft cloth and tucked it against her bosom
before she peered out the door to make sure Andrew wasn't
nearby, then made a dash for the kitchen.

In her mad rush to avoid detection, she cannoned straight
into Jared and almost knocked him down.

He cursed sharply, leaning heavily on his cane as he
grabbed the door for support, and the eyes he turned on Noelle
made her stop short and hold her breath. She'd never seen such
an expression on a man's face. It made her think of guns...

A minute later she wondered if she'd imagined the look in
his eyes. He snapped the door shut and looked at her, unblinking. "What have you got there?"

"It's a kitten," she said, holding it protectively as she

recovered from the cold, merciless anger, now gone, in his blue eyes. But they were only a little less intimidating now. "Andrew told me to put it out. I won't. It's raining again, and this poor wretched little creature is thin and starved and homeless. If it goes, I go with it!" she said, with bravado.

He got his balance back with the cane and straightened. His cold blue eyes slid over the cat and lingered on the firm fullness of her bosom. She was just a girl, he reminded himself, and he was no stranger to a woman's bed. But the pleasure he felt when he looked at her disturbed him.

His gaze lifted to collide with hers. "It will have to live in the kitchen," he said. "Mrs. Pate can keep an eye on it for you."

"I can keep it?" she asked, relieved.

"Yes."

"But Andrew…"

"For God's sake, it's my house. If I say the cat can stay, it can stay."

"There's no need to be so unpleasant," she pointed out. "It's your leg, isn't it?" she added then. "I expect the rain makes it ache more. You should sit down and rest it, Mr. Dunn. It can't be doing you any good to walk around."

His thin lips became even thinner and his eyes narrowed, too. "I'm not infirm."

"It's all right, you know. I didn't mean to be offensive."

"And stop talking to me as if I were in my dotage!"

Her eyebrows both lifted. "My, you are in a nasty temper, aren't you?"

"Miss Brown!"

"One should never meet unkindness with unkindness," she recited. "I'll take the kitten to Mrs. Pate, then. May I tell Andrew that you gave it permission to stay, if he asks why I didn't put it back outside?" she added, not wanting to offend Andrew but determined to help the kitten.

"Tell Andrew what the hell you like!"

"Sir!" She flushed. He didn't apologize for his language or the whip in his voice. After a minute, she continued, "I don't want to make him angry, but it's such a very small kitten." She looked up and met his searching eyes...and felt the ground move under her feet. It was a kind of look that she'd never experienced in her young life.

She wasn't alone. Jared was feeling something similarly profound, but his reaction was typical of a man who wanted no part of entanglement.

"You may have nothing better to do than stand and chat, Miss Brown, but I have work waiting," he said testily.

"Excuse me, then." She moved aside and let him pass, noticing the ungainly gait and the strain on his face. "I could make you some tea—" she began, with compassion.

His head jerked around and the expression on his face put wings on her feet. Whoever said that people grew crotchety with age had been quite accurate, she thought. But at least he'd let her keep the kitten.

Andrew, when told of this decision, was less than pleased. He glared at Noelle.

"I told you to put the thing out, and yet you went to my stepbrother instead. That was underhanded, Noelle."

"A cat will keep the mice down," she said quickly.

"Mice?" He looked around irritably. "I had no idea... Keep the cat, then. I detest mice even more than I detest cats!"

"Thank you, Andrew."

He noticed her adoring glance and it took some of the sting out of Jared's intervention. He moved closer to Noelle, a soft smile on his face. "You're very pretty, little cousin," he remarked. "Very pretty, indeed."

She smiled affectionately. "And you are very handsome," she replied, almost choking on the pleasure of having him pay her compliments.

"You've had little entertainment since you arrived. Would you like to go to a dance with me Friday night? It's a charity affair, very elegant."

"I'd love to go!" she said fervently.

"Then it's a date," he promised her. His hand touched a wisp of hair at her cheek, making her tremble with pleasure. He chuckled at her ready response and dropped his hand. "And I insist that you dance only with me."

She sighed. "That's a promise," she said dreamily.

"Oh," he added, "I left some handwritten orders on the desk in the study. You wouldn't mind typing them for me, would you? I have to go out this evening…a dinner party."

"Of course I'll type them for you," she said fervently, as if she'd walk on hot coals if he wanted her to.

Her devotion made him strut. "Thanks, Noelle," he said, with a wink. "You're a sweet thing."

She walked on clouds all the way out of the room, her fingers brushing the cheek he'd touched. She knew her face must be flushed. Andrew was taking her to a dance!

Then as she gained the hall, it occurred to her that she had no dress grand enough to wear to a society dance. Most of her clothes had been at home in Galveston when the flood struck, and there had never been very many. Since then, she hadn't had any money to buy fabric to sew new things, and her plain skirts and blouses would hardly do for a large social gathering. Andrew wouldn't want to be seen with her in anything she had in her closet. He was impeccable in his attire and expected everyone around him to be equally elegant. He had, in fact, been pointedly critical of her few dresses. What he had to say about her overalls was better left unsaid, and she did her outdoor work when he was out of town.

But that wasn't her only problem. Andrew watched her at the table when she ate, grimacing when she didn't hold her fork right, when she forgot to put her napkin in her lap. Often he grimaced and she didn't know why. She had no knowledge of proper table manners, although she tried to emulate the others at table. She wished she knew how a proper lady was supposed to behave.

Even if she had, it didn't solve the problem of the dress. She didn't have one that wouldn't disgrace him. So she wouldn't be able to go with him, after all. And it felt as if her heart would surely break.

Chapter Three

Andrew's handwriting was atrocious, Noelle thought as she sat before the Remington typewriter at the big oak desk in the study, trying to make out the scrawls on pieces of paper as she typed up his brick orders. She was still slow, but at least her work was professional-looking. Her spelling skills were adequate, and actually much better than Andrew's, she mused.

She was peering down at the pad and didn't notice the door open until she heard the knock of Jared's walking stick against it.

She looked up, startled. "Hello," she said shyly.

He moved into the room, leaving the door open. "What are you doing?"

"Andrew's orders needed typing up, and he was going to be out this evening," she said, with a faint smile.

He didn't smile back. "And I thought slave labor had been outlawed," he drawled.

She stiffened in her chair, looking as starchy as her high ruffled collar. "I most certainly am not slave labor," she said haughtily. "I'm doing Andrew a favor, that's all."

"How often do you do this favor for him?"

Every other night, but she wasn't telling him that! "It's little enough to do, since I'm not paying room and board."

He leaned heavily on the stick. "You aren't naive enough to think my stepbrother pays the bills?" he taunted.

She flushed to her hairline. It embarrassed her that she was living on Jared's charity. And certainly she wasn't doing his typing.

Her scarlet blush made him feel guilty. His lean hand shifted against the cane. "That wasn't kind of me, was it?" he asked. "You earn your crust of bread."

She brightened. "Thank you. I could…type for you, when you open your office, if you like," she offered.

His eyebrows levered up. He hadn't thought that far ahead. He would have an office, surely, but in New York, he and Alistair had employed a male secretary. He wasn't certain that it was quite respectable to offer the job to Noelle. Or that he'd want her that close.

"We can discuss that some other time," he said. He moved toward the desk, so that he could see her handiwork on the white sheet of paper. He took out his glasses case and perched his reading glasses on his nose. He leaned forward and frowned. "You're very accurate," he said.

She hadn't seen him in his glasses before. They seemed to emphasize all his vulnerabilities. They softened her toward him even more. "You sound surprised that I can spell," she said, with an impish grin.

"So it seems." He reached down to pick up one of the forms, his arm brushing her shoulder. She stiffened, and his eyes narrowed. He didn't like her reaction. "Are you afraid that I might contaminate you with my touch?" he asked. His smile was mocking as he met her startled green eyes. "My taste runs to women, not to little girls playing dress up."

She was flustered. "Such a thought never crossed my mind," she exclaimed breathlessly.

"Not even with Andrew?" he taunted.

"Andrew is different," she said. He rattled her. She clasped her hands tightly in her lap. "He's young and—and brave and kind. He's very kind," she repeated.

"Oh, certainly. He's everything I'm not," he said dryly, and took off his reading glasses with a quick, efficient movement of his hands.

"I didn't say that."

"You meant it." He leaned heavily on the cane, his eyes biting into her averted face. It irritated him that she didn't think of him in the same category as Andrew. He could remember women looking at him with fascination, awe, even fear. But Noelle was the first to see him with eyes of pity. He'd noticed it even more when he'd had on his glasses. He wondered if she'd pity the man he really was as much as she pitied the distorted persona.

She shifted delicately away from contact with his long legs. "You're a good deal older than I am," she said.

"I see," he drawled. "I'm an elderly, crippled ruin who needs to be offered warm milk to help him sleep?"

She flushed. "Mr. Dunn!"

He laughed. "When I think of the old days, and how women looked at me then…" he said half to himself. "Perhaps I am old, and growing fanciful, because I can't remember a time when I needed admiration from a marmalade kitten!"

She stood up, too close to him and too angry to care. "I'm not a kitten!"

He deliberately moved closer, threatening, taller and broader than he'd seemed on first acquaintance. At such close range, he towered over her slender form. He smelled of cologne and soap, and she was surprised that she didn't find his nearness intolerable. He was too old, a cripple, citified...

Her eyes lifted and were swallowed whole by his. She couldn't have imagined feeling frozen by a look, but he had her as helpless as if he'd roped her. She looked into those piercing pale blue eyes and couldn't seem to stop looking, while her heart thrust into her throat and her legs seemed to tremble.

"Your face is red," he remarked in a colorless voice. His lean, elegant hand moved to her face and slowly tucked a strand of her hair behind her small ear.

The touch was electric. Andrew's similar contact had made her smile. Jared's fingers made her blood race through her veins, made her mouth swell, made her eyes dilate. The contact ran through her like a lightning flash.

Jared, who knew women, watched her unexpected reaction with an almost clinical scrutiny. He smiled slowly to himself. So she thought she'd given her heart to Andrew, did she? Apparently she was untried and untouched. The thought galvanized him. His jaw clenched and his eyes looked briefly violent.

Noelle moved backward and dropped into her chair, retreating from him. His eyes were hypnotic, threatening. "Don't..." she whispered.

"Don't what?" he asked in a new tone, and without moving.

She swallowed. "I—I don't know," she faltered. "You—you looked as if you might strike me."

He slid his eyes to the frantic, rhythmic ripple of the lace at her throat. "I haven't ever raised my hand to a woman," he said, placing the slightest emphasis on the last word.

Her fine auburn brows drew together. "Or to a man?" she asked absently, implying that he wasn't a fighter at all.

His face closed up into an impassive mask that gave away

nothing. "I noticed you watching my grandmother at table," he said abruptly. "You don't know proper table manners, do you?"

"How dare you!" Impulsively, her fingers closed over the big paperweight on the desk as she glared at him. "Don't you make fun of me!"

The movement of her hand hadn't gone unnoticed. "Or you'll do what?" he challenged, smiling at her. His eyes danced with unholy glee. "Throw that at me? Go ahead," he said, and the glitter in his eyes made him look like a different man.

She hesitated. There was something there, something that warned her not to underestimate him.

"What's the matter?" he persisted. "No guts?"

She drew in her breath. "I'm not afraid of you."

He took a step closer, and she moved the chair back a little farther.

He laughed with pure pleasure and halted his advance, leaning heavily on the cane. "You intrigue me, Miss Brown," he murmured. "I can't say that I've ever met anyone quite like you."

"I can't believe that," she returned, relaxing a little now that she'd put some distance between them. "New York City must be full of women."

"Certainly," he said agreeably. "Elegant, sophisticated women with beautiful clothes and excellent manners and sparkling conversation."

"Everything that I am not," she said quietly, echoing his own earlier words.

"You lack the advantages of wealth," he corrected. His practiced eye ran over her assessingly. "But you have potential. In fact, you have a grace of carriage already. You simply don't have social graces. That isn't your fault."

"How comforting to know it," she said, stung by the

knowledge that he thought her lacking. She was already unsettled because she couldn't accept Andrew's invitation to the dance.

"You misunderstand me. You're young enough to learn," he said.

"And who's going to teach me?" she asked belligerently.

"Andrew?" he suggested dryly.

She flushed. "I couldn't possibly ask Andrew; it would be too humiliating to admit to him that I'm a social moron, even if he already knows it."

He cocked his head and his narrow blue eyes stared at her. "Andrew's opinion means a great deal to you, doesn't it, Miss Brown?"

"Well, yes. It was he who brought me here and gave me a home," she replied.

"That's the only reason?" he probed.

"He's everything a man should be," she said finally, twisting a piece of paper in her hands. "I'm sorry if you don't approve of my admiration for him. I know that my background is nothing special."

He glared at her. "Your background is nothing to me," he said shortly. "Your character is all that concerns me."

"You don't think I have character," she accused. "You think I'm after Andrew because he has money, don't you?"

He chuckled softly. "At first, yes—I did think you might be an opportunist. But you improve on closer acquaintance. I don't think you have a larcenous bone in your body. You aren't the type."

She eyed him with open curiosity. "You'd know the type, wouldn't you?"

His eyes became intent. "What do you mean?"

"You're a lawyer," she replied simply. "You must have defended many men who were guilty of their crimes."

"Not knowingly," he pointed out. "I have too much respect

for the law to dirty my hands helping felons to break it. Although there are plenty of people who consider themselves qualified to be judge and jury," he added.

"You're talking about the lynchings, aren't you? There are a lot of them these days." She put the twisted paper in her hands on the desk and pushed it away. "It's a shame that many accused people don't have a chance at a trial."

"That will change one day," he replied.

"I hope so." She searched his blue eyes curiously. "Why did you decide to come home after so long in New York?" she asked bluntly. "Was it because you thought I was trying to cheat Andrew out of his inheritance?"

Her plainspoken nature amused him. He smiled indulgently and perched himself on the corner of the desk, looking down at her from far too close. "Yes, I think it was," he replied, with equal forthrightness. "But I was tired of practicing pocket-book law, too. The last case I handled was a property dispute. My client was in the wrong, but I didn't find it out until the verdict was handed down and there was some—" he paused "—unpleasantness."

"Someone tried to beat you up?" she asked, wide-eyed.

He almost told her. Surprisingly, he wanted to. But he shrugged. "Something like that," he said, and passed it off.

"You don't like being wrong, do you?" she asked him.

He laughed, annoyed. "I rarely am."

"How conceited," she shot back, but she smiled.

"I know the law." He corrected her faulty impression. "I've been in practice for ten years."

"That's what Andrew said."

He wondered what else his stepbrother had told her about him. Nothing good, he was certain. Andrew didn't like him, and the younger man was apparently taken with Noelle. He wouldn't like an older rival.

"Andrew and I are very different," he pointed out.

"Yes, I know. He's much younger than you, isn't he?"

His jaw tautened. "Not that much younger," he said irritably.

"It's very odd, you know," she said thoughtfully, studying him, "that you look so much older than he does. Shouldn't it be the opposite? I mean, he was in the war and you've spent years sitting in a courtroom. One would think that a soldier, a man who dealt in death, would look older than a well-dressed lawyer who never had to face more than an occasional verbal threat."

His eyes dropped to her long-fingered, elegant hands folded on the desk. She had no idea what his life had been like. She was right, but she didn't know the truth. He'd lived more in his lifetime than Andrew ever would.

"I haven't offended you, have I?" she asked worriedly. "I sometimes speak without thinking."

His eyes shot back up to catch hers. He smiled slowly. "You're not afraid of me. I'm glad. I don't pull my punches, and I won't expect you to. Our association should prove to be an interesting one, with a basis of such honesty." He eased off the edge of the desk and got to his feet. He leaned heavily on the cane, wincing.

"It's an old injury, isn't it?" she asked, standing up, and continued before he could reply. "You must have had a hard time getting around in a big city like New York. It's less crowded here."

She'd gone to open the door for him, and he gave her a glare that disconcerted her with its cold fury.

He reached over, grasped the door's edge and slammed it. The noise made her jump. His expression was even more threatening than the loud noise.

"I don't need doors opened for me, a rocking chair to rest in, warm milk to help me sleep or solicitous exaggerations from a woman who sees me as a cripple!"

She gaped at him. "I thought no such thing about you! I would have opened the door for anyone who—who…" She flushed.

"Anyone who was crippled, isn't that what you meant to say? Spit it out, then."

"All right," she said furiously. "I'd open a door for anyone who was crippled. There! Does it make you happy to have embarrassed me so? Would you rather I pretended that there's nothing wrong with you, when I can plainly see that it hurts you just to stand up?"

He drew in a sharp, angry breath. He leaned ever more heavily on the cane, aware of her slenderness and his superior height as he loomed over her. The injury was temporary. Wouldn't she faint if he told her how he'd acquired it! His eyes gleamed as he debated with himself about doing exactly that.

"I'm sure that a bad leg doesn't have anything at all to do with practicing law, and your grandmother says there isn't anyone at all who's better at it than you are," she continued, unabashed. "I'm sorry if I hurt your feelings, but I like doing things for you."

Both eyebrows shot up in surprise. She'd colored just faintly when she'd said that, and it touched him as few things had in years past. He searched her green eyes far longer than he meant to, and he could see her heartbeat change in the small artery on the side of her throat, where the lace fluttered.

"I mean, I like being of help," she said quickly.

It wasn't quick enough, though. He allowed himself to savor it for a few seconds. Then he laughed at his own assumptions. Her opinion of him certainly precluded any romantic feelings.

"I can open my own doors, nevertheless," he said quietly.

"Very well, Mr. Dunn."

He gave her one last glance, and, with an irritated sound, he opened the door again and went out.

Andrew came in later and peered into the study; Noelle had just finished with the last report. She was putting a hand to her aching back, but she smiled when she saw him.

"I've just finished," she said.

"What a sweetheart you are, Noelle," Andrew said as he picked up the reports and looked through them. "A bit off the lines," he remarked carelessly, "but they'll do, I suppose."

Hours of work, and they'd 'do'? She glared at him. "I spent the entire evening in here," she began.

"Yes, and don't think I don't appreciate it. Now about tomorrow night—"

"I can't go to the dance with you. Thank you all the same for asking me," she said abruptly.

He searched her eyes and then shrugged. "I'm sorry. Another time perhaps?"

"Perhaps."

He chuckled and bent to kiss her on the cheek. "You're a goose," he accused gently. "I wouldn't have asked for anything you didn't want to give me."

"But that's not why," she said, horrified that he had a totally wrong idea of the reason behind her refusal.

He waved her away. "It doesn't matter. Don't worry about it. I'll ask you again," he drawled softly. "Sleep well, Noelle."

He yawned as he strolled back out of the room, still not knowing why she'd refused.

Noelle was upset by his lack of interest about her reasons. His stepbrother would have had the information out of her no matter what it took. She wondered why it irritated her so much that Andrew had been so careless about it. She put up the typewriter, angry that she'd even permitted herself to think about what Jared would have done, and went halfheartedly up to her room.

Chapter Four

Noelle was a little relieved that she'd refused Andrew's invitation to the dance, because she had another problem besides the lack of an appropriate gown to wear. She'd never learned to dance. Her father, a carpenter like her uncle, but also a lay minister, despised dancing and other "sinful pleasures of the flesh," and refused to allow Noelle to attend such functions. She couldn't dance at all.

She was also very unworldly. She'd lived in a house that was little more than a shack, first with her own family and then with her elderly uncle. She'd never experienced indoor plumbing, washing machines, newfangled refrigerators with removable ice trays, or a gas stove, electric lights and a telephone until she came to live in Fort Worth with Andrew's people. She was keenly aware of her limitations. And probably, so was he.

Andrew hadn't been surprised by her gentle refusal to accompany him, and he hadn't wondered why. In fact, he'd regretted his impulsive invitation as soon as he'd made it. Noelle was very attractive, but she was hardly his idea of a cultured companion for a very public evening. Although her speech was passable, she still seemed ignorant of even basic table manners and was uncomfortable among educated, sophisticated people.

He promptly invited Jennifer Beale to be his companion for the evening. Jennifer was a debutante who lived outside town with her father—in a Victorian home even more elegant than the one that Jared had ordered built for his grandmother two years ago. She was beautiful and wealthy and cultured— all the things that poor Noelle was not. He'd met Jennifer by chance at a local dry-goods store and had found her shyness and her beauty enchanting. Since then, he'd made a point of finding out her daily routine, and he made certain that he was somewhere nearby on her trips to town.

She seemed to like him. He certainly liked her. Her father was rich, but he'd started out with nothing. He wouldn't look down on Andrew for not being wealthy. Although the family had started out in the highest echelons of society, Andrew's father had lost the family fortune, and Andrew had found himself dependent on his unpleasant stepbrother for his comfort. He hadn't wanted to go to work, because no male member of his family had ever had to go out to work for a living. But last year, Jared had put his foot down and insisted that Andrew start contributing to his own support.

The job at the brick works had been easily obtained, since the owner had been his father's best friend. But Andrew was surprised to find that the job was challenging and that he seemed to do it rather well. He was apparently a born salesman. He wondered if his father would quite approve of his only son becoming a salaried worker, but it no longer mattered. He enjoyed his job, except for the paperwork. However, Noelle was around to take that off his hands, and he was left with only the pleasantest part of the job—enticing people to buy bricks. He was making a good salary, and his family name made him an asset, because often people would trade with him on the basis of it. The Paige name had also appealed to Jennifer, he thought, because it retained some of its former glory. There were even connections to European royalty, which didn't hurt socially. Mrs. Dunn, Jared's grandmother, was also well respected, but nobody knew anything about the Dunns, since they weren't from Texas. Funny, Andrew thought, how little he really knew about his stepmother and her mother—or about Jared.

If Andrew was impressed with his own background, Terrance Beale wasn't. But Jennifer was entranced, especially by Andrew's tales of his heroism in the Spanish-American War. That had been the key to unlock her heart, and Andrew had set about moving in on it. But she was a sheltered, very innocent girl, and it had bothered Andrew that he wasn't even allowed to hold her hand. He was a man who enjoyed an occasional night in a woman's arms; abstinence was painful. There was no way he could go to one of the local brothels without it getting back to Mr. Beale, who knew people everywhere. But Noelle was right under his own roof, and fascinated by him, and he wanted her. The fly in that ointment was Jared, who, instead of turning a blind, indifferent eye had suddenly developed a personal interest in the girl.

Well, he couldn't be everywhere, Andrew thought irritably. Sooner or later, he'd have Noelle, with or without Jared's approval. Meanwhile, having Miss Beale's affection—and the promise of her father's money (she was, after all, an only child) one day—brightened his outlook immeasurably.

The family kept a carriage and a horse at the local livery for use on special occasions. Andrew was forced to ask

Jared's permission to use it, now that Jared was in residence. It rankled.

Jared agreed, because he had no engagement of his own that evening. "Are you taking Miss Brown?" Jared asked pointedly.

Andrew was glad, given that angry stare, that he could deny it. "No. She refused, and I have to admit that I'm a bit relieved," he added. "She has no social sense, you know, and she dresses like a serving woman. Her one saving grace is that delightful body. She's very well formed, don't you agree?" He smiled.

Jared's eyes narrowed. "I haven't paid that much attention to her body. I'll remind you that she's a guest in our home," he said sternly. "I expect you to treat her with courtesy and respect."

Andrew was surprised by Jared's protective attitude, but he tried not to show it. "Why, of course. But Jared, you must have noticed that she's hardly the sort of woman a man wants to be seen with in public." He laughed. "She's very uncultured. She can't even hold a fork properly."

Jared's unspeaking stance rattled him. In the end, he rushed out with hardly a goodbye.

Jared watched him go with mixed emotions. It had been a long time since any woman's honor had mattered to him. He thought back to his one tragic love affair with cold cynicism. Hadn't he learned how treacherous women were by now? But the thought of seeing Noelle ridiculed was bad enough— without worrying if Andrew would seduce her and throw her aside. It made him angry.

It certainly seemed as if Andrew had seduction in mind. His remarks about Noelle had been frankly personal. And it was all too obvious that Noelle found the younger man fascinating. She was inexperienced and smitten, a combination that would work very well in Andrew's favor. Well, if Noelle was endangered by Andrew because she was uncultured, it was time to think about correcting that flaw. There was one appropriate way, but it was going to be up to Jared to implement it. He cursed himself for having to interfere, but as he'd said, the girl was under his protection.

Andrew had complicated his life enough in the past. Now here he was, putting more obstacles in Jared's path. He'd expected his homecoming to Fort Worth to be uncomplicated. He should have known better. Nothing in his life had ever been uncomplicated, least of all where women were concerned.

The night of the dance arrived and Andrew left before the rest of the family sat down to the supper table. He wanted to avoid Jared, whose black looks were making him uncomfortable. But when Andrew was ushered into the house to escort Miss Beale out to the carriage, he got a look as black as Jared's.

Beale was a self-made man who'd risen to prominence because of a knack for investing his meager savings into profitable ventures. He'd invested in a million-to-one shot that a prospector would find oil in East Texas. His small stake had made him rich when the prospector hit one of the deepest wells at Spindletop. He had money to burn.

But Terrance Beale, who was a widower, considered his elegant blonde, blue-eyed only daughter his greatest asset; he didn't want her head turned by fortune hunters. He numbered Andrew among them. He didn't like Andrew and made no secret of it. He made Andrew nervous.

Beale, a lean and dark-faced man, glared at Andrew without speaking.

"I'll have her home by a reasonable hour, I assure you, sir," Andrew said politely.

"You'd better," Beale, a man of few words, replied. He had eyes that were steely and cold.

Andrew thought absently that he'd hate to make a real enemy of the man.

"Now, Papa," Jennifer Beale chided gently as she joined them, beautiful in her lacy black dress and scarf. "Andrew will take excellent care of me. Don't worry so."

The older man seemed to relax. He smiled and beamed at his daughter, then bent to kiss her soft cheek. "Have a good time."

"Yes, I will. I'll see you later, Papa."

She took Andrew's arm and squeezed it comfortingly. "I've so looked forward to tonight, Andrew," she added, smiling up at him. "It's going to be great fun!"

"Certainly it is," he agreed. She made him feel lordly. Her eyes were as soft as Noelle's, looking up at him from a face that would have graced an art gallery.

Terrance Beale watched them go, his eyes narrowed. He couldn't keep the girl in a glass bottle, but he hated seeing her throw herself away on that tame city boy. She deserved better.

He stuck his hands in his pockets and wandered out to the barn. He had a sick foal and he was worried about it.

Brian Clark, a middle-aged black man with a twisted hand, smiled at him as he approached. Clark had appeared out of the dark one November morning carrying a saddle over one dusty shoulder. He'd asked for a job, and Beale, sizing him up in one long glance, had given it without question. He'd never asked where Clark came from, or why he was on foot. In spite of his handicap, Clark was good with horses and he could gentle the meanest of them. Beale had put him to work taming the remuda to a saddle, and he'd never regretted his snap decision. Clark was kind to Jennifer, too, going out of his way to make sure that her horses were the best kept in the stable.

"How is he?" Beale asked.

The other man ran a lean hand over his short curly hair. There were threads of gray in it, but that scarred face wasn't as old as the eyes in it were. He glanced at Beale without the subservient attitude that some of his race wore like a garment. Clark was surprisingly well educated, and he had the bearing of a man who'd wielded authority. He was an odd man altogether, but Beale had always respected him.

"The foal is worse," Clark replied. "He needs more than my poor efforts for a cure. I think you should call the veterinarian."

Beale nodded. "I'll have Ben Tatum come out first thing tomorrow. Will that be soon enough?"

Clark nodded. "I'll sit up with him tonight."

Beale bent and touched the soft coat of the foal, noting its labored breathing. "You know a lot about horses, Clark."

"Yes, sir, I do," Clark replied, with a faint smile.

Beale straightened, eyeing the other man. "Wouldn't care to tell me how, would you?" he asked, with a gleam in his eyes.

Clark chuckled. "You know I wouldn't, Mr. Beale."

"Guess I do, after six years," came the dry reply. "Keep an eye on him. If he gets worse, come get me."

"I'll do that, Mr. Beale."

Beale nodded. He smiled to himself as he left the barn. He was the only man he'd ever heard Clark address as "sir" or "mister." Despite the insults he sometimes got from temporary cowboys who hired on for roundup, Clark had an innate dignity that kept him out of brawls. He kept his temper when Beale lost his own. Once Beale had knocked a mean cowboy down for cursing the black man, who'd taken a quirt away from him. Clark had chided Beale for his lack of control, and then laughed at the other man's outraged expression. They got along well, despite the disparity in their backgrounds. It occurred to Beale that if his foreman ever quit, he'd probably give the job to Clark. The man had the makings of a first-rate boss. Nobody questioned his orders about the remuda. Not even the white cowboys. Well…most of them, anyway. There were a few who didn't like Clark, especially one bullying middle-aged wrangler named Garmon. He was from Mississippi and he hated blacks. He made remarks that Beale would have decked him for, but Clark simply ignored them. Maybe that was the best way to handle it. Beale tended to be too hot-tempered. He'd led a wild life on the border in his youth, before a pretty young Eastern girl had captured his heart and made him human. He smiled, remembering Allison, Jennifer's mother.

He whistled softly through his teeth as he walked back toward the elegant house, thinking how far he'd come from the adobe shanty where he'd been born fifty-five years past. His life had been a hard one, but he'd overcome obstacles that other men had fallen behind. He was proud of his accomplishments. Most of all, he was proud of Jennifer. What a tragedy that her mother had been killed years ago, and had missed seeing what an elegant beauty their daughter had become. His eyes shifted to a lone grave on a small rise, protected by a wrought-iron fence. He put flowers on the grave twice a week. Sometimes he just went over there and sat, talking to Allison as if she were still alive. It helped get him through rough times. He'd go tomorrow, he thought, and tell her about this Andrew person. He was sure that she'd be as irritated at Jennifer's poor choice of suitors as he was himself.

Andrew didn't relax until he and Jennifer were safely ensconced in the carriage and on their way to the restaurant, where they would have supper before they went on to the dance.

"How lucky I am to have such a pretty companion for

the evening," he said, smiling. "Thank you for coming with me."

"It's my pleasure," she said shyly. She laughed. "Papa is so possessive of me, did you notice? Don't pay him any mind, Andrew. He's just old-fashioned—and he worries about me, especially since Mama died."

"Any man with such a beautiful daughter would worry," Andrew said gently. He searched her eyes hungrily. "Jennifer, I've never met anyone like you."

"Nor I, anyone like you," she replied. "When we met at the dry-goods store, it was as if I'd known you all my life."

"If you hadn't spent the past few years in Europe, you would have." He chuckled. "My family has been here for two generations. The first Paige came over from England. He was the second son of a duke, but he inherited nothing. He made his own fortune here. How incredible that we're only just meeting."

She didn't tell him that her father would never have sanctioned such an association. He didn't like Andrew, and he hadn't liked Andrew's wealthy father, either. He didn't like men who were born with all the advantages and did nothing with them. Andrew had been content to lay about and go into and out of three colleges before he finally took a job—having been forced into it by his stepbrother, gossip said—and went to work. Her father considered Andrew a shiftless layabout, leeching on his stepbrother. Jennifer saw him as a man of vision with great potential. It would only take a caring woman to incite him to great acts, she thought romantically, filled with thoughts of idealistic delight. She smiled at him, lost in dreams.

Andrew smiled back. She made him feel that he could accomplish anything. He still couldn't believe his good fortune in having her accept his invitation to dinner and the dance. God willing, it wouldn't be the last time he escorted her of an evening.

If Andrew was having a good time, Noelle wasn't. She was very quiet at supper, avoiding Jared's curious eyes. She excused herself directly after they ate and went to her room, where she remained for the rest of the night.

The next morning, her withdrawn expression and unusual detachment during breakfast drew more attention from an unexpected quarter. Jared stopped her as she was helping Mrs. Pate clear the table after his grandmother had retired to the drawing room to read.

"You're as unhappy this morning as you were at supper last evening. Why?" he asked bluntly, although he already knew the answer.

She was surprised at the question, and at his perception, but she answered readily enough. "Andrew invited me to the dance last night and I had to refuse him."

"Why?"

She gave him a harsh glare. "Because I had nothing to wear. And even if I had a dress, I—" she cleared her throat "—I can't dance."

Both eyebrows lifted. "Why?" he said again.

"My father considered dancing sinful," she said haughtily.

He smiled faintly. "Probably it is, but even a saint could hardly find anything objectionable about a man's gloved hand on a woman's waist over several layers of fabric."

She flushed. "Nevertheless…"

"He took Miss Beale instead."

"I know that!"

"Your temper is showing, Miss Brown," he said wryly.

"You irritate me, Mr. Dunn. Indeed you do!"

He looked down his elegant nose at her. "You have a sin-
gular lack of tact. You dress poorly. You have no idea how
to behave at table or even in a small gathering of socialites.
You're far too outspoken and high tempered and impatient."

She opened her mouth to rage at him, but he held up a lean
hand.

"But you have a certain potential," he continued. "Elegance
and a soft heart, and a pleasant way of speaking. It might be
possible to...remake you."

"Sir?"

"Remake you." He walked around her slowly, leaning heavily on the cane. "With the proper clothes, and some lessons
in social behavior, you should do well in polite company."

"Sir, I can't afford the proper clothes, and I know nothing
of social—"

He waved away her objections. "Money is no problem,
Miss Brown. I like a challenge."

"Why should you want to do this for me?" she asked.

He shrugged. "I haven't decided where in town I want to
open my practice. I'm having a holiday. But I'm bored, Miss
Brown. You present a temporary distraction that will occupy
my mind and my free time."

"Andrew would realize..."

"He would not, unless you tell him," he replied. He pursed
his lips as he studied her. "It would do Andrew good to have
his lack of foresight pointed out to him. He doesn't consider
possibilities."

The excitement she felt bubbled up into her eyes. "He
might find me attractive, if I were more like the ladies of his
acquaintance."

God forbid, Jared was thinking. But he didn't say it. He
wanted to take Andrew down a peg. He didn't want to hurt
Noelle in the process. On the other hand, he might be saving
her from a fate worse than death. While Andrew wouldn't

hesitate to seduce a woman he considered socially inferior, he'd think twice about giving offense to a woman of culture.

Noelle was nothing to him. But he didn't want to see her hurt, even if she did have a low opinion of him as a man. That was vaguely amusing. He wondered how she would have reacted to him as he had been, before he began to study law. Andrew hid it well, but even now he was intimidated by his stepbrother—and without knowing anything of the past.

She would need a wardrobe and some tutoring in simple parlor manners. His eyes narrowed. He could take her shopping, but that would raise eyebrows. He must be circumspect. His grandmother was too old-fashioned to buy Noelle the kind of clothing she should wear. But there was another woman in the household—moreover, one with good taste in clothes—who would buy what Jared told her to.

"Get Mrs. Pate," he said decisively.

She had an idea why he wanted her. She smiled delightedly and went in search of that lady. When the two of them returned, Jared explained to the housekeeper what he wanted of her.

"Take her to Miss Henderson's dress shop," he instructed, "and have her outfitted—in new styles, not the old-fashioned ones. Then stop by the milliner's and the shoe store. She must have at least two gowns for evening, and a wrap."

Mrs. Pate was staring at him with her mouth faintly ajar.

He gave her a long-suffering look. "She's family, isn't she?" he demanded, and swept an impatient hand toward Noelle. "It's hardly proper to let her walk around like that!"

Noelle drew herself up. Her nice black skirt and spotless white blouse were hardly rags. "'Like that'?" she demanded belligerently. "What do you mean, 'like that'?"

"You're a haughty woman," Jared remarked as he searched her flashing green eyes under her mop of auburn hair in its upswept knot. "Even in outdated clothing, you have the arrogance of royalty."

She took a quick breath. He was offering to help her attract Andrew. She must keep her head and not take offense at every word. "I realize that my clothes are plain. I don't mean to appear ungrateful," she began.

"Good," he retorted. "Then be quiet, Miss Brown, and do what you're told. Take her now, Mrs. Pate, before she has time to think up excuses to stay home."

Mrs. Pate was beginning to get into the spirit of the thing. "Very well, sir."

Noelle hesitated while Mrs. Pate went to get her hat and her light coat, because it was raining again. "Are you sure?" she asked.

He nodded and one blue eye narrowed. "How do you feel about Andrew?"

She caught her breath. "Mr. Dunn—"

"You and I can be honest with each other," he interrupted. "I won't lie to you. I'll expect the same courtesy in return. We have more in common than you might realize, despite the disparity in our ages."

She was surprised by the blunt way he spoke to her, but she felt at home with him, safe, secure, even though he stirred her up inside in unexpected ways.

"I like Andrew. He's dashing and exciting…" She studied him in some confusion. "But I've never known anyone like you," she said slowly.

"I know."

Her eyes went over his face like tracing fingertips, over the dark complexion, the thin eyebrows and steady blue eyes, the straight nose, the high cheekbones and thin mouth with its slightly fuller lower lip, his firm jaw and thrusting chin. He didn't wear a mustache, as Andrew did, in defiance of the fashion. He was extremely good-looking. There was an intelligence in his pale blue eyes that mingled with something dark and reckless and a little frightening, something that was odd in the face of a stoic lawyer. And then, when he smiled at her, there was an expression of faint sensuality that made her toes want to curl up inside her lace-up shoes.

He searched her eyes and then let his own gaze run over her face, from her auburn hair to her soft green eyes, over the faint freckles on her straight nose and the pink sweetness of her full, pretty mouth. He liked its Cupid's bow shape, and the row of even white teeth behind it. She had a nice shape, too, not voluptuous but certainly not slender. She came up to his chin, and he had a strange urge to pull her into his lean body and see how it felt to grind his mouth into the softness of her full lips.

She'd never learned to read a man's expressions, but there was a tension between herself and Jared that made her knees feel wobbly.

"I, uh, I should get my cloak," she said in a voice that wasn't quite steady.

He nodded. He hadn't spoken, but his eyes caught hers and held them, unblinking—for so long that she felt the heat go into her cheeks.

"How old are you, Noelle?" he asked abruptly.

"I—I'm nineteen."

The hand that wasn't holding the cane lifted to a tiny wisp of auburn hair that had escaped her wide bun and was lying against her flushed cheek. He lifted it in his long fingers and gently slid it behind her ear, making the gesture a very sensuous caress. He watched her lips part as her breath escaped, as if she'd been holding it. Her eyes flickered up to his and down to his throat, quickly. The lace at her neck fluttered as her heartbeat raced there. She was attracted to him, there was no longer any doubt in his mind about it.

His fingertip traced the circle of her small ear, from outside to inside, and then down to the tiny lobe.

"Buy something in blue silk," he said, his voice deep and slow and sultry. "Sapphire-blue, mind you, with white lace trim."

"It—it would— My eyes are green," she stammered, hardly realizing what she was saying in the shivery silence.

"I know. But the blue will suit you." His thumb pressed against the artery in her neck and he felt it jump as he touched her skin. His own heart was none too quiet, now. Perhaps he'd been away from women too long, because this child-woman was having a savage effect on him.

She was so shaken that her hands had gone cold where she clutched her skirt in them. Frightened, she stared into his pale eyes and found them glittering down at her from narrowed eyelids, steady and frightening in their single-minded intensity.

The violence of the tension had almost reached snapping point when a door slammed and they both moved back, as if deliberately trying to break some unseen thread that bound them momentarily together.

"I'm grateful for your generosity," she said. Her voice sounded choked.

"It's little enough to do for a member of my family," he said firmly, emphasizing the word.

She didn't look up. What she felt was hardly familial, but she might have misread his expression. She knew little enough about men and their appetites. She might have been imagining his interest. After all, he was much older than she…

"How old are you?" she asked suddenly.

His jaw clenched. "Too old for you, Noelle," he said softly, and abruptly turned away, gripping the cane so hard that his fingers grew white as he walked out of the room.

* * *

The shopping spree was rewarding in the extreme. Noelle had never had such pretty things to wear before. Mindful of Jared's instructions, she did find a dress in sapphire-blue silk, trimmed in white lace and silver bead decoration. She also found a sapphire velvet suit on sale with white ermine trim. She balked at even its marked-down price, but Mrs. Pate didn't bat an eyelid. It would do nicely for next fall and winter, she said, and how it suited Noelle!

Noelle, like most other women, made most of her own clothes. To have store-bought things was new and very exciting, like being part of high society.

She steered Noelle toward the skirts and dresses, and then to the dainty underthings. She bought silk chemises and bloomers and hose, and Noelle felt naughty just handling them.

The milliner's presented an equally exciting experience. Noelle found a sapphire velvet hat that just matched her suit, and two others that went with the lightweight, black-trimmed green suit and the navy-blue-and-white suit she'd bought. Little Miss McAlpine had made the hats herself, creating each one with a flair for design that rivaled Paris. She fitted Noelle and enthused over the way the colors brightened her pretty auburn hair.

The last stop was the shoe shop, where Noelle stood firm about simple black shoes with no frills. Jared had spent quite enough on her, without breaking the bank on shoes that wouldn't even be seen unless she was getting out of a buggy.

"I feel like a princess," she remarked to Mrs. Pate as they went home in the hired carriage. The parcels would be sent on that afternoon from each store.

There was one last stop. Mrs. Pate left a grocery list with

Mr. Haynes at the local market, with instructions to have the food sent out after lunch.

They arrived back at home just in time for Mrs. Pate to start lunch.

Mrs. Dunn and Jared were in the parlor with Andrew when an excited, happy Noelle arrived. She thought of all her lovely purchases and how Andrew would notice how pretty she would look in them.

He glanced up from his newspaper, smiling absently. "There you are! Where have you been, dear girl?"

"I went to town with Mrs. Pate," she said.

"How boring. Come. I'll let you ride to the office with me, if you like. I have to pick up some papers. There's just time before luncheon is served."

"Could I?" she exclaimed, forgetting her resolve to be cool and distant after he so easily replaced her company for the dance.

"Of course." He folded the paper and got up. "We won't be late," he assured his stepbrother and grandmother. "Let me get my hat and coat, Noelle. It seems to be rather wet outside. I'll meet you at the front door in five minutes."

"All right."

He left, and Noelle turned to find Jared watching her with vague amusement.

"They're sending the things on to the house," she said hesitantly.

He nodded. "I hope you found some things you liked," he said carelessly.

"Why, yes. There were two warm-weather suits and a winter suit in sapphire velvet—"

He got up from the sofa, leaning on the cane. "I'm sure Grandmother would enjoy hearing about it when you return. I have to go out."

He passed her without another word, leaving her lost

and confused by the polite snub. The whole thing had been his idea.

When the door closed behind him, Noelle grimaced. "Have I offended him?" she asked.

Mrs. Dunn smiled. "No, dear, of course not. Jared broods. From time to time, he seems very distant, but that's just his nature. He isn't a family man, or a social man. He keeps to himself, just as he did when he was younger. You mustn't take offense at his manner."

"Oh, I don't, not at all. I just wanted to thank him for my things," she explained.

"He knows that you appreciate them. Now run along with Andrew and have a good time."

"Thank you, Mrs. Dunn. Thank you for everything."

Mrs. Dunn waved her away with a smile. But she was concerned. Noelle was a very innocent woman and Andrew was experienced. He could hurt her badly. Her infatuation with him was noticeable, which was not a point in her favor. Andrew thrived on admiration from women. Mrs. Dunn hoped that there would be no complications because of this growing interest.

Andrew was pleasant company, friendly and attentive, and Noelle blossomed under his regard. He held her hand in the carriage while he told her about his sales job with the brick company and how he'd topped their records already. He was hoping for a management position eventually.

"I was an officer in the army, you know," he added, with a smile. "I do know how to get things done."

"I'm sure you do, Andrew," she said huskily.

He smoothed his fingers over her gloved hand and looked deep into her eyes. She adored him, and his attention was flattering. But she felt no thrill when he touched her, and that was puzzling. Jared had only traced his fingers around her ear and she had gone weak in the knees. Of course, Jared was older and experienced. She thought of him with a woman and her face colored. She could almost see him, those blue eyes flashing like summer lightning in his eyes as he held a woman close against his lean body and kissed her to within an inch of her life…

"Are you all right?" Andrew asked, frowning. "You're very flushed."

"It's hot in here, isn't it?" she improvised, fanning with her gloved hand.

Andrew only smiled. He assumed that she was reacting to his closeness, and it made him arrogant. He couldn't touch Jennifer, not if he wanted to win her. But there was nothing stopping him where Noelle was concerned. Nothing except Jared, that was, and what Jared didn't know wouldn't hurt him. "We're almost there," he murmured.

She glanced past him out the window at the row of businesses that graced the long, wide street. "How long have you worked here?" she asked to divert him.

"Since last year," he said, without telling her that Jared had more or less demanded that he find work. "I had hoped to advance much more quickly, but I suppose I'm doing well enough. I must say, I really am in my element with selling, and we have a superior product, too."

"Are there different sorts of bricks, then?" she asked innocently.

He laughed. "Dear girl, there certainly are! And inferior grades can be extremely dangerous when used in construction projects. Why, a building actually fell down in California only weeks ago because the bricks used to build it were fired improperly."

"I had no idea," she said, listening intently. "How very interesting."

"I must educate you in the brick trade," he said, and smiled again at her interest.

The carriage stopped. Andrew helped her out of the cab and paid the driver, then escorted her into the tall brick building that held the headquarters office of James Collier & Sons. He introduced her to the two girls who worked in the front, writing out invoices and taking orders over the telephone.

"It's just like the study at home, isn't it?" Noelle asked excitedly. "It's so modern!"

She was still getting used to the modern equipment, although it felt more familiar to her now. She'd lived in rural areas most of her life. The telephone fascinated her, like so many of the modern gadgets that could be found in most households in Fort Worth nowadays. She did know now how to use a typewriter and a Dictaphone, though. She felt proud of her small accomplishments.

"Compared to some places, I suppose so. We don't have electric streetcars yet, but that sort of progress will come, soon enough."

Andrew took her elbow and guided her into a small cubbyhole of an office, which contained a desk and some war mementos and a framed portrait of himself in his uniform.

"How very handsome!" she exclaimed as she stood before it.

"Thank you. I do miss the uniform at times."

"Your office is very nice," she added, glancing round at the rolltop desk and swivel chair, and the two wing chairs by the potbellied stove, presumably for visitors to sit in.

"It's tiny," he said gruffly, "but someday I hope to have one big enough to suit my needs."

He stuck his hands in his pockets and stood beside the curtained window, studying Noelle in her black skirt and white, high-necked blouse, the old brown cloak wrapped around her for shelter from the rain. She was very dowdy. But she was pretty. If only she had better manners and clothes she would be outstanding.

She turned, catching his eyes on her, and flushed. "The cloak is old," she murmured. "I have a new one, but I didn't have time to put it on. In fact, I have a lot of new clothes," she added.

His eyebrows lifted. "Indeed?"

"Your grandmother insisted," she said, reluctant to mention Jared. He'd told her that Andrew need not know the source of her windfall, and now she was vaguely ashamed not to tell Andrew the truth. Jared had been generous and kind, and she was ignoring his part in her new wardrobe. But to tell Andrew where her things came from...

"Grandmother was right," Andrew agreed. "You are family, after all. What did Jared say?"

"He said that I must have some clothes," she hedged.

He apparently saw no significance in that, assuming that Mrs. Dunn had orchestrated the shopping. "So you should. I will enjoy seeing you in your new things."

She wanted to tell him that she was going to learn how to behave in proper company and how to speak like a lady, but he was already back on his favorite subject: himself.

"As you see, I have my own telephone," he said, gesturing toward the black stick instrument, "and another Dictaphone, just like the one in the study at home."

"Yes, I did notice." Her eyes brightened. "Andrew, I don't suppose you need another girl in your office?" she asked hopefully.

He hesitated. He didn't want Noelle here, of all places, where he hoped to have Miss Beale meet him for lunch once in a while. "I, uh, share a secretary with Mr. Blair, our vice president. Come along and I'll introduce you to him." He picked up a sheaf of papers from his wooden filing cabinet, checked it and then opened the door for Noelle, ignoring her faint blush.

Mr. Blair was an older man, very businesslike and brief. He nodded curtly to her and went about his business. The owner of the firm wasn't in, nor were any of the other executives. Andrew led her back into the outer office and introduced her to Trudy and Jessica, the secretaries. They, at least, were friendly. But it didn't escape Noelle's notice that they were cool until Andrew introduced her as his cousin. Both were young and pretty, and apparently unmarried. Andrew flirted with them gently, which made Noelle feel like an intruder. It embarrassed her that she'd as good as asked him for a job. What a silly thing to do!

"Nice girls," he remarked as they left, having said their goodbyes. "They'd do anything for me, you know."

That had been very obvious. "They seem efficient," she remarked.

"Indeed they are. Charming girls."

He hailed another carriage and put Noelle into it before he joined her, his papers, in their file, clutched in one hand.

"I have to take work home to get it all done," he said, chuckling. "It's a very responsible position. They depend on me."

"I expect you're very good at your job," she said.

He nodded, leaning his head back to close his eyes. He stifled a yawn. "I must keep better hours. Miss Beale is a delightful companion." Before Noelle could bristle, he turned his head and looked at her. "Perhaps next time I ask you to a dance, you will come with me."

"I had nothing to wear," she said shyly.

"Nothing? Why didn't you say so?"

"I was too embarrassed."

"Then what a good thing that my grandmother offered to kit you out," he said, grinning.

She only nodded. It hadn't been that way at all. Jared had noticed her sadness and reacted to it. Andrew hadn't. But he was still the most dashing, exciting man Noelle had ever met. Poor old Jared was hardly anyone's idea of a man of action, after all, even if he did have a strange effect on Noelle's nerves. She might have imagined that, she told herself firmly. Surely it had been pity that had affected her when he stood so close and touched her. She could hardly be attracted to him and in love with Andrew.

Andrew grasped her hand in his and sighed. "I'm very glad that you came to live with us."

"So am I."

He squeezed her hand. "You mustn't mind Jared. He's moody and withdrawn. I hardly know him."

"But you're brothers."

"Stepbrothers. His mother married my father. He was a grown man then, and I was just out of knee pants." He stretched lazily. "We never had the chance to learn anything about each other. He went to law school up North and I finished school and went into the army. We're nothing alike." He glanced at her. "He's very reserved. Almost cold. Do you find him intimidating?"

She only smiled. "A little."

His head shifted. "He isn't to me, of course," he said quickly. "But he has this way of looking at people when he's annoyed; it's rather like having a hole bored into you." He chuckled. "Odd, isn't it? A lawyer with a killer's stare. Perhaps he looks at witnesses like that, and it's why he wins so many cases. I've heard that he has quite a reputation in criminal law. Odd that he'd want to leave a successful partnership in New York to practice law here."

"He's old, isn't he?" Noelle asked.

"Old?" He pursed his lips. "To you, I suppose he is. Thirty-six, I believe."

"Oh." She looked at her skirt and picked off a tiny piece of lint. Thirty-six to her nineteen; of course, she would be twenty in December. That still made him sixteen years older than herself. It was a gap.

"I shall be twenty-eight on my next birthday."

"When is it?" she asked.

"In November," he replied. "And your birthday?"

"In December. I was a Christmas baby, so I was named Noelle," she explained.

He laughed delightedly. "I shall wrap your present in holly." He studied her narrowly and a wicked gleam came into his eyes. "On second thought, I shall wrap it in mistletoe," he teased softly. "And you can kiss me for it."

"Andrew!"

"But we must make certain that Jared doesn't know," he added, teasing, but serious just the same. "We wouldn't want him to send you away, would we? And he might not approve of, shall we say, too much affection between us."

"I shan't say a word," she promised, and then blushed as she thought of the possibilities.

He laughed uproariously at her shocked and delighted expression. He knew that she was his for the asking. It made him feel smug. Women always reacted that way to his flirting. He was handsome and eligible and well to do, and women loved him. It was hardly surprising that Noelle found him fascinating. He liked her, too. But only as a diversion. His mind was already back on the night before, on the delightful Miss Beale and her father's immense fortune.

Chapter Five

The parcels arrived by late afternoon, and Noelle flew upstairs to try on her new things. Her favorite was the blue velvet suit. It was a winter garment that hadn't sold at its original price, and had been marked down for the spring trade. She adored it. Having no knowledge of the fact that most store-bought clothes were fashionable only from season to season, she was certain that she could wear it next fall and winter and it would still look right in style. She had seen drawings of this suit in the local paper and wanted it badly, but its price had been beyond her pocket. The drawings didn't have the striking color of her suit, and despite her misgivings about it, the hue suited not only her hair but her eyes, as well. Jared had been right. It was a color made for her.

She donned the hat that matched it, and the new shoes, and primped before her mirror, making sure not a hair of her coiffure was out of place. She pinched her cheeks to make them rosy and smiled at her reflection. She wasn't beautiful, but her features weren't ugly, either.

Anticipating Andrew's response to her new look, she went downstairs to the living room, where she'd left the family. But when she arrived, only Jared was there.

He looked up and saw her in the doorway, and his features seemed to freeze. She was a vision in the suit, and the color looked as he had imagined it on her. The vivid shade brought her face to vibrant life. He caught his breath.

"Wh-where's Andrew?" she asked, disconcerted by his stare.

The expression left his face. "He took Grandmother to town for some crocheting thread," he replied. "She meant to have Mrs. Pate pick it up this morning when she did the weekly shopping, but she didn't foresee that I would send you with her or that you'd leave so early. She didn't have time to give her the sample to match."

"Oh, I see."

Her expression was now morose and disappointed. She had a parasol that matched the pretty outfit and it was point-down on the floor now.

Jared stood up slowly and walked, with the aid of his cane, to meet her in the doorway.

"You look lovely," he said kindly. "Andrew would certainly tell you so if he were here."

She smiled wanly. "Thank you. And you were right about the color."

"A woman with your pale complexion needs bright colors."

"My face isn't so pale," she said defensively, touching her cheek with a gloved hand.

He lifted an eyebrow. "Not when you pinch your cheeks to make them color," he teased.

She laughed deep in her throat. "You aren't supposed to know that I did that."

His chest rose and fell under his nice gray suit as he studied her. "You have a pronounced drawl," he said.

She bit her lower lip. "I must learn to enunciate."

He shook his head. "The accent is part of you, part of your heritage," he said. "It has a charm all its own."

"But you said that I had a backcountry drawl!"

He smiled. "To someone from New York, anyone in Texas does," he clarified.

"Aren't you from Texas?" she asked him curiously.

The smile faded. "No." He shifted his cane. "This suit is lovely, but impractical for warm weather. Did you buy some things for late spring and summer?"

"Of course, but nothing is as lovely as this," she said. She peeped up at him shyly. "It *is* lovely, isn't it?"

He laughed mockingly. "It isn't the suit that you want me to admire," he taunted softly.

She glowered at him. "You're generous but very disagreeable," she informed him.

"I know too much about women," he said, and for an instant, there was a chilling lack of feeling in his eyes.

Her hand contracted on the handle of the parasol. "You shouldn't speak of such things."

His face lifted. "In the normal course of things, no. But I said that we would be honest with each other."

She stared at him and her thin brows drew together. "I don't understand."

"What don't you understand?"

"Why you…disturb me so," she said reluctantly. "And yet, I feel as if I've known you for a long time. I feel…safe with you."

The iciness left his blue eyes. He moved no closer, yet his presence seemed to envelop her like a cloak. His eyes narrowed as he watched her without speaking, without blinking, in that way that was peculiarly his.

"Are you certain that you feel…safe?" he asked deeply.

She held up a gloved hand in a curious little gesture, like someone warding off an unseen invader.

He caught the hand in his free one, and she felt the pressure through every cell in her body. Holding hands with Andrew in the carriage had been nothing like this. She was drowning in sensations she had never experienced.

Older than she, he understood her feelings as she obviously didn't. He smiled and let go of her hand. "The suit is becoming," he said then, turning away. He didn't have the heart to tell her that it would be out of fashion by the next winter season. Let her enjoy it if it pleased her. "Andrew will find you devastating." He paused, glancing at her over his shoulder. "Have a care, though. Andrew isn't a marrying man."

"Sir!"

"I said that I would be honest with you, Noelle," he reminded her. He stopped in the doorway to the hall. "I've ordered a Gramophone, by the way," he said to surprise her. "When it arrives, I'm going to teach you to dance."

Her heart lifted. "You? But…" Her eyes went silently to his leg.

He laughed. "I see. How, you wonder, is an old, crippled city lawyer going to teach you to dance?"

It was so close to her thoughts that she flushed, giving him the answer he already knew.

He only nodded. "It's just as well that you know so little about me," he said absently, studying her. "I have enough regrets, without adding you to them."

With that puzzling rejoiner, he left her alone in her finery.

In the three weeks that followed, Jared decided on a vacant office downtown and rented it for his practice. He hired carpenters and had it renovated in a style that suited him. He had carpets and curtains and furniture installed, along with the latest office equipment. Then he employed a male secretary to run the office for him when he had to be away. That last act bothered Noelle, who was harboring secret hopes that he might ask her to come to work for him. But he didn't. In fact, he never mentioned the possibility, despite the fact that she still spent two out of every four nights hard at work in the study, typing up letters and doing paperwork for Andrew.

Last of all, Jared had his shingle suspended on a post at the door: JARED DUNN, ATTORNEY-AT-LAW.

Noelle mustered all her nerve to ask Jared about the male secretary as he was leaving the house to go to the office one morning.

"Why did you hire a man for your secretary? Don't you trust women employees?" she asked.

He hesitated at the door, hat in hand, and smiled at her without warmth. "No."

He put on his hat and left.

Noelle commented about it to Mrs. Dunn later, only to find that the older woman understood completely.

"Jared doesn't trust women, not at all," she told Noelle.

"There must be a reason."

She nodded. "An unscrupulous woman was responsible for involving him in a…violent and tragic situation when he was a young man, before he went North to study law. She stole some money and lied about it, and accused a young cowboy of beating her and forcing her to help him steal the money. Because of her, an innocent man died."

She didn't add that Jared had killed the man in question in a gunfight, or that the woman had later confessed that the cowboy wasn't responsible at all for her bruises. She was arrested for her crime. But although the cowboy had been armed and it was a fair fight, Jared blamed himself.

He'd taken to strong drink when he'd learned the truth, and for a few violent months, he'd been a gunman in Kansas. He'd soon left there for an even wilder life on the border, and a twist of fate had sent him to work on the right side of the law. But his mother's sudden illness had called him to Fort Worth, where he had lived with his mother and stepfather and Mrs. Dunn until his mother's death. Andrew, who had been away at boarding school, didn't see the steely-eyed desperado who arrived in Fort Worth on the evening train that fateful day. He wouldn't have recognized that Jared. Mrs. Dunn remembered, though, and was grateful for kindly providence, which had spared her grandson a violent death.

"And now your grandson thinks that all women are unscrupulous," Noelle guessed.

Mrs. Dunn drew her thoughts back to the present. "Perhaps he's learned over the years that honest women exist. But he isn't a ladies' man. Not that he's unattractive to women," she added quickly. "Although at your age, Noelle, you may not see him in the same light that a mature woman would."

In fact, Noelle found herself drawn to Jared unwillingly, and as she spent more time around him, she learned that he was complex and mysterious. She was curious about who he was behind the solemn, stoic expression that he wore constantly. Only his eyes were alive in his face, and there were times when she thought she saw terrible pain in them—not physical pain, either.

His limp was less pronounced now, surprisingly. Perhaps he was disguising his limp for fear that it would affect his clientele, she thought, and then dismissed the thought as frivolous. Possibly the sunny weather had made his leg ache less.

When the Gramophone arrived, she had to wait until he volunteered dance lessons again. He didn't do it immediately, either. He was involved in a meticulous land-swindle case that required long days and Saturday work, as well. She wondered if he'd forgotten his promise to groom her socially. She had to work up the nerve to ask him, but he'd been so busy lately that she hadn't liked to worry him with her problems.

She'd have loved Andrew to teach her those things, and to dance. But it would be less than honorable to ask him when Jared had already volunteered.

But if Jared was distant now, Andrew was, in fact, very attentive. He approved of her new wardrobe and complimented her on each new outfit, although he was strangely hesitant to mention the blue suit she'd purchased on sale. He began to seek her out to talk, but always around the house. He never offered to take her out of an evening, and she knew that he was openly going to theater engagements and dinner with Miss Beale at least once a week.

Jared was too involved in his practice to notice Andrew's sudden preoccupation with making Noelle happy. And when the Gramophone arrived, he put it aside and tried to ignore it. But when he had his office arranged as he liked it, and began to attract his first clients, he became aware that there was a social-club dance upcoming. Andrew had mentioned it, and Noelle had sighed, as if she knew that he wouldn't ask her, finery or no finery. He saw Noelle watching him with curious, hopeful glances for several days before the date of the dance. He couldn't put her off any longer. He wasn't sure if he was sorry or not.

One Friday evening, when Andrew was still out of town on a visit to see a Houston builder and Mrs. Dunn had retired to her room to read, Jared sought out Noelle in the parlor and invited her into the living room.

He was wearing a neat dark blue vested suit. He looked

elegant and rich. Noelle, in her lacy white blouse and dark blue skirt, matched him uncannily.

"Oh, you're going to teach me to dance!" she enthused.

He closed the sliding doors to the living room. "Hopefully. My grandmother finds some of the newer dances sinful."

"I expect you know them all?" she teased.

He glared at her, resting his cane against the wall as he cranked the Gramophone.

"Forgive me," she said demurely, and without a great deal of sincerity.

"A simple two-step is the easiest dance," he told her. He turned as the soft, sweet tune came from the instrument with its huge trumpet speaker. "Come here."

She went to him, thrilling to the deep note of his voice as he waited for her, arms at his side.

"It won't hurt your leg to do this?" she asked.

"Would I volunteer if it did?" he snapped.

She grasped her skirt in both hands with a huffy noise.

"Probably! You and I both know that you wouldn't go back on your word if you knew your leg would break when you tried to dance on it!"

"You know me very well, don't you? Or you think you do," he added coolly.

The look in his eyes made her restless. She dropped her gaze to his chin. "We don't really ever know other people," she replied.

"So it seems." He wasn't wearing gloves. She didn't notice until she felt the strength and heat of his hand at her corseted waist. Even through whalebone stays and the heavy duck fabric of the corset, and the softer muslin of her chemise and her cotton blouse, his touch was disturbing. He was also uncannily strong for such a slender man. At close range, he was much more muscular than he appeared.

"Don't look at your feet," he said curtly when she started to peer down past her long skirt.

"How can I see what I'm doing?" she asked reasonably.

"Dancing is mostly instinct," he said. "Listen to the music and move with it."

She tried, and stepped on his booted foot. She grimaced. "Excuse me."

He sighed irritably and stopped. "Let me lead," he said firmly.

"But I was. I didn't expect you to stop so suddenly."

"I was turning."

"Oh." She listened to the beat and forced her feet to follow. But almost at once, he started toward her, and she tripped on her skirt.

"God almighty, can't you watch where you're putting your damned feet!" he cursed, catching her.

"You have a foul mouth and a nasty temper!" she admonished, breathlessly clutching his hard arms to keep her balance. "This was your suggestion, remember; you offered to teach me to dance. I don't remember begging you to."

He laughed under his breath and his eyes kindled with odd flames. "Your tongue has the fire of your hair in lamplight," he remarked, watching the glow of it. "It's like sunset—gossamer strands, dancing with fiery light."

She felt her breath stop. Her eyes became lost in his.

"That surprises you?" he asked quietly. "A staid, bookwormish attorney should be incapable of flowery prose, is that what you think?"

"You don't seem the sort of man to mince words," she replied evasively. "Or the sort to flatter."

His gaze fell to her soft mouth. "And if I should tell you that it isn't flattery?"

She forced a laugh. "You're teasing, sir."

His arm contracted abruptly, riveting her soft body to his

long, hard one. He looked into her eyes—so close that she
could see the dark blue circles around the pale blue irises.
His body was like warm steel, and the arm enclosing her was
inflexible. He still looked at her mouth, with an intensity that
should have made her apprehensive. It did, but not in a fearful
way.

The feel of his muscular strength was new and electrifying.
When his head started to bend, her heart stopped and then
ran wild.

His mouth poised over hers as he began to move to the
music. She hung there, waiting, breathless. Her feet followed
where his led, while the soft tune enveloped them timelessly.
His breath touched her lips. She could almost taste the mint tea
that had recently graced it, warmly scented. He wore cologne,
because its spicy scent was in her nostrils, too. She watched
his hard mouth hover; her body felt swollen with sensation.
She became boneless, dependent on his strength to keep her
upright as he moved and moved her to the slow, soft beat of
the music.

As it ended, he turned sharply and lowered her against
his side, so that her body was angled across the whole warm,
muscular length of his. And while she clung to him to avoid
falling backward, his head bent, and she felt the threat of his
hard mouth just above hers for one long, sweet, heady second.
If only he would bend, she thought breathlessly, just a fraction
of an inch… If only, if only! Her nails bit into his shoulders
and her lips parted in anticipation.

But he barely hesitated before he drew her back to her feet
and moved away from her, holding her by the waist only for a
few seconds before his arm dropped. He didn't smile. His eyes
searched hers, looking for secrets. She could barely breathe
normally. Her face was flushed, her eyes blank from the brief,
exciting threat of his lips. She looked at him disorientedly,

confused, the lace at her breasts fluttering with the desperation of her heartbeats.

He stared back, unmoving, as the needle dragged against the cartridge with a scratchy sound that repeated unheard.

The sound of the grandfather clock was louder than the static, each beat a heartbeat in the tense silence.

Jared searched her eyes slowly, letting only them touch her. They moved from her flushed face to her mouth, down to the faint tremble of her breasts, the clasp of her hands tight at her waist, over her rounded hips and down the length of the skirt, to the tips of her black shoes under the long ruffle.

An eternity of seconds later, that bold gaze worked its way back up. She hadn't moved. Her lips were parted and her breathing was audible.

"Have you been kissed, Noelle?" he asked.

She shook her head slowly.

He let out a short breath. He looked worried. Puzzled. Confused. Hesitant. One hand clenched at his side. Only then did she notice that his own chest was rising and falling a little roughly.

"You're a guest under my roof," he said huskily. "I can't allow myself to forget it, any more than I can permit such abandon by my stepbrother."

"I—I haven't invited..." she stammered.

"Of course not," he replied quietly. "You're young, Noelle, and very innocent. One of us must act responsibly." He moved to the Gramophone and cut if off. His hand lingered absently on the trumpet. "We'll continue this when we aren't alone," he said.

She flushed as she stared at his long back. It sounded as if he was accusing her of tempting him.

But then he turned—and she saw that she was mistaken. His gaze was intent but not accusing.

He pleased her eyes, she thought as she looked at him. He

had a grace of carriage, an arrogance, that was as different from Andrew's swagger as night was from day. He had the look of authority about him, and it needed no medals on his chest to make it known.

"You're staring," he said softly.

"Forgive me. I…like looking at you," she confessed shyly. "You said that we were to be honest with each other," she added when his eyes narrowed.

He let out a long breath. "So I did." He smiled faintly.

"It didn't hurt your poor leg?" she asked quickly.

He shook his head. "I've had worse than this, you know. It isn't the first…mishap I've ever suffered," he added, biting back the word *bullet,* which had come naturally to his lips before he stopped it.

She straightened her skirt. "Jared, what were you like as a boy?" she asked curiously.

His face stiffened. "Like most boys, I got into mischief as often as possible." He took out his pocket watch and flipped it open. "I have to find a legal precedent among my law books in the study. Excuse me."

She touched his arm lightly as he started to pass her and looked up into his face. "Jared, you said that we'd be honest with each other," she reminded him.

The sound of his name on her lips, heard for the first time, made him hungry. He could feel the heat from her body, she was so close to him. She presented a temptation that was very disturbing to him. Involuntarily his lean fingers went to her throat and moved lightly to her lips. "Say my name again," he said quietly.

Her heart raced. "Jared," she whispered obediently.

He took her small chin between his thumb and forefinger and drew it up so that her lips were poised under his searching gaze. Yes, she would let him kiss her. In fact, the hunger she felt was visible, because she was too young and vulnerable to hide it. And he was tempted. He was more than tempted. He had ached intolerably at the feel of her soft, untouched body in his arms. But stronger than desire, his or hers, was his sense of honor. She was a guest under his roof, deserving of his protection. He had no right to make her feel insecure or uncomfortable because of his advances, even if she did think she wanted them. Honor, he thought, could be trying at times.

With a short, rough breath he released her.

"It's late," he said in a tone so gruff that it was unfamiliar.

Her eyes searched his. She frowned, because her own helpless hunger for him puzzled her. She was shaky all over from his nearness, but his face was like stone.

He turned away from her, seemingly with no regret at all. "Good night, Noelle," he said carelessly.

"Jared," she said weakly, searching for a way to ask him why he was so reluctant to come close to her.

He picked up his cane and leaned on it while he searched her eyes. "There are dark places in my soul," he said unexpectedly, as if he knew what she was thinking. "You know only what I allow you to see. There are things I could never tell you. Be my friend, Noelle. But expect no more than that from me. Your mouth is sweet and it tempts me more than you might realize. But I have nothing to give you. And you have nothing to offer that I haven't had before."

She flushed and drew herself up to her full height. "You needn't sound as if I were flinging myself at you! You're a mature man and I haven't ever known anyone like you before," she began proudly, to explain her helplessness.

He didn't smile. "Yes, I know. You're vulnerable with me and you don't understand why, because you think you're attracted to Andrew. But I don't think that you really want him, Noelle. And that may spare you some heartache."

"Why?"

"Because Andrew wants you."

She felt her cheeks go hot. "He's my friend."

"He wants you," he persisted, narrow-eyed and intent. "Take care that you spend very little time alone with him. He's a gentleman, but only to a point. My stepbrother's something of a rake. I wouldn't see you hurt for all the world."

She frowned. "This is interesting advice from a man who very nearly kissed me!"

"A very chaste encounter, for a man like me," he returned, and there was something dangerous in the set of his head, in his eyes. "You tempt the fall of fire every time you permit me to touch you. Be careful. Scruples are new to me. In the old days, I lived quite well without any, and Fort Worth brings back hard memories."

"You demand honesty from me, but you share nothing of your past with me."

"Total honesty is for lovers," he said bluntly. "And that's something that you and I will never be."

She put a hand to her throat, wide-eyed. "I should certainly think not!" she said, flustered.

"You feel the stirring of the blood in your veins for the first time with me," he continued, ignoring her flush. "I'm flattered. But I want no more madness."

"Is it madness?" she queried.

He laughed shortly. "Isn't it?" He opened the door and went through it. He didn't look back.

It was a trait of his that Noelle had noticed lately. And it wasn't the only one that caught her eye. There were others, like sitting with his back to the wall in any chair he frequented— and asking for a caller's identity before he opened a door. He was an exceptionally cautious man. She wondered what had happened in his past to make him that way. Even as her mind posed the question, she knew with certainty that he would never willingly tell her. He was a man with secrets, and he seemed very adept at keeping them.

Chapter Six

Because he'd been so short with her, almost insulting, while he taught her to dance, Noelle had expected Jared to leave her strictly alone afterward. But that wasn't the case.

In the days that followed, although Jared was still reserved and moody, he spent a surprising amount of time with Noelle— teaching her proper table manners and parlor manners, to the amusement of Mrs. Dunn. No one except Noelle noticed that he insisted that Mrs. Dunn be present while he conducted these "classes."

Fortuitously, Andrew was still out of town on business, which prevented any embarrassing comments from his quarter on Jared's preoccupation with their young houseguest. He'd already explained his motivation to Mrs. Dunn, without going into great detail. She only smiled and gave her wholehearted approval. Like Jared, she, too, was worried by the girl's infatuation with footloose Andrew. Andrew had been unusually attentive to the girl as well, and that was disturbing, especially when Andrew seemed equally bent on the courtship of the eligible Miss Beale.

Usually Mrs. Dunn was present when Jared coached Noelle. But on one occasion, she wasn't.

"No, no, no!" Jared muttered, rocking on his heels with his hands deep in his pockets as he watched her flop in a chair. "Sit like a lady, Noelle," he said. "Gently, and slowly. Don't flop down like a worn-out cowboy."

"And what would a city lawyer know about a cowboy's behavior?" she shot back, exasperated because she couldn't seem to do one single thing to please him today.

He only laughed. "You might be surprised at what I know, and at how I learned it." He looked down at her through narrowed eyelids. The pretty pale blue dress she was wearing had what seemed to him acres of lace, and he found himself wondering how women dressed like that withstood passionate embraces without having the lace torn to shreds.

"What are you thinking?" she asked unexpectedly.

His eyes searched hers. "Nothing of importance," he said. "Try again."

She grimaced impatiently, but she did as he said until he approved of her posture. She sipped her tea delicately and put the thin china cup back in the saucer. "I'm so afraid I'll drop this tiny cup," she confessed.

"If you do, it can be replaced. It's only a cup, Noelle."

"It's a very expensive cup. When I lived at home, we had old thick white mugs to drink from, and our plates didn't match. They were chipped and cracked..." She lifted her eyes. "My dresses were made of flour sacks—and a pair of shoes had to last me for a year or two."

"Not anymore," he reminded her.

"But I don't belong here, don't you see?" she asked plaintively, her big green eyes filled with her uncertainties. "I'm just a country girl. I don't know how to talk to city people.

I must be such a terrible embarrassment to Mrs. Dunn," she added miserably.

"My grandmother is delighted to have you here," he insisted. "So is Andrew."

"But you pay the bills," she replied. "And I came here without your permission, even without your knowledge. They waited weeks to write and tell you that I was here."

"And you think I resent you because of it?"

"Don't you? I irritate you. You can't think I don't know it."

She did irritate him, but not because he begrudged her a home. He studied her trim figure in the dress and her pretty, pale face with growing tension.

"I could go and live with my uncle again," she offered.

"My grandmother would be lost without you," he said carelessly, averting his gaze so that she wouldn't see how disturbed her offer made him. He knew the terrors Galveston held for her.

She felt a relief she didn't dare show. She got up and sat down again, gingerly, before she picked up the cup, very correctly, put it to her lips, sipped and put it down again without a mishap.

He almost laughed at the triumph in her face. She was pretty, he thought, watching her animated expression and the light in her green eyes. She had freckles and soft skin, and he found himself wondering if her skin was that pale all over, that soft milky white...

The thought made his hands clench in his pockets. He took a short breath. "You did that very well," he said. "And I find that your table manners have improved greatly, along with your ability to participate in discussions at table."

"Thanks to your tutoring," she admitted. "Jared, I'm very grateful," she began.

"It's little enough to do. I told you, didn't I, that I have the time."

"You make it," she said, smiling. "I know that you've worked overtime at night to make up for the time you give me, Jared. Your practice is already formidable, after so short a time."

He laughed humorlessly. "It's larger than I expected it would be. But I can take the cases that interest me and put off the others. New York had become tedious, and my practice was limited to cases that involved money and prestige more than justice."

She was surprised and pleased that he could speak to her like this. He was, she had learned over the weeks of his residence, a very private man. He never spoke of the past, even of New York, and when he was with other people, mostly he sat and listened.

"Why did you study law?" she asked.

He lifted an eyebrow and hesitated.

She got to her feet, pausing just in front of him. "It was you who said that we would be honest with each other, always."

"Then be honest with me and tell me why you want to know."

She searched his narrow, pale blue eyes. "You suspect me of hidden motives," she said unexpectedly, and watched him react with a frown. "Yes, that's why you say so little about yourself. You don't trust anyone—especially women."

He stood unmoving, his face as rigid as his stance.

"Do you think that after all you've done for me I would ever seek to harm you in any way?" she asked. "I owe you so much, Jared."

"You owe me nothing," he said tautly. "I do what pleases me, no more. Your...education is a pastime to me, and the help you give more than pays your way. I expect nothing in return. Least of all do I expect a pretended interest in my life."

She flushed scarlet. "It isn't pretended!" she said hotly.

"No?" He smiled, and it was not a pleasant smile. "But isn't it Andrew whose past should interest you?"

She put her hands on her hips in a very unladylike way and glared up at him. "Andrew would probably faint with terror if I even asked about his past. No doubt his is full of mangled dead bodies on a battlefield and scores of pretty women in his bed!"

Only when his eyebrows lifted and he began to laugh did she realize how unconventional her remarks were.

She clapped a hand over her mouth. The action brought attention to her horrified green eyes.

He wasn't shocked, as another man might have been. He laughed, because her unconventional response delighted him. He leaned closer. "And do you know what a man *does* with a pretty woman in his bed, Noelle?" he asked outrageously.

She actually cried out with embarrassment. Red-faced, she turned to run, but he caught her arm with steely fingers and pulled her back to him.

"That was unforgivable!" she raged at him. Her eyes were as livid as her cheeks.

"No doubt," he agreed lazily. He let go of her. "But you always forgive me, don't you, Noelle?"

"God knows why!"

He nodded complacently and checked his pocket watch. "We have less than thirty minutes before dinner will be on the table. Would you like me to teach you to waltz?"

"In thirty minutes?" she asked, calming slowly from her emotional upheaval.

He chuckled. "I can teach you the steps. After that, you'll only need practice." The smile faded. "And that, I can't offer."

"Your leg hurts you when you stand on it for a long time," she said. "I've noticed."

"Why?"

She couldn't answer. She found herself watching him all the time, and her own fascination disturbed her. Surely it was because he was her tutor, her mentor, her helper. He'd been kind to her—when he gave no impression of kindness toward the world at large. In fact, Andrew was often scathing about his stepbrother and some of the cases he'd won. Andrew talked about Jared as if he had no heart and no conscience. But that couldn't be true.

He moved a little jerkily to the Gramophone. "The waltz is an elegant dance. It requires concentration, however, and stamina."

"You seem to be able to concentrate even in the noisiest situations," she commented.

"A learned reflex. One can rarely find sufficient peace and quiet in the modern world to reflect on a case." He cranked the instrument and started the music.

When he turned, Noelle was right behind him. "Ideally," he added as his left hand encircled her trim waist, "your partner would be wearing gloves."

"Ideally, so would I," she replied.

He smiled, nodding as he indicated the first step. "Follow my lead. This isn't so different from the two-step you've already mastered, but it's more complex—Noelle, wait until I turn before you try to!"

She had stumbled a little and caught him off balance. He grimaced as he straightened.

"Oh, I'm so clumsy! I'm sorry. Did I hurt your leg?" she asked plaintively.

"No," he said through his teeth. "Try again."

She knew he was lying. He was stiff as he moved her slowly to the rhythm and took her through the turns, teaching her how to move gracefully. But less than five minutes later, the strain was telling on him.

She stopped. "You did hurt your leg. Oh, Jared, I'm sorry. It must be like teaching a cow to dance."

He glared at her as he rubbed the soreness at his kneecap. "I'm not an invalid," he murmured irritably.

"Please sit down," she pleaded. Her concern melted his stubborn resolve not to be pampered. He permitted her to lead him to an armchair; he sank gratefully down into it, stretching the offending leg to ease the pain.

"Can't I get you something to take for it? Do you have medicines?"

"Medicines." His pale eyes stabbed into hers. "Medical men love their potions," he said shortly. "They wanted to give me opiates to ease the pain…and create an addiction. Is that really what you think I need?"

She wrung her hands. "No. But what, then?"

He drew in a strained breath and his eyes closed. "Do you know how to pour a shot glass full of whiskey?"

"Yes, of course. My uncle used it medicinally. He was subject to colds."

He would have made some dry comment about that, but he was hurting too much. "In the cupboard, in the study," he prompted.

She went to fetch it, uncaring if the whole household saw her toting alcoholic spirits around. Poor Jared. He must be in severe pain, but he would never quit. She wondered how long he'd suffered, and if it had hampered him in his career, because his grandmother had said that he traveled a great deal before settling here in Fort Worth.

None of the servants were around when she went back down the hall to the living room with the small shot glass full of amber whiskey.

She closed the door—just in case his grandmother came down from her room.

He was sprawled in the chair, his teeth still gritted together.

She sank to the floor beside the chair, her skirt spreading around her, and handed him the small glass.

"Thank you." He held it to his lips and downed it in one swallow. Noelle had smelled it—and wondered how one could drink something so noxious. It smelled worse than liniment. His hand dropped to his side and she took the glass from him.

Curious, she dipped a finger into the drop at the bottom and put it to her lips.

"Oh," she exclaimed, making a face, "what a terrible taste!"

He glanced down at her, feeling the warm glow from the alcohol wash over him as he smiled at her expression. "Why, you sot!" he said teasingly.

She gasped indignantly and looked up at him. "I am not!"

"Give me that."

She handed the shot glass back. "Uncle let me taste his, but it wasn't as terrible as this," she said defensively. "At least his had honey and lemon to temper it."

"A toddy," he said. He sat up, grimacing, but the pain was easing. He leaned over to where Noelle sat at his feet on the spotless throw rug, her skirts all around her.

"I'm sorry," she said, with genuine concern, as she looked up at him. "It must have hurt terribly when I tripped."

"Pain is a fact of life," he said simply. "I've lived with it for a long time."

Which meant that the injury had to be an old one, she thought, not realizing that he spoke figuratively.

"Can I get you anything else?" she asked.

He shook his head. "I'm all right." His eyes slid over her and he had to fight a growing urge to pull her up between his splayed legs and press her body into his. "Get up, for God's sake," he muttered irritably.

"Of course." She caught the arm of the chair to give her some leverage, but she stumbled over her skirt and muttered a word she'd heard her uncle say. Then she gasped as Jared's arms spared her a fall.

He stood up, too, taking her with him, and he was laughing.

She realized then what she'd said and gasped. "Oh!" she cried, horrified.

Without counting the cost, he pulled her against him and wrapped her up tight in his arms, rocking her with rough affection, despite the throbbing pain in his leg.

"Wicked, wicked girl," he said into her ear. "It will take all my patience to turn you into a lady."

She felt the beat of his heart under her ear. But she felt, also, the steely strength of his body, which was not so obvious at a distance. He was warm and hard, and he smelled nice. She felt his warm breath in her hair. Closer, she felt the sudden tensing of her own body as the feel of his chest under her flattened hands made her hungry to touch him under his clothing. She stiffened, frowning at her shocking thought.

He felt her reaction and lifted his head to see what had caused it. Her wide, curious, searching eyes met his squarely; he felt her heartbeat race.

The amusement left his face as rigid as ever, but his eyes were alive in it, glittering with emotions too long suppressed. His hands at her back became exploring, caressing, so that even through the whalebone stays they were warm and welcome.

Her breath came in short gasps. Her hands pressed flat against his broad chest, where his silky vest covered his spotless cotton shirt. Under it, she could feel his heartbeat quicken, his breathing grow rough.

His hands slid to her waist, and, while he held her eyes

relentlessly, up her sides, her rib cage, to her underarms. His thumbs just touched the edges of her firm breasts, and while she was burning from that light, outrageous pressure, he urged her arms up around his neck.

She started to speak, but he shook his head.

His arms slid around her again and he pulled her gently, so that her body came to rest completely against his. Then his arms contracted, ever so slowly, until he was openly embracing her. She felt her body swell, burn, throb. Her lips parted. She had never experienced anything so overwhelming, so sweet.

His eyes fell to her parted lips and lingered there hungrily while the sudden chiming of the grandfather clock in the hall signaled the dinner hour.

"This is unpardonable," he said stiffly, and began to release her inch by inch. "In the old days, a shot of whiskey was less affecting to me. Or perhaps it is my advancing age that makes my head spin so."

He had moved her away from him while he spoke. She was not at all embarrassed by the frank, hungry embrace. She was puzzled, because her own hunger was inexplicable. She searched his eyes. "You didn't mean it?" she asked softly.

His jaw clenched and he breathed audibly through his nostrils. "You're a guest in my home," he said.

"And if you offended me, sir, I should say so," she replied quietly. "You've never offended me, in any way."

"Noelle, you're a child," he said harshly. "A green girl with no more knowledge of men than I have of Paris hats."

"Well, if I need teaching—" She started to say something utterly unforgivable, thought first and blushed angrily.

He saw the words forming on her lips. "No," he said curtly. "That I won't teach you. If you want lessons in that area, get them from Andrew. He's the object of this exercise, isn't he?"

His sarcastic tone made her angry. It wasn't enough that he'd teased her into making an idiot of herself, now he was making her sound as if she'd flung herself at him!

She glowered at him. "I can't put a foot right with you, can I? And just what conceit made you think that I'd ask a decrepit old milksop like you to give me lessons in love?" she added furiously, pushing back her disheveled hair with a trembling hand.

"Ah," he said, with a wicked smile. "The truth at last."

"You stuffed shirt of a city lawyer!" she cried. "You lazy, spineless bookworm!"

His eyebrows lifted. "You do have a nasty temper," he pointed out, more amused than insulted.

She stomped her foot. "I hate you!"

He only looked at her, his pale eyes sparkling with humor... and something much deeper.

"If I were a man, I'd strike you down!" she raged.

"All this because I didn't kiss you?" he asked outrageously.

She went scarlet. "As if I would permit—as if I ever even thought of—as if—!"

He moved closer, and her voice died away as she watched him approach. She didn't move, her face flaming, almost in tears at the intensity of emotion that had her in its clutches. And despite her anger, she reacted as she always did to his nearness, with helpless delight.

He stopped in front of her. His lean hands went up to cup her oval face. He tilted it up to his and searched her wet eyes.

"Perhaps I've been too protective. We are, after all, kinfolk...of a sort," he said as he bent. "Surely it isn't indiscreet to exchange a chaste kiss with a distant cousin of my stepbrother's."

She shivered at the sensuous note in his deep voice. Her

fingers dug into the lapels of his jacket. Her eyes watched his hard, thin mouth come closer and begin to part. Then it hesitated, just hovering, so near that she could taste coffee on his warm breath while he deliberated whether or not to take that final, irrevocable step.

Her expression decided for him. She stared at him with rapt hunger. "Oh, Jared," she whispered weakly. "Don't stop. Please don't tease me again. I think…that I…shall die if you stop now."

His hands contracted until they were almost painful. "I think that I would, too, Noelle," he ground out.

He coaxed her face up to his; he blurred in her sight as his warm mouth suddenly bit into hers, twisting, demanding, insistent. She'd never known a kiss from a man at all. Her dreams of it had been vague, tender ones. The reality was violent, even a little frightening. His mouth was hard and tasted of whiskey. It was very intimate to feel it almost inside her own, and she moaned and jerked with the starkness of its possession.

He felt the movement and stopped at once, lifting his mouth from hers to search her face. Her soft lips were swollen and she was less hungry now than intimidated.

"Did I frighten you?" he asked gently. "Forgive me. It's been…a long time." He bent again and now his hands were caressing, not imprisoning, on her face. And his mouth was soft, slow, sensuous as it traced and nibbled around her warm lips.

She caught her breath. This was more like her dreams. But the face in them had been Andrew's, not this stoic, mature man's. Yet, she had no such pleasure from Andrew's touch. It was disturbing to consider.

She had no resistance to him. Her rigid posture relaxed more with each insistent brush of his mouth over hers and she melted into his body. Then, and only then, did his mouth open, pressing her soft lips apart, so that he could take full possession of it with his lips and his teeth and his tongue.

She gasped at the things he did to her mouth. She should be shocked, outraged, indignant. She should slap him.

His hands had gone to her hips and pulled them into his, and she felt something that she had never expected to experience. Her whole body felt breathless with delight. She was innocent, but what had happened to him was unmistakable, even to a green girl. She did, after all, have girlfriends who were married and told her the most shocking things.

She stiffened, because it was unthinkable to permit him such a liberty, and her hands pushed at his chest.

"Gently," he whispered. His hands moved up to her waist and he let her move away, but not very far. "Look at me, Noelle."

"Oh, I...can't!" she moaned, embarrassed.

But his hand came up to tip her chin, so that she was forced to meet his glittery eyes.

"And now you know what can happen between a man and a woman, and how quickly."

She swallowed. "Was that...why you did it?"

His thumb rubbed slowly over her swollen lower lip. He watched it. "We both wanted to know how it would feel," he said finally. "Now we do. But such experiments are best not repeated. I told you before—I have nothing to give. There's nothing of love left in me."

Her fingers reached up hesitantly to his face. He didn't jerk back, so she explored the straight nose, the thick brows, the high cheekbones, the thin, hard mouth, the stubborn chin. There was a faint stubble there already, although she was certain that he had shaved only that morning. It was exciting to touch him. Her hand continued up into the thick, cool strands of his wavy black hair.

"I'll be twenty in December," she said huskily. "And you're thirty-six. Andrew told me."

His hand caught her wrist roughly. His eyes were dangerous. "My age is of no concern to you. And what happened is best forgotten."

She searched his cold eyes. "It was my first experience of a man," she said gently. "It's unlikely that I can forget it."

Not a muscle moved in his face. He let go of her. "And equally unlikely that I shall remember it." He smiled cruelly. "You were not my first experience."

Inexplicably, her hand came up quickly. He caught it just in the instant before it collided with his hard cheek.

Shocked at her own behavior, she jerked her hand back. "I… Forgive me."

He didn't say another word. The surprise he felt was only for a second visible in his pale eyes. He watched her, unspeaking, while she backed away from him.

She was barely aware of the scratch of the Gramophone still going, very slowly, and of voices down the hall. She stared at Jared with her uncertainties in her face.

He didn't ask why she should be so offended that she wasn't the first woman he'd kissed. He knew the answer, and so did she.

"We met at the wrong time," he said, in a clipped tone, deep with restraint.

"I've asked you for nothing," she whispered.

"And that's what I'll give you," he replied. "Nothing." He laughed coldly. "Go and dress for dinner, Noelle. Tomorrow we'll both have forgotten that this even happened."

She turned away, shaking. He made it sound inconsequential, yet her whole life had just changed. She paused in the doorway and looked back at him, standing there in his vested gray suit, looking faintly ruffled and sensuous—and more masculine than any man she'd ever known. He looked, in fact, dangerous. She wondered how she could ever have thought him a bookworm or a milksop. No man had such a physique and such strength when he only sat behind a desk, and that leg didn't even slow him down.

Her eyes searched his, sending a thrill of pleasure down to her toes. She opened the door quickly and went out into the hall. Her heart was beating so hard that it shook her, and she was grateful that she made it to her room before anyone could see her swollen lips and the turmoil in her eyes. She wondered how she was going to sit across from Jared at the table and pretend that nothing had changed between them.

Chapter Seven

Andrew returned from his latest selling trip and promptly asked Noelle to the upcoming dance. She didn't feel confident with only a few dance lessons under her belt, but she did have a nice dress and she was more confident about her parlor manners. She accepted with delight, although the invitation wasn't as exciting as she had thought it would be. She liked Andrew very much. But he stirred no response in her in any physical way. She was infatuated with him, but it was only emotional. She couldn't understand why Andrew left her cold and a man like Jared, his total opposite, could stir her to madness with the lightest touch.

Not that Jared seemed interested in doing that. She hadn't slept for days, remembering the warm passion of his hard mouth and her own hunger to know the taste and feel of it on her own. Her response had frightened her, and apparently it had alienated him, because he hadn't spoken directly to her since it happened, during their ill-fated waltz.

Well, he was too old for her and too stuffy, she kept telling herself. She didn't want the attentions of such a man in the first place. But then her mouth would tingle and she would remember the way it had felt when his tongue eased into it. And she would go hot under her clothing.

It embarrassed her to have such a physical reaction to Jared Dunn, who was certainly not romantically interested in her and had even told her so. Since their last encounter, he spoke to her only when necessary, and not in any way that could be construed as personal. He was polite, but remote.

Andrew had never noticed any familiarity between the two of them, but he had questioned Jared's intervention weeks before, about the cat. Later, he decided that he was being fanciful and it was likely the mice had prompted it. Not that he'd actually seen any mice.

The cat, meanwhile, was thriving. Noelle had bathed and groomed him, and after he was properly fed, he'd turned into a neat and inoffensive house pet. Mrs. Pate kept him in the kitchen with her, where he had a comfortable wooden crate to sleep in at night and could be let out the back door when he needed to go outside.

Like the cat, Noelle had gained a little weight and was content in her surroundings. She read to Mrs. Dunn and performed small services for her. When she wasn't doing that, she was helping wherever she was needed—mostly doing Andrew's paperwork. It became obvious to the family that she was no stranger to hard work, nor did she mind it.

Even Andrew, who was growing more attracted by the day to young Jennifer Beale, had to admit that Noelle filled a gap in the household. If only he could keep her out of those overalls she wore when she worked in the vegetable garden and the flower beds! Her continued mode of dress there, despite Mrs. Dunn's admonitions, was a source of worry to him. Neighbors occasionally caught glimpses of a dirt-stained Noelle in pants, rushing around with a hoe, and made sly mention of it to the lady of the house. Andrew found it embarrassing.

"Those overalls fit her much too tightly—and she rolls them up to her knees," he muttered to his grandmother. "It is so unladylike! You must speak with her about it."

"I have tried," Mrs. Dunn said solemnly. "She smiles and nods in agreement, and then she rushes back out with the hoe the minute Henry gets a little behind in his weeding."

"Perhaps he would get less behind if he drank less whiskey," Andrew said.

She sighed. "Yes, I know. I had thought about having Jared speak to him."

"I shall speak to him," Andrew said arrogantly. "I have, after all, been the man of the house for some time while my stepbrother was putting on airs in New York City!"

Mrs. Dunn turned toward him. "If I were you," she warned gently, "I wouldn't take that tone of voice with him. There are many things you don't know about Jared."

He scoffed. "He's a city lawyer, a dandy. Why, I imagine that he did fall off a horse and that is the cause of his injury. Imagine that. I rode from the time I was a boy."

Mrs. Dunn had to bite down hard on a quick reply. She didn't want to say anything to Andrew about Jared's past. It would make things very difficult for him if accounts of his past sins caught up with him now.

"Noelle is to accompany me to the Benevolent Society dance Friday evening," Andrew said then. "Will you join us?"

"I had planned to do so. I would like you to try and persuade Jared to come, also. He has had no recreation of any sort since he began his practice again, and he works much too hard. Imagine, we hardly ever see him at table."

Andrew started to remark that it suited him very well not to have that stoic, inhibiting presence at the head of the table, *his* table. But he only smiled. "He undoubtedly has much work to catch up on. And it will take time for him to gain a suitable practice here. He is used to a much bigger clientele."

"Well, Andrew, I've heard that he's much in demand already," she said. "His reputation in law has preceded him."

"No doubt it is exaggerated," Andrew said shortly. He looked at his pocket watch and snapped it shut. "I must go. I have an appointment. Can I bring you anything back?"

"No, dear boy." She smiled. "You're good to me, Andrew. I'm sorry that you and Jared are so dissimilar. It would have been better if you had things in common."

"I was a career soldier, with combat experience," he reminded her. "Hardly in the same league with a civilized practitioner of law in a major city." He laughed. "Jared and I get along well enough."

"Still…"

He bent and kissed her cheek. "I'll return soon." He glanced toward the backyard. Through the window, he could see Noelle with her hoe, in those blasted overalls, in full view of the neighbors, and he grimaced. "Could you speak to Noelle?"

"I shall."

"Thank you."

He went out the front, almost knocking into Jared. "Why… you're home early," he said, surprised.

Jared glowered at him. "And you're in a hurry, aren't you?"

He grimaced, glancing around. "Miss Beale asked me to drive her to a social appointment. Her father's out of town and she detests a hired carriage."

Jared searched the younger man's eyes, his level gaze unnerving. "I thought you found our Noelle more interesting."

He cleared his throat. "Well, I do. But, frankly, Jared, she's becoming an embarrassment." The look on his stepbrother's face made him uneasy. "Excuse me, I must hurry."

Jared hesitated. Then he stepped to one side and let the younger man pass, but not without a studious glare. Embarrassment, indeed! It was unjust, somehow, that such a lovely and tragic young woman should be so resistible to the one man she wanted.

He walked into the living room, where his grandmother looked equally broody.

"Andrew wishes me to speak to Noelle again," she said grimly, "about the gardening. Jared, perhaps it would make more of an impression on her if you spoke to her. Really, he is correct. She should be more circumspect."

He tossed his hat onto the hat rack and shrugged. "I can hardly see that it matters if she gets pleasure from digging in the dirt."

"In overalls?" she muttered. "You're far too unconventional yourself, my boy," Mrs. Dunn said. "I know the penalties that can befall a woman. You don't. One indiscretion can lead to another. I shouldn't like there to be any question of Noelle's reputation or character while she's in our care."

"Very well."

He walked toward the back porch. The cane wasn't really necessary. His leg was healing well, although he had a slight limp because it was sore. But he liked the feel of the cold silver wolf head in his lean hand and the security the black cane gave him. He didn't wear a sidearm, but the cane would be a handy weapon if he required one. He laughed silently at his own whimsy. He was a cautious man since New Mexico. Perhaps too cautious, especially where Noelle was concerned. Oddly, the more he avoided her, the more he was attracted to her.

She was stooped over a tomato plant, weeding carefully around its base. She was sweating because it was late spring and warm, even in the overalls with their rolled-up legs. His eyes studied her slender calves with quiet appreciation. It was outrageous for a woman to display so much of her pretty legs, but he had to admit that he liked looking at them. Wisps of sleek auburn hair had escaped from her high coiffure. Her slender hands were dirt-streaked and there were smudges of fresh earth around the hem of her overalls. But to Jared, even with those flaws, she was lovely. He leaned on the cane and watched her intently, his pale eyes on the graceful way she moved, on the lovely curve of her body as she bent over the plants, on those white, elegant legs...

Noelle paused in the midst of her labors, feeling eyes on her. She turned and caught her breath at the sight of Jared standing so close by. Her hand, unthinking, went to the lace at her throat and left a smudge on the white fabric.

"Did I startle you?" he asked quietly. "Forgive me."

She let her hand fall, oblivious to the smudge. "Did you come to chastise me?"

He lifted an eyebrow and smiled faintly. "Everyone seems to think that I should."

She grimaced. "I'm not ladylike," she muttered. "It pleases me to work with my hands, to weed and plant and harvest, and skirts get in my way. Perhaps I am unconventional, but how can working God's earth be shameful?"

He couldn't understand why himself, so it was impossible to give her an answer. He moved closer, resplendent in a navy blue suit and an immaculate shirt and tie. He eyed her overalls. "It isn't what you're doing so much as what you're wearing, Noelle," he remarked, touching the legs of the overalls with his cane. "You have dirt on your legs."

"They'll wash," she said, with soft belligerence.

"Noelle, you're a rebel," he commented. "A renegade. Have you no concern for your reputation?"

"But I've done nothing wrong," she argued plaintively, looking up into his pale eyes. Her own were captured there, held—caressed—by a look so intent that it made her toes curl up inside her high-topped shoes. She didn't dare let herself remember how it had felt when he'd kissed her so ardently.

"Ladies don't show their legs in this manner," he said gently.

"Gentlemen don't curse in front of ladies," she countered, recalling his first words to her weeks ago.

He laughed mirthlessly. "Did I ever claim to be one?"

She brushed at a streak of dirt near her hip. "No, nor did I claim to be a great lady." She hit at her pant legs irritably. "Oh, Jared. I'm hopeless. I have no social conversation, I like to do unladylike things..." She bit her lower lip. "It was Andrew who asked you to speak to me, wasn't it? I saw him glaring out the window at me earlier. I'm not good enough for him," she groaned.

"It was my grandmother who asked me to speak with you," he countered, and hated himself for protecting the hateful Andrew. "She's concerned. The neighbors are talking, it seems," he added dryly.

She dropped the hoe and looked down to where it lay in the rich dirt. "See how fertile the soil is," she remarked sadly. "Rich and loamy. It will grow exquisite vegetables." She looked up accusingly. "Henry drinks," she said shortly. "He has no time to take care of these seedlings."

"I'll speak with Henry as well, and if he doesn't make a firm pledge of temperance, I'll hire someone in his place."

"Would you?" she asked animatedly.

He sighed heavily. "If that's what it takes to have peace, yes. You and your cursed vegetables, Noelle!"

She smiled. "You like vegetables. I notice that you prefer them to meat at table...most of the time..." Her voice trailed off as she realized what she was admitting.

"You watch me," he said.

She colored. "You intimidate me!" she said, defending herself.

He shook his head slowly.

"You imagine things. I have no need to devote my attention to you, sir," she continued. "Surely you know that it is Andrew whom I find interesting. He is a soldier and an intelligent, responsible, dashing young man."

He nodded. His eyes narrowed on her face and he looked at her until the slow color rose into her cheeks and fear came into her wide green eyes.

"Andrew is all the things that I am not," he said quietly. "And it doesn't surprise me that he fascinates you. But have a care, Noelle. A man who wishes only to change you has nothing to give you."

"I don't mind changing myself for the better. I wouldn't want him to be ashamed of me. And you're hardly the appropriate person to encourage me to be unconventional, sir."

He chuckled deeply at that blatant misconception, but he didn't challenge it. "Perhaps not. I find the sight of you with a hoe…appealing." He stared at her legs so long that she flushed. He straightened. "But to please my grandmother, wear skirts and leave the gardening to the servants."

She sighed. "I'll make an effort."

He searched her sad face. "Andrew mentioned that he's taking you to the Benevolent Society dance Friday evening."

"Yes." She patted at her hair. "And no doubt I'll slurp my punch, or spill some down one of the matron's backs, or trip and knock over someone in the band!"

He smiled at her description. "Andrew will see that you make no social faux pas," he assured her.

She looked up at him. "Are you going?"

He hesitated.

She moved closer, drawn by some alien force. She stared up into his shuttered eyes. "Please."

His jaw tautened and something flared under his thick lashes that made her step away.

"You needn't look so violent," she said defensively. "You've worked very hard of late. I only thought that some recreation might improve you."

"I require no such recreation," he muttered. "Nor do I need to parade around for the benefit of the social matrons of the community who are openly shopping for sons-in-law at such functions."

"But you are old," she began, flushed. Then she stammered. "Well, not—not exactly old…"

"You'll level that charge at me once too often," he said after a moment's daunting silence. "In some circumstances, age can be an advantage rather than a drawback."

"Sir?"

He didn't speak. He only stared at her with narrowed eyes until his meaning penetrated, and then she gasped. "Sir!"

His hard, thin lips pursed. "I should be ashamed," he said almost to himself. "Forgive me, Noelle."

"You rake!" she said unexpectedly.

He raised an eyebrow. "As you yourself said, I'm old. A man can hardly attain my advanced years without learning something of…life."

She gripped her overalls tightly. "It's unseemly for you to speak to me like this."

"How conventional you sound for a young woman brazenly displaying so much of her legs in the garden!"

Her lower lip jutted. "Mr. Dunn!"

"All right." He held up a hand. "But put the hoe up, won't you? My grandmother will give me the wrong end of the buggy whip if I fail her a second time."

She smiled with exasperation. "Jared, you're a trial to me."

He smiled, and his eyes were teasing. "How grown-up you sound, Noelle," he said. "Yet you're green. Very green."

There were secrets in his eyes as he looked at her. She felt a surge of emotion that made her tingle all over. She was reckless when she was with him. She had feelings that she didn't want to acknowledge at all, and she had to remember that Jared wanted nothing to do with her. Andrew was the recipient of her affections. Why could she not remember that when she was within five feet of this man? Why did he alone have the power to weaken her?

"I shall be twenty in December," she told him.

"So old? We'll have to have a social evening to celebrate." He looked up at the sky. It was darkening. "Come along, Noelle. I think we may have a shower."

"The hoe…"

"Leave it," he said irritably, but she bent down and picked it up defiantly, carrying it into the small implement shed before she rejoined him.

She clasped her hands at her waist as he gave her a hard look before he turned. She walked back to the house with him in a stiff silence.

"You delight in defying me, don't you?" he asked curtly.

"Forgive me, but you seem to delight in giving orders." She peeped up at him. "Are you certain that you were never in the army?"

"At one time I was an officer in the Texas Rangers," he said surprisingly. "Over near El Paso."

She stopped dead. "But…no one ever mentioned it."

He stopped, too, and turned toward her. His pale eyes glittered down at her. "No one else knows, except my grandmother. I share more with her than with anyone. She went with my mother to Fort Worth while I remained…farther north. I drifted down to El Paso and took work as a Ranger, just briefly. A few months afterward, I was called to my mother's deathbed. I went to Harvard then, to read law. My mother had saved a little to help me go."

"Andrew's father did not?"

"No. He died just before she did. He was a soldier, too, during the War Between the States. He retired as a colonel."

"How interesting. And your father?"

His face was as closed as the implement-shed door. "I never talk about the past. What I've told you is more than Andrew knows. We didn't meet until my mother's funeral."

He turned and put his hand on the brass doorknob. Hers rested over it, and he threw it off, whirling to look at her with eyes that made her breath catch in her throat.

"I'm…sorry," she exclaimed, shocked by the violence of the action and the look on his face.

"Never touch me," he said under his breath. "Never!"

She backed away from him, wide-eyed.

He took a quick breath and opened the door, muttering as he opened it and went inside, leaving her to follow or not as he stormed back down the hall to the study. The feel of her soft hand had all but undone him. After the passion he'd shared with her once, his body was attuned to her. When he was near her, it grew taut with tense desire. He could never fulfill the hunger she kindled in him, and he was frustrated and confused by the thoughts in his mind. Then she had touched him and his body had gone rigid with arousal. He could hardly admit such a thing, but to allow her to come any closer might have had disastrous consequences. She was Andrew's concern, not his. Why in God's name could he not remember that?

He slammed the door of the study behind him. Noelle passed it carefully and walked rapidly back to the staircase. Mrs. Dunn saw her through the open living room door and called to her.

She was curious about the heat in Noelle's face and the tears she thought she saw in her eyes.

"Was Jared unpleasant?" she asked regretfully. "Forgive

me, Noelle. I only wanted to spare you any more gossip. I should have spoken myself. If Jared upset you, I am sorry."

"He said that he would make sure Henry did the work properly," Noelle said assuringly. "Forgive me for troubling you. I meant no offense. I have much to learn."

"I hope to help you learn it without the pain I suffered," the older woman said quietly. "Gossip can be deadly, my girl. I know."

"I'll be more circumspect," Noelle promised. "I don't want to violate your hospitality, or cause you any trouble." She hesitated. "Mrs. Dunn, I could go back and stay with my uncle."

The older woman joined her in the hall. "My dear, it would grieve me to lose you now," she said, with genuine fondness. "I do not mean to hurt you. We have neighbors with reckless tongues, and I am sensitive—more sensitive than most, per-haps—to being the object of so much unwanted interest."

"And I have been most uncooperative," Noelle said sadly. She smiled and kissed the elderly cheek. "Forgive me. I'll try harder. And Jared…did not upset me," she added. "We simply disagree a great deal. He's a most difficult man."

"Yes. But he's kind to those he loves."

Which certainly didn't include Noelle, she thought miser-ably. He was frequently unkind to her.

The night of the dance, Noelle wore her pretty sapphire silk dress with the white lace and satin trim and silver but-tons. She tried a new style with her hair, in ringlets around her face and big curls held back by a sapphire ribbon. She wasn't beautiful, but she did look attractive, and the gown fit well in the nicest, most decent way. She had a pretty velvet hooded cloak to wear with it, and her new black shoes.

Mrs. Dunn was wearing black velvet with black satin trim. She looked very elegant. Andrew, in his dark evening clothes, was incredibly handsome. He smiled at Noelle and offered her one arm while he extended the other elbow to Mrs. Dunn.

"It seems that I shall have you two beautiful ladies to myself this evening." He chuckled. "Jared is working late, again."

Noelle would not for the world have admitted, even to herself, how disappointing that statement was.

"I can't think that he will be missed," she said flippantly. "In fact, the evening has just improved."

"I agree," Andrew said. "He is a most unhumorous man. Come, then. Let's be off."

He helped them into the waiting carriage and entertained them with stories of his comrades in the Philippines all the way to the town hall, where the dance was being held.

The decorations followed a spring motif, with paper flowers and lovely cut-flower arrangements. The band played waltzes while the assembled personages, almost a *who's who* of the Fort Worth social register, drank punch and nibbled canapés and talked about modern evils and what could be done to correct them.

"I thought this was to be a banquet followed by a dance," Andrew confided to a radiant Noelle while they danced very correctly around the room. "I shall starve."

Noelle wouldn't admit that she was hungry, too, but she was. Jared had cost her her appetite for the past few days. But now, dancing with Andrew, she felt more cheerful than she had in a long time. Her dress was very up-to-date and people were treating her as good company. No one remarked about her presence except in a positive way, and Andrew had to avoid several young men who looked with interest in her direction. Ironically, their interest enhanced his, so that the lovely Miss Beale, who had come with a socially acceptable young man from Dallas, glared at him angrily from across the room.

Noelle noticed the girl's animosity with interest. Miss Beale was very pretty—prettier than Noelle, certainly. But Andrew was ignoring her, and very blatantly.

"Miss Beale is piqued," she remarked as he swung her around to the rhythm of the waltz.

"Is she?" he remarked, sounding indifferent. In fact, he was excited, because up until now most of the interest had been on Andrew's part. Miss Beale had been like a princess flattered by a commoner's interest. He had deliberately refrained from asking her to partner him, to see what her reaction would be. It was more than he'd dared hope for. Tonight, she was very obviously jealous, and he was intrigued to have two young women vying for his affections.

While Miss Beale was pretty, Noelle was unconsciously seductive and sensuous. His gloved hand on her waist made no improper moves, but all the time he danced with her, he wondered how it would feel to slide his hand up to her pert, firm breasts and smooth over the silk that covered them. The thought of it made him dizzy with pleasure. He found Noelle exciting.

Because of it, he was more attentive than he had ever been, fetching punch and little cakes for her and giving her his undivided attention. During intermission, he sat with her on the side of the room where chairs lined the wall and talked about his adventures—both abroad and since he'd left the army. It never occurred to Noelle that he evinced no interest whatsoever in her past or present, or in her life. He asked no questions about her, made no comments about her home or her family. He knew little about her and apparently was content for it to be so.

Forcibly she was reminded that Jared had a way of peering into every cranny and crook of her life. He knew more about her than any other member of the household, and yet he had no apparent interest in her. In fact, she recalled painfully, he could not even bear to have her touch his hand. That shattering discovery had hurt her. It was really no surprise when he didn't come tonight. Apparently she was now repulsive to him, for reasons she couldn't begin to fathom.

"You're very pensive tonight, my dear," Andrew remarked as she finished the last of her punch.

"I'm sorry," she said, smiling. "I was just enjoying the music," she lied.

"It is rather good, isn't it? We had a regimental band that was truly superb," he recalled. "I wish you could have heard it. I do miss the service, Noelle. Civilian life is not the same."

"Why did you leave it?" she asked.

"Because there's so little for an army to do in peacetime," he replied, sighing. "What a pity."

She started to reply when his head turned and he uttered a short, amused laugh.

"Well, look at that," he exclaimed. "So he did decide to come. And what a charming companion he has brought with him."

Noelle turned in her chair to look—and was just in time to see Jared entering, resplendent in evening clothes, with the most beautiful blonde woman Noelle had ever seen on his arm. She fought down a surge of jealousy, reminding herself that she was Andrew's companion and that she had no right to resent Jared bringing a woman with him. He was single, was he not? All the same, she felt a sense of possessiveness about Andrew's stepbrother that was out of character and totally without reason.

"Lovely, is she not?" Andrew asked. "The eligible Miss Amanda Doyle. Her father is a railroad baron, and he and his wife are unimaginably protective of their three daughters." He didn't add that Miss Doyle had rejected his suit rather brutally. "I could hardly imagine Jared with such a young and wealthy debutante. He must have hidden depths, if he has impressed her."

Chapter Eight

It took all Noelle's willpower to keep from blurting out that she knew there was more to Jared than met the eye. It was painful to remember how hungry she'd been in his arms. It was more painful to know that he was aware of her helpless desire, her response. Perhaps bringing the beautiful Miss Doyle was his way of emphasizing that he had no use whatsoever for a young, very green country girl from Galveston. He was a cultured, wealthy and intelligent city man who would never marry beneath him.

"You look very pale," Andrew said, with some concern. "Here, Noelle. Do you want to sit down?"

"No, thank you," she said huskily. She smiled up at him. "I'd like to dance again, Andrew."

He held her very correctly and began to waltz her around the crowded room. He danced with expertise, and he was very handsome. Noelle knew that other women were watching her with envy. Andrew in evening clothes was the epitome of a cultured gentleman.

But even though she was flattered at being his escort, there was a deep hurt inside her when she looked toward Jared. If Andrew was handsome, Jared was striking in evening wear. Just the sight of him made Noelle's knees weak. He was attentive to the Doyle woman, very correct, but smiling and faintly affectionate. He held her arm possessively as he introduced her to his grandmother, and the way he looked at her made Noelle feel cold and alone.

"I had no idea that you could dance so well, Noelle," Andrew said when the waltz ended. "I'm surprised."

She was, too. Andrew was a practiced dancer and she wasn't. She could hardly tell him that her expertise was a gift from his stepbrother. Andrew resented Jared, for reasons she didn't understand.

Her eyes flickered again to Jared and Miss Doyle, and she found him watching her from across the room. When he saw her, he smiled mockingly. Yes, she thought as she averted her eyes, it was deliberate. He'd come here with that lovely debutante to make a point, and his attentiveness was only part of that plan. What she didn't understand was why it hurt so much.

"Let's go and see Jared's lady," Andrew said, drawing her along with him. "I've only once had the pleasure of making her acquaintance. Her father is very well-known hereabouts, and although his main source of wealth is the railroads, he also invests in the building trade. He'd be a useful contact," he added. He was putting on a merry face, but it was hurting him to see his own Miss Jennifer Beale with another man. Consequently he was much more attentive to Noelle than he would have been, and Jennifer pointedly ignored him as he led Noelle to where his stepbrother was standing with Miss Doyle and his grandmother.

Noelle went reluctantly. She didn't want to meet Miss Doyle. It was going to hurt even more than it already did. But she put on her best polite smile and tried to remember that it was Andrew to whom she was attracted, not Jared. The Doyle woman looked to be in her mid-twenties, too, which made her more his own age.

She clutched Andrew's arm closer and fanned gently with the blue, black and red Oriental silk fan Mrs. Dunn had loaned her to go with her elegant sapphire silk gown. Jared had paid for the gown and taught her to dance—and to become socially acceptable. She was his creature, but he'd lost interest in her. He was telling her so without a word.

Jared watched her approach him with Andrew, and the look on her face disturbed him. He'd met Miss Doyle at a civic-betterment meeting and her parents had immediately pushed her at him. A rich New York attorney was a good catch for a young woman of good family. He'd asked her to the dance tonight only to show Noelle that he had no real interest in their young houseguest, but his idea was backfiring. This was hurting Noelle. It was just a date, nothing serious or binding, but Noelle's big green eyes were wounded and he felt badly about that. He'd recalled over and over again his action the last time they'd been together, when he'd thrown her hand away from his and made her think he found her touch repulsive. He didn't understand himself lately. He wanted her passionately, but she was a green girl—and besides, her heart belonged to Andrew.

As Andrew joined his stepbrother, the lovely but snippy Miss Doyle gave Noelle a contemptuous stare and clung tighter to Jared's arm. She barely glanced at Andrew, as if she didn't know him at all.

"This is Noelle Brown," Mrs. Dunn was saying. "Noelle, this is Miss Amanda Doyle. Her family has been here for two generations."

"I'm very pleased to make your acquaintance, Miss Doyle," Noelle said politely.

Miss Doyle didn't smile back. She only nodded. "Hello, Andrew," she added, with a faint smile. "Nice to see you again."

Andrew nodded graciously. "And you, Miss Doyle." He drew Noelle's hand tight in his. "Noelle and I are just sitting out this dance. We're exhausted."

Jared's eyes flashed as he noted Noelle's pallid face. "Don't keep Noelle out late," he said curtly. "She isn't used to long evenings."

Miss Doyle fanned herself frantically. She lifted a thin eyebrow and smiled condescendingly. "Noelle. Now where have I heard that name? Oh, yes. You do the gardening for Mrs. Dunn, I believe, and in your bloomers. How scandalous!" she said sweetly, adding, "Mrs. Hardy is an old friend of my mother's. She lives at the corner, just beyond Andrew's house."

Mrs. Hardy had been gossiping. Noelle's green eyes met Miss Doyle's unblinkingly. There was a bit of a rumor she'd heard in one of the shops about this woman. She smiled with cool nerve. "And I believe that you were recently engaged to a young man who represented himself as an official of a rival railroad company of your father's? How *did* his trial come out, by the way?"

It was a faux pas of the first order. Miss Doyle looked near to a faint. Her face went so white that she resembled a bleached bedsheet. Voices started to murmur loudly all around her.

"Let us dance, Noelle," Andrew said quickly. He dragged her away and back to the dance floor, and she went only reluctantly. That silly woman, passing on gossip, making her out to be a hussy! Her green eyes blazed with anger, and she noticed that Jared refused to look at her. Probably he was furious at what she had said, and she didn't care.

Andrew was shocked. "My dear," he began gently, "one simply doesn't mention such things in polite company."

"But she made fun of me, Andrew," she said indignantly. "She told everyone that I was your gardener!"

"If you will continue to potter in the garden dressed like a—a…well, you must expect such gossip," he said irritably.

It was, she decided, a good thing that she was no longer blindly infatuated with him. She had already learned that he was, for all his swagger, the most conventional member of the family. Even more so than his grandmother. It amused her that Jared found her antics less shocking—when he looked and acted so straitlaced.

He wasn't laughing tonight, though. She was sure that he would read her a lecture after the dance was over about her unspeakable behavior. And she would deserve it, she admitted. She had let her temper make an idiot of her—and embarrassed Mrs. Dunn and especially Jared—who had been so good to her. Not that the haughty Miss Doyle didn't deserve to be put down, she thought belligerently. Even if she had invited comment with her puttering, it was hardly Miss Doyle's place to tell the world about it.

It was malicious, and unfounded. Why should the woman want to embarrass her? She hadn't ever met her until tonight. It seemed odd that she would want to attack a total stranger. Jared hadn't defended her, either. She remembered again the way he'd thrown off her hand at their last meeting and she felt miserable.

She sighed. Andrew heard the faint sound and felt guilty for having been so stern with her.

"You're new to such situations," he said soothingly. "It takes practice to behave well in polite society. I'll take you out more often, Noelle," he decided impulsively. "If I teach you proper behavior, you'll fare better."

"How kind of you to think of it, Andrew," she said. She didn't look up. There was no need to let him know how angry she was. The woman had attacked her first, after all.

Andrew grimaced. "And here comes Jared."

She didn't look up, except to stare at a spotless white shirt under a tuxedo and black tie that appeared beside Andrew. She heard Jared's terse apology, followed by his request to dance with Noelle.

"Could we wait a bit, old chap?" Andrew began, with smiling arrogance.

"No, we couldn't, old chap," Jared replied, with a cold smile.

Andrew found those blue eyes chilling at close range. Jared made him feel cowardly. He handed Noelle over without protest.

"Age hath its privileges, dear girl," Andrew said maliciously, with a meaningful glance at his stepbrother. He kissed her gloved hand with a flourish and relinquished her without another word.

Noelle felt Jared's gloved hand at her waist, the other clasping her own. He moved her fluidly to the music, staring straight above her head.

"Go ahead," she muttered, with a glare in the general direction of Miss Doyle, who was surrounded by friends who gossiped behind their silk fans while gaping over them at Noelle. "Lecture me. Andrew said that I should expect it. I've disgraced the family."

"Parts of it," he admitted.

She stared at his nice, neat black tie. "She made me look a fool, because I like to grow things."

His hand tightened on hers, although not a sign of sympathy

showed in his hard face. "Nevertheless, it was unkind of you to bring back a painful memory to her."

She nibbled her lower lip thoughtfully. "Did he go to jail?" she asked, with irrepressible curiosity.

"Yes, for impersonating a railroad official and extorting money in that guise. Her father was out of town at the time, or he'd have been found out sooner. But the subject embarrasses Miss Doyle."

"Miss Doyle is a—"

"Noelle!" he said disapprovingly.

She stiffened. "I don't like your world. People in it are hypocrites. Look at them," she invited, inclining her head toward the beautiful girls that surrounded Miss Doyle, "gossiping about me. Mrs. Hardy has no doubt told them that I come from a poor background and am not fit to associate with them. How dare she insult me so!"

He was trying desperately not to laugh. He whirled her around to the rhythm and groaned at the pressure on his leg.

"There, see what you've done!" she said, stopping at once as her bad temper gave way to concern for him. "You should be sitting down, not trying to prove how fit you are."

He glared into her green eyes. "I need no advice from you, miss."

"Yes, you do. You won't listen to anyone else. Mrs. Dunn said that you'd been on your feet for two days in court this week, and you wouldn't let any of the other attorneys in town assist you. For heaven's sake, your leg must be killing you."

It was. He hated having her know it. His dark brows drew together over dangerously glittering pale blue eyes. "I don't need a nurse."

She sighed angrily. "Go ahead, then, make it worse. Then you can get your sweet Miss Doyle to bring you whiskey to ease the ache!"

He stared down at her with more conflicting emotions raging inside him than he'd ever felt in his life.

She glared up at him. "And should you be touching me, after all? You do loathe my hands, don't you? I'm certain that you think I'll poison you. But we're wearing gloves, aren't we? Perhaps that makes me more acceptable."

He didn't reply. He could never explain why he'd thrown off her hand that day in the kitchen.

She stopped in the middle of the floor, sick with humiliation and bad temper. "I'll ask Andrew to take me home. I don't want to stay here any longer. Please make my apologies to Miss Doyle. Regardless of what she said, I suppose that it was wrong of me to embarrass her. But then, I have no breeding, have I?"

She turned before he could say a word and made a beeline back to Andrew. "I feel unwell," she said huskily. "Please, could you take me home?"

"Of course," he said. It was difficult not to show his relief. Miss Doyle was still glaring in their direction, and his own Miss Jennifer Beale was looking livid herself. Noelle's presence was embarrassing him in more ways than one. "Let's go at once."

He took her arm and escorted her around to make her apologies to her host and say good night to Mrs. Dunn. She didn't speak to Jared. In fact, she didn't even look at him.

"What a very odd houseguest you have, Jared," Miss Doyle commented coolly as she watched Noelle leave with Andrew. "She has no manners at all, has she?"

Jared was watching her leave, too, his hands in his pockets and all sorts of protective impulses prickling inside him. "She's a child," he said quietly, turning back to Miss Doyle. His eyes narrowed. "And your comment was in extremely poor taste. One hardly expects such tasteless remarks from a woman of your class. I'm disappointed in you, Amanda. I thought you were above such petty behavior."

She gaped at him. He'd spoken loudly enough so that the girls standing around her heard him. They looked uncomfortable, and she colored. "Jared, Mrs. Hardy told me—"

"Noelle is my cousin," he said, emphasizing the word. "I don't take kindly to derogatory remarks about members of my family. From anyone."

Miss Doyle fanned herself furiously. She was more embarrassed than she could ever remember being. "Please, Jared. I meant no harm. It was an innocent remark, truly it was. You must forgive me."

"Gossip is unforgivable," he said harshly. He looked at the other women coldly. "I find women who practice it repulsive."

There were gasps and choking sounds, and a rapid movement of feet. If he'd been in a better mood, he might have been amused at the reaction his remark brought. But Noelle had left with Andrew, and he was furious that Amanda had given his stepbrother an excuse to be alone with her.

"Please excuse me," he said stiffly.

His blue eyes were cold as they met Amanda Doyle's. She didn't need an advertisement to know that her chances of landing this moneyed fish had gone awry.

If she'd had hopes, he spent the rest of the time thwarting them. He danced with Jennifer Beale and several of the matrons present, but he deliberately refused to dance with Amanda the rest of the evening, which was remarked upon. Amanda seemed only then to realize that she'd driven Jared away with her insensitive remarks about his precious cousin. And not only Jared. Other men present, also outraged by her, left her on the sidelines, as well. By the time Jared took Miss Doyle home, she was the subject of more gossip than Noelle had been. And he wasn't sorry.

* * *

Andrew took Noelle home, pausing in the hall just long enough to make sure that she was all right.

"I hate leaving you here alone," he said sadly. "Noelle, it isn't your fault. I wouldn't have had you embarrassed tonight for all the world. That Doyle woman is a viper."

He was defending her for once, even if he'd waited to do it in private. It made her feel warm. Jared hadn't defended her at all. She smiled up at him. "You're kind, Andrew," she said. "Thank you."

He moved restlessly. "You'll be all right?"

"Mrs. Pate is here," she reminded him. "I'll go to bed. It was a lovely dance."

"You were lovely," he said softly. "You are lovely." He pulled her to him, kissing her very gently on the lips. He smiled at her shy hesitation and kissed her again, hard this time, and with ardor.

She didn't fight him, but she didn't respond, either. How odd that she felt no tingle, no spark, when she'd dreamed of his kisses for so long. He lifted his head and touched her cheek softly. "You have no knowledge of this, have you?" he asked, with arrogance. "It doesn't matter. A shop-soiled girl has no appeal whatsoever. You're like a rose in bud, Noelle. I find you delightful."

She smiled halfheartedly. She was surprised. She'd wanted Andrew to kiss her for months. Now he had, and she felt nothing at all. The touch of his mouth, while not unpleasant, struck no chord within her. She wasn't even breathing quickly.

He patted her shoulder affectionately. "Sleep well, my dear. Tomorrow, we might go to the theater. There's a new vaudeville troupe in town."

"That would be nice, Andrew."

He winked at her and smiled. "Good night. Sleep well."

He closed the door behind him and whistled merrily on his way back to the carriage. Noelle was delightful to kiss.

But all the way back to the party, he was thinking about Jennifer Beale's jealousy. It delighted him that she was beginning to care for him. He would play his cards very carefully, but her fortune would spare him the indignity of daily work. It was a prospect he desired greatly. And she was pretty enough, and somewhat more pliable than Noelle—although Noelle truly was a joy in his arms. Ah, well, there was no law that said a man, even a married man, couldn't have a bit on the side.

The house was quiet. It was very late, and the others had long since come home. But Noelle still couldn't sleep. She deplored her bad behavior, however merited. She felt guilty about what she'd said to Jared's woman friend and about making things more difficult for Mrs. Dunn. She was a guest here. She must stop embarrassing the family.

She wondered if a warm drink might not help her to settle. On second thought, a shot of that whiskey Jared had savored might be even better. Feeling utterly wicked now, she pulled her ruffled, lacy pink-and-white wrapper around her, with her auburn hair loose and full around her shoulders, and crept downstairs.

The house was dark, but she had eyes like a cat. She felt her way into the parlor. Light from the streetlight near the house illuminated the cabinet where the whiskey was kept.

She pulled out the squat bottle and a small glass and carefully poured a tiny measure into it. She put the bottle away and then stood, trying to get the liquid past her nose.

A faint sound made her turn. There was a tall, shadowy figure in the doorway, and she gasped, holding her throat. The shot glass almost upended. She righted it in the nick of time.

The door closed. The gaslight beside the door was turned on, and Jared stood there in his long burgundy robe, staring at her from a hard, alert face. He looked as if he hadn't slept, either, although his dark hair was tousled. The robe was pulled tight, but it left a tiny sliver of his chest bare. It was dark, and not from the sun, and covered with thick hair. Noelle had never seen a man in such a state of undress. She was uneasy, and only then did it occur to her that she was standing up in only her nightgown and a flimsy robe, with bare feet and loose hair; every line of her body was outlined.

Jared hadn't missed that. His pale eyes were intent on her body, and the look in them made her take a step backward, even though he hadn't moved.

"Are you really afraid of me?" he asked quietly.

She clutched the shot glass to her bosom. "It isn't decent for me to be seen like this by a man," she said.

"Or for me to be seen like this by a woman," he replied. His hands were deep in the pockets of the robe. He stared at her for a long time, until she felt her knees wobble under her.

She broke the silence. "You were the one who said I needed to be more conventional."

"It would behoove us both to be." He noticed, belatedly, the small glass in her hands. "Have I driven you to drink?" he asked, with sudden amusement.

"I couldn't sleep," she replied. "I thought…if it was strong enough to ease your pain, it might make me sleep."

He smiled mockingly. "Unused as you are to it, you might not wake until noon."

She smiled back, a little shyly. His eyes traced her long auburn hair over her shoulders. It reached to her waist, and it looked like silk in the light.

"I've never seen you with your hair down," he remarked.

"I only loosen it to sleep," she said. She touched a strand of it nervously.

"I've wondered how it would look hanging down your back like that."

She dropped her eyes to the glass in her hand. "Was Miss Doyle very upset?"

"No." He didn't mention his treatment of her, which had caused her some difficulty. "Nevertheless, you should have been more circumspect with your remarks."

"Yes."

He stepped away from the door and moved closer. Her breath increased with each step, and when he was just in front of her, she couldn't drag her eyes away from the opening of his robe. The garment was long enough to reach to his ankles, and she wondered recklessly if he wore anything beneath it. She didn't dare ask. He was intimidating enough in the folds of the robe.

"Why did you insult her, Noelle?"

Her fingers had gone white gripping the shot glass. "She insulted me first. Besides, we've already agreed that I'm uncivilized. Jared, I must go upstairs now. This is—this is very unconventional."

"You really are afraid of me, aren't you?" he asked softly, reading her thoughts. "Don't you know that I'd never hurt you, in any way?"

She lifted her eyes to his. "Of course I know it," she said heavily. "But, Jared…"

"Were you jealous of Amanda Doyle?" he asked quietly.

Her indrawn breath was audible. "Why—what a question!"

"Do you know why I took her to the dance?"

"Of—of course," she stammered. "To show me that I was of no consequence in your life."

He nodded solemnly. "That was what I meant to do. It didn't occur to me that she might attack you. It must have ruined the evening for you."

"It didn't matter. Those are hardly the sort of folk I'm used to," she confessed. "Jared, is it really so bad that I wear overalls and dig in the garden?" she asked miserably, looking up into his eyes.

"Of course not," he said. "I don't mind wagging tongues any more than you do. But Andrew and my grandmother are more circumspect that we are, and it disturbs them. It's best that you leave the gardening to Henry."

She sighed. "Oh, very well. It's just that I have so few pleasures." She smiled with sad memories. "My mother always kept a kitchen garden and a rose garden. My earliest memories are of working in it with her. It brings me peace, because it's like being with her again."

"I'm sorry," he said genuinely. He touched her cheek lightly, reaching past it to grasp a strand of her hair and smooth it through his fingers. "Your hair feels like silk, Noelle. And you carry the scent of roses about your body."

She felt her heartbeat increase and grow erratic. "I have a milled soap…that smells like roses." He was too close. Her eyes glanced off his bare chest where the robe parted, flickering nervously up to his face.

He laughed shortly, without humor. One lean hand came up to take the shot glass out of her hand. He put it on the table beside them and caught her by the shoulders, gently pulling her to him.

"Jared, no," she whispered, pushing at him. But her hand slipped into his robe, against the thick hair over his heart, and she froze in position.

His own breath caught. He grasped her hand and pushed it closer, holding it to his bare flesh, so that she could feel the thunder of his heart. He moved it down to the hard nipple and pressed her damp, warm palm to it; his heartbeat began to race.

"This is unwise," she whispered shakily.

"Of course it is." His own hand went to the soft collar of her robe, held precariously in place by her free hand. "Let go," he said softly.

"Why?"

His mouth brushed over her eyelids. "So that I can do something ungentlemanly to you."

She bit her lower lip, but his caressing fingers traced up and down her throat until they made her blood run hot. Inevitably, she released her stranglehold on the fabric; he smiled faintly at her temple as his hand went inside, underneath her gown, to the soft, rose-petal skin just above her collarbone, and began to trace it lightly.

She began to tremble then. His arm went around her, holding her upright. He drew her against him so that his arm supported her, and while he looked into her eyes, his fingers slowly moved down until they touched her naked breast.

She moaned in shock and anguish and pleasure. His warm, strong hand covered her firm breast completely. His thumb worked its way over the nipple and made it peak and ache. He caught his breath at the exquisite softness of her skin, at her headlong response. She slumped a little, and his arm contracted to hold her while his hand moved on her soft body.

And still his eyes looked into hers, held them, caressed them. But then he bent and kissed her eyelids until they closed. She shivered with each new caress, and she leaned against him helplessly as his mouth fitted itself slowly to hers and the magic worked a spell on her.

Her hand smoothed slowly over his chest, her fingers tangling in the thick hair, testing its wiriness, loving the hard, warm muscles under it.

He groaned suddenly and lifted his mouth from hers. His eyes fixed on hers; she saw him fight for the control he'd almost lost.

"What do you do to me?" he whispered half-angrily. "I

had no intention of…" He looked down at his hand inside her robe, inside her gown. He made a sound deep in his throat and suddenly pulled the fabric down, baring her taut breast to his eyes. He caught his breath, ignoring her frantic haste to cover herself.

He was paler, his face rigid, his eyes blazing with desire. He stared, entranced, at the perfect contours of the breast he'd revealed as she trembled. "My God," he breathed huskily. "No!" he snapped when she tried to pull the edges together. He stayed her hand. "No. Let me look, Noelle," he said roughly. He traced, softly, around the ruby-red nipple, onto the milky-white flesh with a tiny scattering of freckles. The nipple went erect. She gasped, and he laughed, deep in his throat.

"You mustn't!" she choked, fighting him.

He let go of the gown and robe so that she could pull them back in place. She flushed, trembling.

"There's no need to be embarrassed by this," he said gently. "You're lovely, Noelle—a sight to grace a man's memory until he goes down into the dark."

She stopped clawing at the gown and stared at him, transfixed.

"Can you bear so much honesty?" he asked quietly as he released her. "I find you exquisite. And it flatters me beyond bearing that you allowed me to touch you, to look at you, in such a way."

She caught the robe tight. She should be embarrassed, ashamed, frightened, outraged. But she couldn't focus on any one emotion.

He smiled, and it was the most tender smile she ever remembered seeing on his face. "Your skin is like milk," he said gently. "But even your breasts are freckled, like your pretty nose."

She flushed to her hairline. "I should never have permitted—" she began.

He put his forefinger to her lips, stilling them. "No one will ever know it happened, except the two of us, Noelle," he promised quietly. "You should know by now that I keep secrets well."

She felt a little more secure. He was hardly a gossip. But she was shy with him now, having given him a view of her body that no one else had ever had.

He reached for the shot of whiskey and handed it to her. "Let me see you drink it."

She lifted it to her lips and threw her head back, downing it in one gulp. It made her deathly ill and started her coughing. She thought she would choke, and then her body felt as if it were on fire, starting with her throat.

He laughed deep in his own throat as he calmed her. Then the warmth raced through her veins and she felt hot, burning inside. She blinked, swaying a little, and took a deep breath.

"Shall I carry you upstairs?" he asked mockingly.

She found her voice, but with difficulty. "That would be interesting. We should both go pitching down headfirst, with your gimpy leg to hold us up."

He grinned at the mischief in her face. "Possibly so."

She put a hand to her mouth. "Forgive me. The alcohol has loosened my tongue beyond repair."

"You speak as if I were a lifelong cripple. It's a temporary injury," he said lightly. "Didn't you know?"

She shook her head.

"All the same, if I carried you into your bedroom, I might lose my head."

"As you just did?" she asked demurely.

He smiled. "Noelle, what happened was very innocent, although you're probably too green to realize it." He leaned down. "And if you hope to remain that way, you'd better leave. Now."

There was a sensual threat in his deep voice that made her

legs move. She tugged the robe closer and looked back at him from the door, her eyes huge in her face.

"Did you touch her like that?" she asked abruptly.

He shook his head. "It wouldn't have occurred to me to try," he said, with genuine surprise. "I don't feel that sort of attraction to her."

She had to fight down a smile. "I see." She averted her gaze.

"Do you?" He put his hands in the pockets of his robe. "I'm seventeen years your senior. It's a great gap. And there are still too many secrets between us."

Her eyes ran over him with new knowledge, new familiarity. He was devastating to her, handsome and virile and constantly surprising. "If you told me those secrets, there wouldn't be any more to keep."

He smiled. "You tempt me. But trust comes hard. It comes very hard."

"A woman betrayed you, is that what happened?"

Her words brought back the pain and grief of the past; all the hunger she'd kindled was suddenly quelled. He walked to the door and opened it for her.

"You said that you'd always be honest with me," she reminded him.

"As honest as I can be," he said agreeably. He searched her wide eyes; his face softened magically. "Will you sleep now?"

"I'll try." She hesitated. "Does your leg hurt?"

He smiled dryly. "A little."

"Whiskey kills pain and dulls the brain."

"Is that why you let me touch you?" he teased softly. "Because of the whiskey?"

"Certainly."

"Liar." He made the word a caress.

She only smiled, making her way quickly to the staircase.

Fortunately the rest of the household was asleep. She had enough on her conscience already without adding a new scandal to it. She didn't dare look back. But she felt Jared's eyes all the way to the top of the staircase, and when she lay down, she went to sleep at once…with tingling memories of his lean hands and his hard mouth.

But with the morning, instead of the sweet memories, regret hit her in the stomach. She woke with stark anguish as her behavior of the night before paraded itself in her sober mind.

Chapter Nine

Noelle wasn't certain that she could sit at the breakfast table with Jared without blushing. And he was there when she went downstairs, sitting lazily at the head of the table. He didn't glower at her. In fact, his gaze was speculative and curious. She sat down uncomfortably, feeling naked and shy.

Andrew came in, talking to Mrs. Dunn. "Ah, there you are," he said to Noelle, smiling rakishly. "Did you sleep well?"

"Very well," she said, and didn't dare look in Jared's direction.

Andrew laughed deep in his throat, remembering the kisses he'd exchanged with her at the door. He looked at her with intimacy. And Jared saw it and felt his blood begin to rise.

Noelle glanced at Andrew and blushed, and that ignited something in Jared that he hadn't felt since his youth.

Unaware of it, Noelle reached for a biscuit and smiled at Andrew. "Did you enjoy the rest of the dance?" she asked.

"I would have enjoyed it more had you remained," he

said gallantly. "You dance divinely, Noelle. Where did you learn?"

"Indeed," Jared added as he spooned scrambled eggs onto his china plate, his pale eyes on the plate. "Where *did* you learn?"

"I was tutored," Noelle said carefully. "By a relative," she added quickly.

"He taught you very well," Andrew said obliviously, and with a smile.

"He's very experienced," Noelle replied. She glanced angrily at Jared.

"A relative, you say?" Andrew said, thinking. "Do I know him?"

"No," she said flatly. It was no lie. Andrew knew as little about Jared as most strangers.

"Well, you're very light on your feet, and your gown was the envy of several young ladies," he added, with a grimace. "If only Miss Doyle had not—"

Jared looked up. "Miss Doyle will not be mentioned," he said firmly.

"She was very unkind to Noelle," Andrew replied sadly. "She's jealous of you, of course, even of a distant relation—"

"I said," Jared repeated levelly, unblinking, "that we will not discuss her."

Now the words were a threat. Andrew laughed nervously and buttered a biscuit. "If you please. Noelle, what did you think of the music?"

"It was very nice," she replied. She ate a mouthful of egg, furious at Jared. How could he be so two-faced, she wondered angrily, as to hang on Miss Doyle and then come home and make passionate love to Noelle right in the living room!

"Noelle, you look disturbed," Mrs. Dunn commented.

She looked up, red in the face. "Oh…I was merely

thinking about…well…" She looked straight at Jared. "About gossip."

"Hardly surprising," Jared said, without hesitation. "Since you seem to have a penchant for attracting it."

"I know someone else who does, too."

His pale blue eyes narrowed. "You have no sense of propriety."

"And you have no manners!"

"If I had them, madam, they would be wasted on a termagant like you!"

"How dare you call me names!"

His eyes were flashing like blue lightning, and her own were greener than bottle glass. She clutched her napkin angrily.

"Noelle!" Mrs. Dunn laughed nervously, looking from one to the other. "Jared! Please!"

He didn't look away. Neither did Noelle. They glared at each other.

"The theater is tonight," Andrew interrupted quickly. "Noelle, we should leave this afternoon by six o'clock. We can have dinner at Monaco's."

She had to drag her angry eyes away from Jared's face. She looked at Andrew and smiled sweetly. "I should like that."

"Have you another new dress to dazzle me with?" he teased.

"Oh, yes. A lovely green one," she replied—and then remembered that Jared had paid for it and suffered twinges of guilt for her behavior. She hadn't meant to trade insults with him so hotly that it drew attention to them. Amazing that only last night they had been nearly as close as lovers, and now they seemed to be bitter enemies without any visible cause.

Jared put down his napkin and got to his feet. He didn't say a word, except to nod to his grandmother before he left the room. His half-eaten breakfast was still on his plate.

"Why are you and Jared so violent with each other?" Andrew asked.

"He doesn't like me," she muttered. "He thinks that I'm too outrageous."

"That isn't true," Mrs. Dunn said gently. "Noelle, he's very fond of you. Not that it was very evident just now…"

"It was my fault, and I apologize," Andrew said gallantly. "I should never have said that about Amanda Doyle." He chuckled. "Perhaps Jared is in a bad mood because Miss Doyle didn't kiss him good night. She's very circumspect, and her parents are quite protective, they say, although they seem to approve of Jared."

Jared was courting the woman? Noelle's heart felt leaden. Well, what had she expected? But it seemed so horrible for Jared to court Miss Doyle and make love to Noelle behind her back.

"You will enjoy this comedy at the theater," Andrew assured Noelle. "We'll forget the unpleasantness of this morning."

"Of course we shall," she agreed.

But it played on her mind all day. She hated being at loggerheads with Jared, who had been kinder to her than anyone. But she didn't know how to apologize. She didn't even know who started it. Jared was unhappy with her, and she didn't know why.

She played with the kitten in the kitchen and looked out the back window at the garden. Henry was pottering among the vegetables, but without any care for the small seedlings. It was like letting an ax murderer loose among them. She glowered at him. If only she didn't have to be decorous! In some ways, it was better when she was living in poverty in Galveston. At least there, nosy neighbors didn't watch her every move with malice.

Mrs. Hardy was on her back porch, watering her leafy

plants. The woman had nothing that flowered, and Noelle thought wickedly that they probably shriveled from the woman's malignant presence. She probably curdled milk, too.

"Oh, I am wicked," she told the kitten, and went back to dragging the string for him.

Later, she put on the green silk gown with its white lace trim and arranged her hair in its puffy high coiffure. She had no jewelry to wear with it, but the dress didn't really require it. She had a lacy black mantilla to keep her warm. She draped it around her slender neck and stared at her reflection with little real appreciation. Jared had bought the dress, and she had been unkind to him. Not that his behavior had been any better, but she regretted her lapse. She would have to apologize. Despite their differences, he was in a strange way the best friend she had. At least he was as long as she didn't think too hard about the feel of his mouth and the tenderness of his hands. He was old, she kept telling herself, and crippled and bookish. She was much better suited to young, dashing Andrew. And perhaps she could learn to appreciate his touch as she did Jared's.

Andrew took her to dinner at Monaco's and he was delightful company. He regaled her with stories of his week's business and the people he'd met in his travels. He found people fascinating, and it was obvious that he enjoyed them. Noelle was more reticent, more withdrawn. In fact, she was like Jared, who conducted business quite well but who kept to himself at other times. His private life was all too private. He had hinted at dark secrets, and no one in the family seemed to know much about him—not even his grandmother. She wondered what kind of life he had led. He might have been very poor, as she had been. Or he might have been crippled in a fight over the woman in his past.

No. He'd told her that his injury was recent and temporary. She wondered how he got it.

"Do you know anything about Jared's childhood?" she asked suddenly.

Andrew's eyebrows went up. "Jared?" He blinked thoughtfully. "Well, no. As I once mentioned, I had very little to do with him. He was seldom here, and we never spent time together. He does not speak of his early life."

"I had noticed." She traced the fine lace collar of her dress with her fingers. "He had Mrs. Pate take me shopping," she said after a minute. "He said that I had nothing proper to wear, and that he did not want a relative of his to attract unkind comment." She looked up suddenly and saw a strange look on his face. "I should have mentioned it before."

"How unusual, that Jared would care," he commented. His eyes narrowed. So Jared was interested in his young cousin. That would explain his anger this morning. He understood now. He had brought Noelle home—and the kisses he had shared with her were insinuated by the way Andrew addressed her. Jared had noticed, and he had become jealous. Did she know? He studied her thoroughly. No. She did not seem to understand at all. Jared had attacked her and she had retaliated. That she was disturbed by the argument was also evident.

He sat back in his chair with a calculating smile. He had never found himself the rival of his stepbrother in any way. It had irritated him that Jared should come home to Fort Worth and immediately become a social success because of his impeccable reputation as a criminal attorney. Andrew was younger, more handsome and more debonair. But Jared had the community in thrall and Andrew had been pushed aside for him on guest list after guest list. And last night, Jared had counted the social coup of the season by escorting one of the most beautiful women in Fort Worth to a dance—one, moreover, who'd rejected Andrew.

But it was Noelle who had his eye, and it was obvious to the whole family that Noelle wanted Andrew. Even Mrs.

Dunn had remarked on Noelle's infatuation. He was secretly delighted, because he had something that Jared wanted. He had Noelle's heart.

He wasn't sure that he really wanted it. She was more accomplished than she had been, she was pretty and sweet and pleasant to be around. But she had drawbacks, like that flash-fire temper and her inclination to do unladylike things. He could always change her to suit him, though, if he ever got around to thoughts of marriage. He was not yet thirty, and that lay far in the future.

His eyes dropped to her bodice and lingered there while he pretended to look at his crystal water glass. It would be interesting to see how she reacted to real lovemaking. He might find her more receptive to him than he'd first thought. A little dalliance was, after all, permissible to a bachelor. And cutting Jared out was appealing.

"However you came by the dress, you look lovely in it," he told her.

She smiled. "Thank you, Andrew. You are very dashing yourself."

He smoothed his mustache and studied her quietly. "But the next time you need new clothes, let me assume the bill."

"Andrew!"

"I don't like having you receive things from my stepbrother," he continued. "It's his house, and I live there. But you are my responsibility, not his. I assumed that responsibility when I asked you to come and live with Grandmother and me."

"Yes, and I'm more grateful than you know—" she began.

"Let me finish." He looked very stern. "Jared is very taken with Miss Doyle," he lied, noticing how Noelle's face closed up. "I think that he may eventually marry her. If this is the case, then he shouldn't do anything that would seem less than proper. Buying your clothing isn't quite proper for a man when he's considering becoming engaged, Noelle."

She flushed. Her hand went to her throat. Jared hadn't told her about any engagement. And he had held her, kissed her. Her face grew hard. Had he been playing, then? Was it a last fling before he gave Miss Doyle a ring?

"He was angry because I insulted her by bringing up that scandal in her past," she said, thinking aloud. "But it was Miss Doyle who insulted me first."

"She thought you a rival for his affections," he said, chuckling. "Imagine that, when you are only Jared's cousin. And mine, of course."

Only his cousin. She could picture Jared with that beautiful woman in his arms, kissing her as he'd kissed Noelle the night before, making her moan with shocked passion. She swallowed. Her body felt tight and hot even with the memory. Jared might not be a man of action, but he had a way with women that was not immediately evident when one saw him in public. And a man did not gain such experience with only one woman. Even in her naïveté she knew that.

"Did he tell you…that he was considering Miss Doyle for his wife?" she asked.

His eyes were on his plate. "Certainly."

She hated the emptiness inside her. She had no claim on Jared. But she was possessive about him, without knowing why. He had been kind to her. Surely that was all. After all, she had been infatuated with Andrew since her first glimpse of him.

She looked up now, studying his handsome face with quick, interested eyes. He was very handsome, she admitted, and good company. But when he touched her, why did she feel no excitement, no surge of emotion?

"We get along well, don't we?" he asked, smiling.

She nodded. They did. They never argued like cats and dogs or had flare-ups like she and Jared did.

"I think that we may be well suited," he said. "Time will tell." He sat up. "Finish your dessert, dear girl. We mustn't be late for the curtain."

The play was from the New York stage, with actors who made Noelle alternately laugh and cry. It was billed as a comedy, but it was poignant just the same. She watched it raptly, and thought how much Jared would have enjoyed it. Andrew seemed interested, but the poignant parts went right past him. He was not a sensitive man. Probably being in the army for so long had affected him.

Jared had mentioned a brief stint with the Texas Rangers. She wondered if he had done other law-enforcement work, and how dangerous it might have been for him. She lifted her head with sudden enlightenment. Jared had been a Texas Ranger. That meant that he had to know how to use a gun, how to ride, how to confront and handle violent men. Why, how could that have escaped her all this time? She hadn't really thought about what he'd told her. She'd called him a milksop. Her cheeks grew hot.

"What's wrong?" Andrew asked as the play finished and they walked toward the theater entrance. "You looked very sad at the end of the play."

"I was only thinking." She looked at him. "Does Jared ride?" she asked suddenly.

The question surprised him. He laughed aloud. "Ride? Heavens, he fell off a horse and hurt his leg!"

"Did he tell you that?" she persisted.

He shrugged. "No. But it's logical, isn't it? He's a city man and he was recently on a case in New Mexico, my grandmother said. Probably he had to ride a horse to get to the courthouse and it threw him."

She was sure that Jared hadn't fallen off any horse. But she only smiled. "Of course," she agreed pleasantly. "I'm sorry that I argued with him. I shall have to be less unkind. I do owe him a great deal. And I must apologize to Miss Doyle also." She glowered. "If she's to become a member of the family, she'll have to be treated kindly."

"She's very beautiful."

She nodded sadly. "Yes, indeed." It hurt her to think of Jared with the woman.

It wasn't really late when they returned home. In fact, someone was visiting, because Noelle heard voices coming behind the closed living room door. She started toward it, but Andrew caught her hand and tugged her toward the parlor.

He put a finger to his lips and smiled conspiratorially.

He drew her into the parlor and closed the door, chuckling at her expression. "Do you want to sit around and listen to female complaints for an hour or more?"

"Not really," she confessed, and smiled back.

"Good. Would you like a cordial?"

"Yes, please."

He poured her one, and she tried not to remember as she looked around the room that Jared had been in here with her only last night in a state of undress.

When Andrew handed her the small cordial glass she had to forcibly evict the startling memories that made her body tingle.

He had a brandy snifter with only a small portion of the bottom filled. He warmed it in his hands while Noelle sipped her drink and walked idly past the bookshelf, looking at the titles.

"A great many of these are law books," she remarked.

"Yes. Jared has moved most of his books to his office, but

he likes to keep these here. I had to remove my collection of first editions to accommodate them," he muttered.

"First editions? What were they?" she asked, interested.

"I have no idea," he said, smiling. "I invested in them, that's all. I hate taking the time to read books."

"But what a waste!"

He shrugged. "I'm a man of action, my dear," he reminded her. "Not a bookworm."

He was referring to Jared. She was sure of it. But she didn't reply.

He watched her for a long time. Finally he put his brandy snifter down and took her half-empty glass from her hands. He put it beside his glass and turned off the lights. Then he pulled her toward him.

Jared had done much the same the night before. But Noelle's whole body had clenched with need at the first glance of his pale eyes. Andrew was already holding her, and she felt nothing. Nothing at all.

"Don't worry," he whispered, smiling as he bent to kiss her. "I mean you no insult. But I do so love the taste of your mouth, Noelle. It excites me to hold so innocent a woman in my arms."

She started to speak, but his mouth covered hers hungrily, and he began to kiss her, confident his advances would be welcome.

His mouth was warm and wet and she did not like the way his tongue kept poking inside her lips. He might be a good soldier, but his talent as a lover was limited.

Noelle's hands pushed gently at his chest. It had released her immediately from Jared, but Andrew was made of different stuff. He clasped her to his body with both arms and his mouth became insistent. One hand slid quickly down her body and caught her skirt, pulling it up so that his hand could find her leg. He reached above her garter-held cotton hose to her thigh, where the long legs of her ruffled muslin bloomers reached.

She gasped and pushed, but he kept right on, her skirt hiked to reveal much of her leg.

"Relax," he said huskily. "Relax, there is nothing…to be afraid of."

He bent suddenly and put his open mouth right on her breast.

And while they stood like that, Noelle protesting, Andrew with one hand up her skirt and his mouth covering the whole thrust of her breast, the parlor door suddenly opened.

There was no time to react. Mrs. Dunn and Mrs. Hardy, who had come to borrow a history of Fort Worth for a Daughters of the American Revolution article she was researching, stood in the doorway with the light from the hall behind them and their mouths wide-open, gasping at the sight that met their shocked, horrified eyes. It was dim in the room, and Andrew was in the shadows, but Noelle wasn't. There was enough light to see that her skirt was pulled up and a man's head was at her breast.

And to make it worse, Jared had just come into the hall. He was behind them, but not too far away to miss the couple silhouetted against the window. Noelle thought that as long as she lived, she would never forget the way he looked at them.

Andrew had kept his back to the door, sliding farther into the shadows, but Noelle stood there like an accused prisoner. The damage was done.

"I will…speak to you…presently." Mrs. Dunn choked. She herded the gaping Mrs. Hardy out the door so quickly that she didn't see Jared standing in the doorway of the living room. The women's muted, stiff voices resounded down the hall before they went out onto the porch, closing the door behind them.

When he heard the voices retreat, Andrew came out of the shadows and stopped dead as his stepbrother came through the doorway.

"Jared." Andrew laughed nervously, holding out both hands. "Surely you understand. We forgot ourselves in a moment of passion."

Jared didn't speak. Not one word. He was looking at Noelle with eyes she couldn't meet.

"It's a misunderstanding," Andrew continued, glancing at Noelle in something like panic. His fair complexion was very red and he looked frightened. He'd never thought to be discovered in such a scandalous position, and with a woman who hadn't even wanted his embraces. "Noelle, tell him!" he pleaded.

She was shaking, from revulsion as well as shock and sick fear. "It was…a mistake," she whispered.

"One you'll both have to pay for," Jared said finally, his voice as cold as his eyes. "I won't have my grandmother subjected to this sort of scandal. Mrs. Hardy's proclivity for gossip is well-known to you. If you had to sport with each other, you might have had the decency to make certain you wouldn't be discovered."

Noelle felt closer to a faint than ever before in her life. Her face was paper white. She couldn't manage a single word through her tight throat.

Andrew looked haunted. "What shall we do?" he said.

"Do? You'll get married," Jared said mercilessly. He smiled, but it wasn't a pleasant smile. "And the sooner, the better."

"Married? I can't marry Noelle!" Andrew burst out. He glanced at her and grimaced. "Forgive me, Noelle, but marriage is out of the question. Why, we're cousins, Jared. Yes, that's it! We're blood relations. There would be talk…"

"Oh, there certainly will be talk," Jared agreed. He didn't move. "You'll do the honorable thing if I have to escort you down the aisle at gunpoint." And at that moment he looked capable of it.

Andrew, who'd underestimated the older man at every turn, found himself in a corner without hope of escape. He didn't want to marry Noelle, but Jared was looking murderous.

"You've ruined her," Jared accused.

Andrew stared at him. And then, at once, he understood. Jared thought that he'd compromised Noelle, that this was only an indication of the intimacy of their relationship.

He was as angry as Jared. He wouldn't be forced into marriage. He wouldn't!

"Can one ruin a fallen flower?" Andrew demanded indignantly.

Noelle's lips fell open. "Andrew!" she said, gasping. "Oh, how could you? How could you insinuate such a vile thing about me?"

"Forgive me, Noelle, but a man must be honest when he's threatened with an unwanted marriage," Andrew said stiffly. Jared looked briefly uncertain, and Andrew's confidence grew. "I won't marry her," he told Jared. "I want a chaste woman for my bride, not a soiled one. She permitted my touch, after all. She is nothing but a slut—"

The words broke on Jared's fist. The older man decked Andrew with no effort at all and landed him on his back on the floor. Jared moved slowly toward him, with that unblinking stare that had unmanned Andrew once before.

"Jared, no!" he cried, holding up both arms defensively.

"Get up," Jared said coldly. His fists were clenched at his sides and he wasn't limping.

Andrew rolled away and got to his feet, retreating to the desk. He didn't look like anyone's idea of a war hero. He looked more like a frightened boy in the grip of a schoolmaster.

Noelle walked to the door.

"Come back here," Jared said venomously.

She didn't stop or turn to look at him. She opened the door.

"I won't marry Andrew," she said, and still didn't look at him. "He's lying. I've done nothing with him, or any other man, that would ruin me—and what occurred just now was forced on me."

"A convenient excuse," Jared drawled contemptuously. "And I know better," he added meaningfully, watching her face tauten at the insinuation of how well he knew her physical response to ardor. "But it won't save you. You'll marry Andrew or I'll throw you both out of my house."

"There'll be no need to throw me out," she said huskily, wounded to the bone. "I shall pack immediately. My uncle will give me a home." She went through the open door and up the staircase, determined not to let him see her cry. Andrew's lies made everything so much worse. And now Mrs. Hardy would have plenty of things to gossip about. Poor Mrs. Dunn!·

Chapter Ten

Noelle couldn't remember ever feeling so miserable. Andrew had made her out to be a loose woman, Jared believed her capable of sporting with any man at all, and Mrs. Dunn would probably never speak to her again. Worse, the terrible Mrs. Hardy would gleefully spread news of Noelle's downfall around the city to anyone who would listen.

She put her few possessions into her nice valise and looked wistfully at the pretty things Jared had bought her, still hanging in the chifforobe against the wall. She didn't want things from a man who could think her so vile a woman. He wouldn't even listen to her explanation. He'd judged her and found her guilty from Andrew's cowardly lie. His contempt hurt more than the threat of having her good name ruined in the community.

With her cloak around her, dressed in the familiar white blouse and black skirt, with a simple wide-brimmed black hat on her head, she left the room she'd occupied for so many months and made her way down the staircase.

Andrew was nowhere in sight. He was probably nursing the cheek Jared had hit. She was surprised that Jared had done that when he held her in such contempt, but she was pleased that Andrew had at least some small retribution for the lie he'd told. She'd idolized Andrew until the first time Jared had kissed her. How strange, she thought, that Andrew was everything Jared was not, and yet it was Jared whose admiration and attention she craved. What a tragedy that it should have taken this to make her realize that she had no affection at all for Andrew!

With her head high she went straight to the front door and opened it. She had no money, no train ticket, no place to go except her uncle's and no way to get there. But she was too proud to ask the family for help. She would wait tables, if she had to, or cook in a kitchen or get a job as a housekeeper and earn her way back to East Texas. She'd starve before she'd ask Jared for help now.

But as she opened the door and started onto the porch, a steely, merciless hand caught her by the upper arm and dragged her back into the house. The valise was taken from her and tossed aside; the door was closed.

She jerked away from Jared with hatred in her green eyes. "Don't you touch me!" she hissed.

"Why deny me what you dole out to other men?" he asked, still in a quiet rage at what he'd seen.

She rubbed the arm he'd gripped and stared at him accusingly. "Andrew lied," she said flatly. "I wasn't encouraging him, I was trying to get away. Or do you think I welcome such blatant advances from a man?" And then she remembered how eagerly she'd responded to Jared and blushed furiously.

He mistook that flush for guilt. His pale eyes narrowed. They were unblinking, steady, frightening in that lean, rigid face. "How easily you lie," he remarked in a deep, soft undertone. "Women are treacherous at best. I'd actually forgotten how treacherous until tonight."

Her hands clenched at her sides. "Believe what you like, then, Mr. Dunn," she said formally. "I want to go now."

"Where?" he asked angrily. "It's the middle of the night, and you have no money."

"I'll earn it!"

Her haughtiness outraged him. He couldn't get the picture of her with Andrew out of his mind. Every time he thought of it, he hated them both. It didn't occur to him to wonder why. "And where will you work to earn money?" he demanded. He smiled coldly. "In a brothel?"

Her gasp was followed by a furious upswing of her hand, which he caught effortlessly. She'd never been able to land a slap on that arrogant face. He was incredibly quick.

He threw her hand down. "Will you never learn?" he muttered. "A lady doesn't indulge in brawls."

"I'm no lady," she said, stinging from his remarks. "And you're no gentleman!" Tears of pain and loss stung her eyes, although she was too proud to shed them. Her eyes widened, trying to hold them back.

But he saw the shimmer and he felt bad about the things he was saying to her. She loved Andrew. Everyone knew it. Andrew had seduced her and now he was trying to make it sound as if she were no better than a prostitute. He was furious, but not quite furious enough to believe that of her. She had a sweet, passionate nature but she'd been untouched when he first took her into his arms. Whatever had occurred with Andrew had been very recent, because the shy, half-frightened girl to whom he'd made gentle love had not been a fallen woman.

He stuck his hands in his pockets to keep from grabbing her and shaking the truth out of her.

"Why should I care what you say?" she asked huskily. "After all, Andrew's made me out to be no better than I should be. Perhaps you think I'm only fit for a brothel…" Her voice broke and a single tear escaped her eye.

That did it. With a soft groan, he reached for her, pulling her roughly against his broad chest, wrapping her up tightly in his arms. "I can't bear to see you cry," he ground out at her ear. "Stop it."

She hit his chest, trying to stem the hot tears. "I'm not…a fallen woman," she bit off.

"For God's sake!" He pressed her face closer. "Did I say that you were?" he demanded.

"You said I could go to a brothel," she said tearfully.

He sighed heavily. "Noelle," he bit off. His cheek nuzzled hers. "Noelle," he whispered huskily. "I didn't mean it."

He rocked her in his arms until the sobs died away. Then he handed her a handkerchief and watched broodingly while she dried the tears. His hands were back in his pockets again and he watched her steadily.

She hated that intense stare. She didn't know what he was thinking. He said that he hadn't meant it, about calling her a loose woman, but he thought less of her. She knew it.

"I've reacted badly," he said after a minute, having regained the control she nearly cost him with her unexpected vulnerability. "What you do with Andrew is, after all, your business. But the two of you have created a scandal. Mrs. Hardy will have it all over town that you and Andrew were in a state of dishabille in a room, alone. By the time she's finished exaggerating it, you'll have been found in bed together."

She bit her lower lip hard and lifted her chin. "Will you lend me the price of a train ticket to Galveston?" she asked proudly.

"And if you leave, what then?" he demanded. "What about

my grandmother? Have you considered what the scandal will do to her life, while you're safely away?"

"I don't want to marry Andrew," she said harshly. "He lied!"

"Oh, what does it matter?" he burst out. His pale blue eyes were unyielding. "It's common knowledge that you worship him. I can't hold you in contempt for giving way to your feelings for him, when it was so obvious that he shared your hunger."

"But we did nothing," she persisted. "Jared, he—"

"I don't want to know any more," he said wearily. "You and Andrew can work this out together. But you must marry. A scandal of this sort is unthinkable. My grandmother has a weak heart. I can't allow her to suffer the sort of notoriety she'll be subjected to if this is unresolved. I think you have some idea of the effect gossip has on her already."

From her gardening, she thought miserably. Yes, she knew that Mrs. Dunn had suffered from the gossip started by Mrs. Hardy.

"I don't want to marry Andrew," she repeated.

He laughed coldly. "What you want doesn't matter."

She clasped her hands in front of her. "You sound so superior," she said quietly, lifting her eyes to his. "And yet you made love to me when you were all but engaged to Miss Doyle."

His eyebrows lifted. "Engaged?" he exclaimed.

The door to the living room opened and Andrew came out into the hall. He was glowering and red-faced, and through the open door, Noelle could see little Mrs. Dunn sitting bowed and tearful on the sofa.

Andrew glared at Jared and fingered his bruised cheek. "There was no reason to hit me," he began.

Jared, still angry, turned toward him in a threatening way, and Andrew actually backed up.

"No reason?" he asked, nodding toward Mrs. Dunn. "What would you call that? You've disgraced us. You have the morals of a rutting pig."

Andrew inhaled sharply. "You have no right to speak to me like that!"

"The hell I haven't. This is my house," Jared reminded him. "You puffed-up little dandy, who do you think you are?"

Andrew grew redder. He glared at Noelle. "She tempted me," he accused, and then averted his eyes from the look on her face.

"And you couldn't resist her," Jared drawled.

"No, I couldn't. She's very attractive," he admitted, "and she hung on my every word. She watched me all the time. How could a man not react to such admiration from a pretty woman?"

Jared knew this to be true, and so did Noelle. She wanted to say that she had found Andrew less attractive with each day she spent in his company, but Jared's expression was uncompromising. He might comfort her, but he wouldn't believe her.

She stared at Andrew with bitter resentment. He made it sound so logical. And yet it hadn't been that way at all. He'd forced his unwanted attentions on her and now he was denying it—and Jared wouldn't believe her. Why should he, though? Jared had no feelings for her, unless it was one of mild physical attraction. He himself had no scruples about kissing her in dark rooms at night, but he was outraged when Andrew did the same thing. She could hardly say that.

"You must see that marriage would be a grave mistake," Andrew said, pleading with his stepbrother. Then laughing, he said, "It was only a kiss, after all."

"You insinuated that it was much more," Jared reminded him.

Andrew cleared his throat. He couldn't brand himself a

liar, nor could he make an already bad situation worse. "I'm only human," he said then, to save face.

Jared's eyes were using other adjectives to describe the pretentious man facing him. Andrew put on airs and pretended to be a war hero, when Jared knew for a fact that the younger man had held down a desk job in the Philippines and had never been in combat. He had kept his silence because it was no concern of his if Andrew wanted to play toy soldier. But Noelle and other women took that swaggering hero image at face value, and it had led to Noelle's downfall.

"I can't marry you," Andrew told Noelle. "I'm sorry. You're very pretty and I'm fond of you, but you're not the sort of wife I want. I had been seeing Miss Beale," he reminded her, wincing at Jared's expression.

"And despite that, you toyed with Noelle's affections," the older man accused.

"She invited it!" Andrew raged. "It's unspeakable to say so, but she teased me until I was wild. Surely you're man enough to understand that."

Jared lifted an eyebrow. His stepbrother was probably voicing the collective notion of what he appeared to be. He didn't really mind. But he did mind Andrew's determination to leave Noelle in the lurch. It was a very serious matter. If there was no marriage, the scandal would be unbelievable.

"I'll go to Dallas and work out of our office there," Andrew announced firmly. "I can arrange that very easily. Perhaps when I'm gone, the gossip will die down."

"Do you think so?" Jared asked mockingly.

"It's no longer my concern. I'm sorry for the embarrassment to Grandmother, but I'm not willing to sacrifice my entire life to stem gossip when none of this was my fault."

He nodded curtly and stepped warily around Jared, quickly moving out the door. He didn't spare Noelle even a glance.

When it closed behind him, Jared was left with Noelle

in the hall. A subdued, worried Mrs. Dunn came out of the living room.

"Whatever shall we do?" she moaned. "Mrs. Hardy was shocked and livid with outrage. She'll tell everyone. And now Andrew has run away in the middle of the night!"

"There's only one thing that can be done." Jared didn't look at Noelle as he spoke, but his posture became even more rigid. "I'll marry her myself."

"Never!" Noelle burst out furiously. "I wouldn't marry you if you came with a trunkload of gold sovereigns!"

He looked at her without speaking, one eyebrow lifted.

"Yes," Mrs. Dunn said, ignoring the red-faced girl. "Yes, that would be an ideal solution, Jared. Mrs. Hardy didn't really see anyone except Noelle. Andrew was in the shadows with his back to the door, and Mrs. Hardy didn't see you at all, because you came up behind us after she had seen Noelle. It was dark in the room and she got only a glimpse, and while she and I started toward the front door, you went quickly into the room with them and closed the door." She was nodding as she considered it. "Yes, we might convince her that she saw you instead of Andrew with Noelle."

"It doesn't matter what anyone will think, because I won't marry you," Noelle told the tall man belligerently, even as her heart ran wild at just the thought of being Jared's wife.

He lifted his chin arrogantly. "You have no choice in the matter," he said. "It was your behavior that landed us in this mess."

"I didn't do it all by myself! And Andrew lied," she said. She stomped her foot furiously. "Why won't you believe me? He pawed me!"

"You invited it," Jared said mercilessly. His pale eyes blazed at her. "For weeks you've been his shadow, doing his paperwork at night, hanging on his every word, staring at him adoringly. He's a man. What did you expect?"

She shivered with revulsion at the memory of Andrew's wet mouth on hers. "Even if I am partially to blame, he had no right to make me sound like a loose woman," she said passionately. "He's a cad!"

"Pretending rage will do us no good," he replied indifferently. "You'll marry me as soon as we can arrange the ceremony."

"Why are you willing to sacrifice yourself?" she demanded. "And won't your precious Miss Doyle slash her wrists if you leave her in the lurch?"

"Miss Doyle is none of your concern," he said flatly. "As for the sacrifice, surely you know that I'd do anything to spare my grandmother further pain."

Noelle looked at the older woman and her rage melted away. Poor little Mrs. Dunn was paper white, and her small body was more stooped than usual with age and dejection. It didn't take much guesswork to know that Mrs. Hardy would have a field day about the scandal.

Jared saw the expression on Noelle's face and knew that he'd won. He couldn't permit a scandal of this sort to put his grandmother in her grave. She'd been his anchor all his life. He would have done anything for her—even marry a soiled dove like Noelle. He thought back to the first kiss he'd shared with Noelle and his heart hurt. She'd been innocent then, he was certain of it. But she'd wanted Andrew, not Jared. And judging by the familiarity and intimacy with which Andrew had been handling her in the study, she'd been in Andrew's bed. He was sick at the thought.

"It won't be so terrible a thing, Noelle," Mrs. Dunn said gently. "You must save your reputation. And ours. Think what the scandal would do to Jared's law practice."

That hadn't occurred to her. Jared might be well-known in New York, but he was only just getting started here. A scandal might cost him business.

"My practice isn't what concerns me," Jared said. He was leaning against the wall, looking worn and irritated. "If Noelle's reputation can be salvaged, that must be our first priority."

She looked down at her feet. What he meant was his grandmother's. He was being gallant, something that her dashing Andrew wasn't.

He shouldered away from the wall. "Can you make the arrangements, or shall I have my secretary make them?" he asked his grandmother.

"I can't see Adrian being quite that efficient, Jared. I'll be happy to do it," Mrs. Dunn said proudly. She touched Noelle's shoulder lightly. "Don't look so sad, child. None of us is perfect. God forgives."

God might, but Jared looked as if he never would. Mrs. Dunn went back into the living room, mumbling to herself about invitations and a minister.

"Your hero had feet of clay, didn't he?" Jared taunted, with a twisted smile. "He ran like a chased rabbit."

She swallowed. "He isn't what he seemed to be," she said faintly.

"No one is. Not even you. I thought you were a model of purity, of all the virtues," he said shortly. "But you're a dark angel, Noelle. You've disappointed me."

She drew in an indignant breath. "Perhaps I did lead Andrew to believe that his attentions would be welcome," she confessed tautly. "But he made advances that I neither encouraged nor wanted. Believe that if you believe nothing else good about me."

"What I believe is irrelevant," he said carelessly. "I hope that you don't expect to share my bed," he added softly, lest his grandmother hear. "Despite your attractions, I have no desire for my stepbrother's leavings."

She shuddered with pent-up rage. Her face, drawn and

white, was as tight as her clenched hands. "Nor have I any desire to be intimate with a man who thinks of me as a soiled woman!"

He inclined his head mockingly. "So long as we understand each other," he said politely.

She stared at his back when he left her, wishing she had a heavy object to heave at it. Oh, she could refuse to marry him; she could leave and go home to East Texas. There might be a way she could borrow the money. But it would leave poor Mrs. Dunn in an untenable position—and might cost her her life. Noelle *had* encouraged Andrew, but she hadn't realized how distasteful his attentions would be. She'd loved the touch of Jared's hands and mouth, she'd gloried in the look on his face when he held her. She'd expected that, and more, when Andrew kissed her. But she'd felt only revulsion for the handsome blond ex-soldier.

The reason for her inexplicable emotions confounded her. Why, Jared was much older than she was, and mocking, and half the time he acted as if he hated her. He was withdrawn, moody, stoic. Yet, he'd been so kind to her. No one in her life, except her late parents, had ever treated her so tenderly.

Not anymore, though. His contempt was so obvious as to be tangible. He'd marry her for Mrs. Dunn's sake, but never for his own. He wanted the elegant Miss Doyle.

She bit her lower lip hard. What a terrible situation it was, for all of them. And the only solution was a marriage that would make everyone miserable.

Wedding plans were made and announced, and not a minute too soon. Already people were whispering every time they saw Noelle with Mrs. Dunn anywhere in town. Fort Worth was big, and getting bigger, but people knew one another just the same. The local newspaper carried news of who was visiting in each hotel, and the society page was full of cheerful gossip about local people. Fort Worth was a small town that grew, retaining all the intimacy of its past, so that it was more like family than community.

But family could be cruel when scandals broke, and every time Mrs. Dunn's lower lip trembled from the malicious, loud gossip, Noelle felt guilty.

When the wedding announcement made it into print in the *Fort Worth Morning Register,* Mrs. Pate came home from the market with a basketful of meat, coffee and flour, and a smug smile.

"There, that's given them something to gnaw on, the vicious old gossips," Mrs. Pate said when she greeted Noelle, who was stringing beans at the table.

"What has?" Noelle asked.

"The wedding announcement. Now it's said that Mrs. Hardy got it all backward, and who she saw was you and Mr. Jared spooning. In fact," she added, with a laugh, "they're saying that you'd just got engaged when Mrs. Dunn and Mrs. Hardy walked in on you."

Noelle picked up another bean. She wasn't feeling elated, as Mrs. Pate was. "At least perhaps they won't whisper so much around Mrs. Dunn now. It's been hard on her. I've feared for her heart."

"I wouldn't worry so much. She's a tough old bird," Mrs. Pate said heartily. "I remember when she first came here with Mr. Jared's dear mother," she added wistfully. "Why, she had to be hog-tied so that she'd stay out of the flower garden with that hoe."

Noelle's gasp was audible.

Mrs. Pate pursed her lips and stared at Noelle whimsically over her glasses. "Didn't know that, did you? Ah, she had the tongues wagging, she did. That's why she made such a fuss about you."

"I've behaved shamefully," Noelle said. "I've embarrassed

everyone ever since I came here, and now I've made us notorious."

"Mr. Andrew helped," she said curtly. "Imagine him, running like a yellow dog and leaving Mr. Jared to make it right. It's always been that way, too. Why, Mr. Jared's bailed him out of more scrapes over the years, and never complained. He had to pay one time to keep Andrew out of jail over some vandalism he did downtown."

Noelle's hands stilled. "You're very fond of Jared, aren't you?" she asked.

Mrs. Pate nodded. Overhead, the ceiling fan spun merrily, its faint *burr* pleasant in the late morning. Sun filtered through the curtains, making patterns on the wooden kitchen table where Noelle was working.

"Mrs. Pate, may I ask you something?"

"Why, of course, dear."

"Is Andrew really a war hero?" she asked gently.

"No more than I am," came the terse reply. "He was a clerk in the supply depot in the Philippines," she scoffed. "Never even shot a gun. And here he comes home swaggering and bragging about his service to his country and all these fine deeds he did. Huh!"

"Was Jared in the service?"

She nodded. "He never spoke of it," she said. "He was in the reserves. His unit was called up and he went to Cuba with some of his friends."

"Is that where his leg was hurt?" she asked.

"No."

"Do you know how it was hurt?"

"Yes." She studied Noelle's face. "It's for him to tell you that. He's a very private man, is Mr. Jared. What I know, I don't talk about. That's why I'm still employed here."

"Forgive me, I didn't mean to pry. It's just that I know so little about him."

"Plenty of time to learn, after you're married." She paused in her unpacking of the shopping bag to look at Noelle. "All you need to know is that he's ten times the man Mr. Andrew is. He doesn't swagger or brag. But he doesn't run, either. Never has."

Noelle went back to her beans.

The wedding gown was the most glorious garment Noelle had ever seen in her life. She hadn't wanted something so elegant, but Jared had insisted.

"Those gossiping old biddies aren't going to make a verbal meal out of you," he said when she protested the expense of sending to New York for an imported Paris wedding gown. "You're going to have an original, and it's going to be the most expensive one there is."

"Is this really necessary—just to make a point?" she asked.

"Yes."

She gnawed her lower lip. "I could still go away."

"You aren't going anywhere…except to church to be married," he said shortly.

The dress had arrived days later, matching exactly the measurements that Noelle's local dressmaker had provided, and when she unpacked it from its huge box, she was astonished at the yards and yards of imported lace that trimmed it.

"Brussels lace," Mrs. Dunn had exclaimed. "Oh, how exquisite, Noelle! No one will ever forget how you look in it."

Noelle touched the lace. It was delicate and pretty. But she was marrying for all the wrong reasons. The joyous occasion she'd dreamed of since girlhood was tarnished, and she looked ahead to sadness and grief. A loveless marriage would be a sort of hell.

Chapter Eleven

Jared viewed his approaching marriage with the same resignation that a man facing a firing squad would feel. He hated being forced by social convention to marry a woman for whom he had only contempt—his stepbrother's fallen angel.

He knew that women were treacherous, but Noelle had melted in his arms, welcomed his kisses. And despite her headlong response, she'd gone from his arms to Andrew's in less than a day.

Not that he cared, he told himself firmly. He'd felt sorry for her at first, but that was all. The unwanted physical attraction he felt for her was unexpected, but it changed nothing. He should have been firmer; he should have insisted that Andrew do the honorable thing. Yet, somehow, he couldn't bear the thought of seeing Noelle married to his stepbrother. That was why he hadn't protested Andrew's defection.

He scowled out the window as he pondered his own strange

behavior. He didn't understand why the woman should have become so important to him. She was much too young for him, in the first place, and she'd been in love with Andrew for months. She might feel desire for Jared, but it had been made obvious to him that she felt it for Andrew, as well. And she loved Andrew. It was folly to marry her, scandal or no scandal. But there was his grandmother, he told himself, finding reason after reason that made the marriage logical. It didn't occur to him that he was justifying it to himself because he wanted Noelle any way he could get her.

A knock on the door interrupted his train of thought. "Mr. Dunn, there's a man to see you, sir," his secretary, Adrian, told him.

"Send him in."

Adrian stood aside to let a tall black man in a worn suit enter the room. The black man had his hat in his hand, and he looked tired and out of humor. But he didn't look at his feet or stumble over apologies for interrupting the attorney without an appointment.

"Mr. Dunn?"

"I am."

"I am Brian Clark," the black man told him. "I would like you to represent me."

"On what charge?"

The man lifted his chin proudly. "On a charge of robbery and assault, sir. I expect to be arrested momentarily."

Jared's eyebrows lifted. There was a noise outside the office, muffled voices coming closer, a door opening and closing. Louder voices in the outer office. A thud. And then a knock on the door.

It opened, and Jared stared at the uniformed police officer and the city police detective beside him. The policeman had jurisdiction over the crime, because the robbery had occurred inside town. The city detective, who wore a low-slung sidearm, was obviously along in case there was any trouble.

"Sorry, sir," Adrian apologized. "They refused to wait until I announced them."

Jared waved him away with a lean hand. He moved toward them, at the same time maneuvering himself in front of Brian Clark. He took off his reading glasses. "May I help you?"

"We want that colored man," the policeman said. "He stole a hundred dollars from old man Ted Marlowe at the dry-goods store—knocked him over the head with a pistol barrel and left him for dead. Doc says it's a miracle he's still alive, but he ain't conscious yet. He's in a coma. Doc says he may not live."

"Have you evidence to support a warrant?"

The officer stared at him. "I beg your pardon?"

"I won't surrender Mr. Clark until you produce a warrant for his arrest, stating the charges against him. You're an officer of the court, as I am. I operate by the book. As every public official should," he added, with a cold smile.

"Well, I never did," the city detective, Sims, said heavily. "You're going to protect that…" and he used an epithet that made the black man cringe.

"His name is Clark," Jared corrected. "It's easy enough to say."

Sims snorted. "He beat and robbed an old storekeeper— old Mr. Marlowe—and you want to keep us from arresting him?"

"Arrest him. But get a warrant first."

The police officer hesitated, but he didn't like Jared's stance any more than he liked that threatening blue stare. He'd heard things about this lawyer fellow from New York from the judge that he hadn't quite believed. Until now.

"I'll be right back," he said curtly. "You make sure he's here when I return."

"He will be," Jared said easily. "An innocent man doesn't need to run."

The policeman made a rough sound at that and motioned the city detective, a tall, foxy man who was also his friend, to follow him. The door closed.

The black man let out a heavy breath. "You took a chance, Mr. Dunn."

"Not a very big one. I had the law on my side. Sit down."

Brian Clark slid into a chair and sat with his long legs splayed, his face drawn with pain.

"They said Ted Marlowe was robbed. Why do they think you did it?" Jared asked. He tossed his glasses on the brief he'd been reading and perched himself on the edge of his desk.

"I was set up, Mr. Dunn," came the quiet reply. "There's a man at Beale's ranch, where I work, who hates me. He's tried for months to make trouble for me. He got liquored up last night and said he was never going to let me have the foreman's job out at Beale's. He said he'd see to it, no matter what he had to do."

"The man's name?"

Clark lifted his face. "I won't tell you that," he said. "He's a fellow cowboy."

Jared gaped at him. "For the love of God, are you out of your mind? If you know who he is, you have to tell me."

"I can't."

"Good God, do you want to be lynched?" Jared persisted, cold-eyed. "You know what happens to men of your race these days for any suspected crime."

"I do, indeed." The man smiled faintly. "But this is a point of honor. I can tell you that he made his intentions quite clear to everyone present. That's as far as I'm prepared to go."

"You didn't rob the store?"

"No, sir. I did not."

Jared glared at him. *Honor.* It was a word he knew very

well. He'd lived his life by it. But he wasn't sure that, in Clark's position, he would have given a damn about it. Not when his life hung in the balance.

It wouldn't go easy for Clark, either. Old man Marlowe was well-known and well-liked, and his assailant would not have an easy time of it. The case would be controversial and dangerous. Jared liked it already.

"You're being square with me? You didn't do it?" he asked the man.

Brian looked at him straight on. "No, sir. I didn't. I've killed men, but I've never been one to drink or steal. I was a cavalry officer before I left the service to go to work for Mr. Beale. I've never robbed anyone, and I like Mr. Marlowe."

"Cavalry?" Jared asked. "Which unit?"

"Tenth."

"Ah. The Buffalo Soldiers."

The black head inclined. "Our regiment has a proud history," he said. "We're men of honor. It would go against the grain for me to do something so dastardly as to rob a man and beat him half to death in the process."

"Will Mr. Beale stand by you?" Jared asked.

The black man smiled. "I'm afraid so, and things won't be easy if he does," he murmured. "He's an honorable man, so he won't desert me. But his support won't go well with the townspeople, either."

"If you're innocent, someone else is guilty. Old man Marlowe is well-liked around here. I remember hearing people tell stories about him when my mother first moved here. You could be lynched before we can get to trial."

Clark's long fingers went to his throat. He grimaced. "Plenty of my race have been, whether or not they were guilty." He shrugged. "I haven't got much money. I'll owe you—all my life if it takes that long to pay you back. I've heard a lot about you in town. They say you're the best lawyer in these parts. Take my case. Defend me. I didn't do it."

Jared smiled. "You have a way with words, Mr. Clark."

"Will you defend me?"

"Oh, yes," he replied, getting up from the desk. "I'd decided that two minutes after you walked in the door. You don't act guilty enough to warrant lynching."

Clark nodded and smiled. "Thank you, sir." He extended his hand, and Jared shook it. At the same time, he noticed the other hand, gnarled and useless, hanging at the man's side.

Angry voices sounded outside the office again, along with the thud of booted feet on the wooden sidewalk.

"They're back again," Jared remarked.

"I have to go with them, I know. They won't let me be lynched, will they?" he added worriedly.

"Not if I can help it."

The door opened and the police officer and Sims entered the room with a warrant, which Sims handed abruptly to Jared.

"That makes it legal, so you come with us, boy," the skinny city detective told the black man, grabbing him roughly by the neck. "You're going to lodge in the city jail until we hang you."

"He's not a boy," Jared said icily. "And no cavalry officer deserves to be treated like that. Unhand him."

"Cavalry officer?" Sims, the detective, drawled. "Him?"

"Tenth Cavalry," Jared replied. He turned his attention to the stoic policeman. "He surrendered himself to me, and I'll represent him at trial. Furthermore, I won't expect to find any marks of violence on him."

He was making the police officer think. Despite the nativistic tenor of the times, which made anyone nonwhite a legitimate target for scorn, he was planning to run against the sheriff in the next election and he'd heard that Jared had friends in high places in government. He didn't want to risk his future job on a city detective's brutality. Sims, the skinny one, had a reputation for being overly rough with Mexicans and blacks. He also fancied himself a gunman—wore his holster low on his thigh and liked to draw his Colt with little or no provocation. The police chief had found him troublesome ever since he'd been hired.

"Let him loose, Sims," he told the man. "Right now."

Sims jerked his hand away with a puzzled scowl.

"Put the handcuffs on him," the policeman instructed.

Sims complied, with muttered complaints about nursing criminals.

"I like old man Marlowe," the policeman said. "He's been robbed and beaten to his knees, and I have three witnesses who saw this man come running out of the store with a small bag just before Ted Marlowe was found."

"I was there to pick up some supplies for Mr. Beale. But I left long before they say that robbery happened. I wasn't even in town when it happened," Clark said. "And I had no small bag."

"Really? Well, John Garmon says you did," came the reply. "He wanted to come after you with us, because he thinks the world of Marlowe."

"He'd better keep his distance," Jared said coldly.

"And what will you do if he don't?" Sims drawled. "A pretty city feller like you."

Jared put his hands in his pockets and looked at the man. That level, cold blue stare was utterly fearless and faintly threatening. "Take care that you don't have to find out what I'll do."

Sims fancied himself a fighter, but he shrugged uncomfortably and moved away. "Come on, you black thief." He dragged Clark out the door.

"You take a lot on yourself, Mr. Dunn," the police officer

said quietly when Sims had taken the prisoner away. "Sims
was a gunman in Arizona, and he's bad-tempered."

"Oh, I'm impressed," Jared drawled.

The policeman muttered and went out the door, warrant in
hand.

The trial gave Mrs. Hardy and her friends something else
to gossip about, but Mrs. Dunn was even more worried when
she read in the paper that Jared was defending the black man
accused of robbing and beating poor old Ted Marlowe.

"He's such a kind man," Mrs. Dunn said at the dinner table.
"Poor Mr. Marlowe."

"I agree," Jared said. "But I think the real thief should be
caught, and it isn't my client."

"How do you know?" she persisted.

"Because if he has a motive, I can't find it," Jared
replied.

"Maybe he has one that you don't know about," Mrs. Dunn
said. She grimaced. "Oh, Jared. This case is dangerous—you
know it is. Why did you accept it?"

"He asked me to represent him. He's a former cavalry officer. There is such a thing as fellow feeling."

Noelle, who had listened quietly, and uneasily, turned to
look at her future husband. "Were you…in the cavalry?"

He nodded. "I did a lot of things in my checkered past. I
served in the army twice."

Her green eyes searched his pale ones. "I don't know much
about you," she said, thinking aloud.

"There's nothing much that you need to know," he said
coolly. "You're marrying me for the protection of my name,
not for love."

Until he said it, she hadn't realized it—but she was marrying him for love. It was unexpected and shocking to face
the fact that all this time—when she'd thought Andrew was

the end of the rainbow—Jared held her heart in the palm of his hand. Why else had she worried about him, watched him, responded with delight to his kisses, hung at his mouth like a slave? Oh, how horrible to know it now, when he hated her, when his contempt was visible every time he looked at her. And he was going to marry her, give her his name, only to save her reputation. He felt nothing for her. He couldn't have made it more plain.

"You look unwell," Jared said curtly.

She couldn't look at him. Not yet. "I have a headache," she said huskily.

"Shouldn't you lie down in a darkened room until it eases?" Mrs. Dunn asked worriedly. "I have a powder that might help, Noelle."

She shook her head. "I think that lying down will be enough," she said. She got up from the table, her meal uneaten. "Excuse me."

Jared watched her go with cold eyes.

"The wedding is next Saturday," Mrs. Dunn said. "It's nerves, I think, that make her so restless. She'll feel better once the ceremony is over. Jared, this case…you must be very careful. I don't want you injured over the fate of a cowboy."

"A black cowboy," he emphasized.

She chuckled. "Oh, you know I have no ill feeling toward people because they're of a different race."

"Yes, I know," he replied, smiling. "It was you who taught me that all people are of value, a lesson that was reinforced at Harvard." He shook his head. "This nativism is disturbing. There's so much violent hatred against immigrants, against people with any noticeable differences. And this at a time when we have become so conscious of the poor treatment of mental illness, and criminals, and even vagrants in our society—and are working to correct these problems. It seems incongruous to attack social evils such as slums and overcrowding and at the same time attack the immigrants who must suffer them."

"A question philosophers have often asked, I'm certain. Eat your roast beef, dear boy."

"In a moment. I have to see about Noelle. She'll be my responsibility from now on."

"Leave the door open, if you please," Mrs. Dunn murmured dryly.

He chuckled at her tone. "There won't be anything to see, I assure you," he added. "I have no such interest in Miss Brown."

He was lying, but his grandmother didn't know it. He walked upstairs and down the hall to Noelle's room. He tapped at the door and went in.

She was lying on the spotless bedspread, unmoving. She'd stiffened at his entrance, but now she was very still.

He moved to the end of the brass bedstead and rested his hand on it. Not that he needed the support. He hardly limped at all now, and had long since dispensed with the cane.

"Do you have a headache, or an attack of conscience?" he asked coldly.

She pulled herself into a sitting position and lifted her legs over the side of the bed. She folded her hands over her long skirt before she answered.

"I have the beginnings of a headache," she said, prevaricating.

"Why?"

Because I've suddenly discovered that I love you most desperately, she thought with wonder. But she didn't say it. She didn't look up, either. She really couldn't meet those piercing pale blue eyes just yet.

"It's not long until the wedding," she remarked.

"No, it isn't. And you have cold feet, is that it?"

Her hands clenched tighter. "Do you?"

He shrugged. "Nothing will change if we marry," he said idly. "Except that you'll share my name and people will have one thing less to gossip about."

"This black man whom you're to represent, is it a dangerous case?"

"Why should that matter to you?" he demanded. "I'm the one in the line of fire. No one's going to shoot you because I'm defending him."

She looked up then, with her worry on her face. "It isn't for myself that I'm afraid."

He drew in a short breath. "My grandmother is tougher than you imagine. She has no qualms about my client."

"She has a bad heart, and this case will certainly be controversial."

"What would you have me do, Noelle," he asked quietly, "give an innocent man up to the gallows to spare my grandmother more gossip?"

"I thought that you were marrying me to accomplish that."

"The sort of gossip you represent is more dangerous to her than this case, I assure you," he said. "She's acutely aware of her social standing and fearful of anything that might jeopardize it. But a murder trial will only excite her and make her read the papers—and try to shake more details out of me." He smiled faintly. "You don't know her. She isn't what she seems."

"No one is what they seem," she said, looking at her hands.

He studied her down-bent head. She seemed thinner. The worry and shame of the past weeks had honed her down. She still worked like a draft horse around the house, helping wherever she was needed. Her one concession had been to stay out of the garden. Henry was doing a better job, because Jared had insisted that he must. She played with her kitten and sewed and embroidered things for Mrs. Dunn. But she was reclusive now and unnaturally quiet.

"Noelle, how you've changed," he remarked.

"For the better, I hope," she replied calmly.

"I'm not sure."

She smoothed her skirt and got to her feet. "My headache is better. I'll help Mrs. Pate with the dishes."

She started past him, but he caught her by the waist and slowly pulled her to him.

He'd been unkind to her. She should protest, flee, slap him, scream in outrage. She did none of those things. His hand came up to brush back the loosened wisps of her hair, and she closed her eyes at the glory of his touch.

He felt that helpless response and reacted to it with cold fury. Was she so enslaved by her physical needs that any man would do, even him?

"Are you missing Andrew?" he asked, with a mocking smile. He tilted her eyes up to his. "Shall I lock the door, Noelle, and roll you onto the bed and give you what you need?"

The crudity of the statement burned her cheeks and made her want to hit out.

"I need nothing from you," she said in a choking tone.

"No?" He caught her chin in his lean hand and lifted it. His mouth crushed down over hers, parting her lips, burrowing, caressing, until she was helpless.

Her body, starved for his touch for weeks, responded predictably by melting into the length of him without restraint. Her mouth opened, surprising him into deepening the kiss.

He groaned and his arms enfolded her, tightening, demanding. She reached up to hold him closer and felt her breasts flatten against the broad, hard chest as the kiss went on and on, burning into her like hot steel. She trembled at the intensity of it, at the ardor that left her shaking all over before he abruptly released her and all but threw her away from him.

She sat down heavily on the bed, too weak in the knees to even stand, and looked up at him with wide eyes and swollen lips.

"It seems that any man will do," he said cruelly. "You're an easy mark, aren't you? So easy that I find you totally undesirable. You won't have to lock your bedroom door against me when we marry. But," he added as he moved to the door, "perhaps I might have to lock mine!"

He smiled mockingly and gave her a curt little bow before he went out and closed the door with a snap.

"You...vicious bastard!" she shouted after him.

She grabbed up a small dish from the bedside table and flung it at the door with all her might. It shattered loudly and fell in colorful shards. She looked around for something else, but there was only the lamp and heavy furniture. She cried aloud, furious at her response and his sarcasm. She hadn't asked him to kiss her! And he wouldn't have to lock his door, because she wouldn't want to get leprosy from touching him!

She was screaming these sentiments at the closed door. Outside it, a coldly angry Jared hesitated just briefly before he controlled himself and continued on down the hall. She had a vicious temper and a mouth that needed washing out with lye soap. She couldn't know how the word she'd hurled through the door had once pained him, since it was true—he had no father. Even his mother hadn't known the identity of the man who raped her and left her pregnant. The word had been the worst kind of insult in his youth. It still stung when he heard it.

But in all fairness, he knew that he'd provoked her to that show of rage. He shouldn't have been so cruel to her. It was just that the fever he shared in her arms made him vulnerable and angry. He didn't want to be so hungry for a woman his stepbrother had seduced and abandoned, for a woman, moreover, who was in love with another man. That weakness he felt for her wounded his pride.

She denied letting Andrew seduce her. But if she loved Andrew, it was natural that she'd want him. Had she or hadn't she slept in Andrew's bed? His eyes narrowed as he contemplated the question. There was only one way he could find out. His whole body went hot at the thought of a naked Noelle in his bed. If tonight had been any indication of her state of mind, she would welcome him.

But it was odd that she should find him physically irresistible when she was in love with his stepbrother. It had been that way from the beginning, from the first time he'd kissed her. She'd talked about Andrew, blushed when his name was mentioned, poked around for any little tidbit of information about the dashing blond man with the mustache. Yet that same infatuated girl would melt into Jared's arms the minute he touched her, hang hungrily at his lips waiting for his kisses, even permit him to touch her under her gown, to look at her there.

He couldn't understand why she would do that, unless she really was loose in her morals. But she hadn't flirted with other men. At the dance she'd attended with Andrew, she'd only danced with Andrew and Jared, and she hadn't smiled at or teased any of the eligible young men present.

He went to his own room with all his unanswered questions rippling in his mind. He didn't sleep well because of them. When dawn poured in through the curtains, he was no closer to an answer. But his temper hadn't quite cooled, either, from the insult she'd given him.

Noelle, meanwhile, had tossed and turned with vengeance on her mind. She was going to make Jared pay for his cruelty, one way or the other. She didn't know how just yet, but she was going to pay him back for every low remark he'd made about her. And when she finished with him, the despicable Andrew was going to be next on her list!

Chapter Twelve

Noelle and Jared were married in the First Methodist Church. Noelle's gown reached to her toes in layer upon layer of delicate Brussels lace with mauve and pink and blue ribbons interlaced, and a matching bouquet of silk flowers. Her veil was massive, trailing out behind her over the train of her oyster silk wedding gown. She wore no hat, only delicate ribbons in her upswept hair, which were pinned in the bun of her hair to secure the long veil. The ribbons matched those in her bouquet. Her gloves were of the same pretty lace as the gown's trim. She looked faintly haughty with her auburn hair gleaming from the sunlight as she walked down the aisle on the arm of the minister's brother, who had offered to give her away.

She was sorry that her parents and brothers were gone, for she had no family save Mrs. Dunn to see her wed. Her uncle had wired that he couldn't attend the wedding because of his back, but he did send congratulations. Andrew was her cousin, but, of course, he would not attend. She couldn't look at Jared as she walked slowly down the aisle. It was like being offered heaven while standing on shifting rocks over hell.

He'd barely spoken to her since the night they'd argued and he'd kissed her. She'd called him a name that made her flush in retrospect. She was sorry for it, but she hadn't been able to find any way to apologize. That he was still angry had been hard to ignore. He'd avoided her except in company, and he'd only spoken to her when it had been necessary. He didn't look at her even when she approached the altar. He stood straight and unbending, his face like stone.

She was given over to Jared as the piano played the familiar strains of the "Wedding March" and the minister slowly went through the marriage service. The church was full, partly because of the gossip and partly because of Jared's controversial client in the upcoming trial. Most of these people were curiosity seekers, including Mrs. Hardy in the first row. Her presence incensed Noelle, but there was nothing she could do about it—short of flinging the woman out one of the long ceiling-to-floor windows—unthinkable behavior in a church.

The two questions were asked and answered. The minister smiled and pronounced them man and wife, inviting a cool, unsmiling Jared to kiss the bride.

Jared looked down his nose at her for a long moment. His eyes went over the thick veil that concealed her eyes and mouth. He'd been furious with her beyond all imagining, because she'd used a word that wounded him. But now, looking down at her pale, sad face, pride of possession suddenly took precedence. She was his. She might love Andrew, but she'd married him, Jared Dunn, instead.

Slowly he eased the veil back from her face; the significance of what he was doing went right through him. He was seeing her as no other man ever had, ever would—he was seeing her for the first time as a bride.

Wonderingly his thin lips turned up in a smile so tender that her breath caught audibly. It was as if they were alone in the world. While the audience sat, spellbound, Jared framed her oval face in his lean, strong hands and very slowly bent to her mouth.

She saw his lips part as they met hers, felt his warm breath against them. He kissed her with breathless tenderness, as if it were the first time. She stood there entranced, and the poignancy of it made her sob, made tears form in her eyes.

He heard the sound. It brought him back from the brief fool's paradise he'd entered. He lifted his head at once and the coldness came back into his eyes.

He knew what had prompted the tears. She'd just realized that Andrew was forever out of her reach. She was crying over Andrew, in church, at her own wedding.

He bit back the words he wanted to say. His eyes said them for him. She averted hers even before he abruptly released her, and, taking her arm, escorted her down the aisle, past the wedding guests and out the door.

When they were on the sidewalk, he let go of her arm and looked down at her with cold eyes. "You lie beautifully with your mouth. What silky promises, 'to love and obey and forsake all others.' Ha!"

Her mind was still spinning. One second he'd been kissing her, almost like a man in love. And here he was spitting poison at her.

"I—I don't understand," she faltered.

"Don't you?" he asked coldly.

He escorted her quickly to the gaily decorated carriage, put her inside with a minimum of fuss, moved her skirts into it, slammed the door and motioned to the driver to take her home. The startled man complied. Jared didn't look in at Noelle. He turned on his heel, put his hands angrily in the pockets of his best trousers and walked angrily down the street toward his office.

Behind him, wedding guests filed out into the sunlight, having missed the most exciting part of the wedding. The carriage, and Jared, were out of sight by the time they left their pews, talking excitedly about the bridegroom's exquisitely tender kiss for the bride. No one saw Noelle go home alone in the carriage.

Mrs. Dunn received all the congratulations, beaming, and went home in a carriage by herself. She smiled with delight. Now the tongues would stop wagging and she could stop being the object of attention everywhere she went in town.

She went on to her dressmaker's house for a fitting, confident that Noelle and Jared were probably making up. They would work things out now that they were married. Surely they would, if the way Jared had kissed Noelle was any indication.

But when she arrived, much later, and went into the house, she met a morose Mrs. Pate.

"Why, what's wrong with you? That's no face to wear after a wedding!"

Mrs. Pate glowered at her. "No? The bride came home alone, in tears, and the bridegroom hasn't set foot in the house all afternoon. I believe that he is at his office, working as usual."

Mrs. Dunn's eyes widened. "They left the church together. They've just married—" she began.

"Unwillingly," Mrs. Pate said, cutting in. "He thinks that she has been intimate with his stepbrother."

"Oh, dear. I do wonder…" Mrs. Dunn began uncomfortably.

"I wash all the sheets and all the clothes," Mrs. Pate said bluntly. "And I can tell you quite frankly that nothing of that sort has been going on in this house!"

Mrs. Dunn went red and gasped.

"Thought you should know," Mrs. Pate said, with a jerk of her head, and walked away, leaving the older lady to compose herself.

Noelle took off her wedding gown and her lovely veil and repacked them in the box they'd occupied since their arrival. She was married. She wore a gold band that Jared had placed on her finger. But nothing had changed. Nothing at all. Jared didn't want her, and he'd just made it crystal clear.

Well, to be fair, she'd called him a foul name and thrown things at the door. But he'd deserved it, the rake! She hoped that he would lock his door against her tonight, she mused wickedly, and that everyone heard him do it. Perhaps she could put on some shocking nightgown, stand outside his door and beg to be let in, with everyone watching and laughing because he locked her out.

It might have been funny, but she loved him. He would never love her or want her, and there would never be a child. That was the saddest thing of all. She loved children. She'd loved her young brothers. Caring for them had never been a chore. She'd often thought that she would have her own children one day, and when she first came to Fort Worth, she'd pictured handsome Andrew as their father. But that picture had rapidly faded. Now, she saw little dark-haired boys with pale blue eyes instead, but they were hopeless fantasies. Jared didn't want her for his wife. He might even leave Fort Worth and go back to New York to escape her.

She sat down heavily on the bed, in her chemise and corset and bloomers, as she considered the terrible thought. All she would be left with was the protection of his name and an income about which she knew nothing.

There was this trial, of course. He couldn't leave until it was over. And remembering what Mrs. Dunn had said, she grew worried for Jared. Tempers ran hot during such trials. Suppose someone tried to shoot him? He was an elegant city attorney. Although he had been a Texas Ranger, and apparently a cavalry soldier, in his youth, he was older now. And he had that gimpy leg, although she had noticed that he limped hardly at all anymore and didn't use the cane.

She fingered the ruffle on the legs of her bloomers with a grimace. They were muslin. She'd put away the pretty silk things Mrs. Pate had helped her buy because she wanted nothing Jared had paid for. Anyway, she thought brazenly, it wasn't as if he'd ever see them.

She dressed in her usual dark skirt and white blouse, buttoned it up at the throat, put on her thick hose and garters, and laced up her shoes. Then she put her hair up and went downstairs. It was just another day, she told herself. Getting married was incidental, and no grand occasion. If Jared could treat it so lightly as to go back to work, so could she! He need not think she would sit in her room weeping because of his rejection.

She went to the kitchen to offer Mrs. Pate some help with the evening meal and found her missing. But Henry was out in the garden, with a bottle of whiskey. He was drinking and hoeing up her prize tomato plants, which now had little tomatoes on them, and he was laughing at his butchery!

It was the last straw, in a day liberally filled with them. She jerked open the door and marched outside. She didn't care if Mrs. Hardy and the entire block of neighbors saw her.

She picked up a bucket and threw it with all her might in Henry's direction.

It landed on his foot. He stopped what he was doing and gaped at her with eyes so round they looked like saucers. The half-empty bottle of whiskey dangled in his hand at his side, against his overalls.

"You drunken idiot!" she raged, moving in for the kill. "Dig up my tomato plants just as they begin to bear, will you? You snake in the grass!"

Her hand whipped out and dragged the whiskey bottle from his hand. She upended it, brandishing it at him as she spilled its contents all over the ground.

"If you want this, sir, then have it!" And she waded in, holding the bottle over her head like a bat.

He screamed at the top of his lungs. Then he turned and lit out across the yard as if a pack of rabid dogs was chasing him. He ran with his arms over his head across two yards, including Mrs. Hardy's, with Noelle hot on his trail, running as fast as she could, shouting threats and waving the empty bottle over her head.

Noelle ran out of breath at the corner and stopped, breathing heavily, just off the dirt road. Two carriages had stopped dead at the sight of the middle-aged man in a beaten hat and overalls running away from a slender woman brandishing a whiskey bottle. He ran right into the road, threatening the horses and his own person, jumped a hedge and kept going.

"You're fired!" Noelle raged after him. "If you come back, I shall shoot you—and no gardener in Fort Worth will convict me!"

There was a shout of laughter from one of the carriages. She turned, embarrassed now that her anger had diminished, flushed and tucked the bottle against her skirt so that it was less obvious. It had been an upsetting day.

She walked angrily back across the yards, pausing to glare at Mrs. Hardy, whose mouth had fallen open.

"Now you have something else to gossip about, you poisonous old biddy," she told the elderly woman. "Go and see if you can't find some more lives to ruin with your wagging tongue, and then see how long it takes before God catches up with you! Sitting in church, so smug and self-righteous, when you're the biggest hypocrite in the city! Shame on you!" she added, shaking a furious finger at the woman.

Mrs. Hardy looked as if she might swoon. Her hand was at her throat, clutching.

Noelle ignored her and kept on walking. She fancied that she left a trail of fire wherever her feet touched, all the way home.

It was unfortunate that Jared should be standing on the back porch, watching, when she came up to the yard.

She threw the whiskey bottle at his feet, where it landed with a hollow thud in the dirt.

"He killed my tomato plants!" she raged, red-faced and disheveled. "You said that you would speak to him, and look how much good it did!"

He was staring at her. "Where did you get this whiskey bottle?" he asked.

"From Henry. He'd already consumed half of it. I took it away from him and chased him to the street." She stared at him indignantly. "I only regret that I couldn't get close enough to hit him with it! Mrs. Hardy was on her porch, and I told her what I thought of her, as well." She put her hands on her hips and blew a wisp of auburn hair away from her mouth. "Now, I'm going to tell you what I think of you."

He leaned against the porch with his arms folded and the oddest faint smile on his lips. He made a gesture of invitation with one hand.

"I'm not a loose woman," she began, uncaring if the whole world should hear. "You may think whatever you like, and you may lock your bedroom door at night if you feel I'm a threat to you. I did nothing that I'm ashamed of, and I won't apologize. Furthermore," she added, "if I feel like working in this garden, in overalls, I'll do it, regardless of how many neighbors find it scandalous." She had raised her voice, looking pointedly toward Mrs. Hardy's back porch, where a shadow moved.

She glared at her husband. "And how dare you leave me at the church to find my own way home on my wedding day?"

He whistled softly, his eyes lingering on her livid face. "How dare I, indeed," he agreed, which was as close as he could come to expressing the guilt that had brought him home so early in the day.

She pushed her loose hair away angrily. "I didn't mean to call you such a vile name, Jared," she muttered, lowering her eyes for the first time. "It was very wrong of me, and I'm ashamed for doing it."

She had wound down. He left the porch and approached her, stopping an arm's length away. "Do you know why it made me so mad?"

"Because I was so nasty," she said.

He shook his head. His sigh was audible. "Because I *am* a bastard, Noelle, and everyone knew it when I was a boy. My mother was attacked by some unknown man in Dodge City. I was the result."

"Jared!"

Her shock was expected, but not the sudden sympathy in her eyes, the compassion.

"I do beg your pardon most humbly," she said, with regret in her green eyes. "I'd never have said such a thing, regardless of how angry I was, had I known."

She made him feel small and ashamed. His eyes narrowed on her face. "There are a lot of things in my past that I can't share with you. This one is known only to my grandmother and myself."

She moved a little closer. "You're very secretive," she said. She looked up. "Have you other secrets that you're willing to share?" she asked softly.

His breath caught in his throat. She was full of surprises. He found himself thinking about her at the damnedest times— like this morning, when he should have been working on the new case. A man's freedom, if not his life, was at stake, and he'd paced his office remembering the stricken look on No-elle's face when he walked away from her outside the church. It had driven him home—into an unfolding scene that he'd never forget. Henry's hysterical retreat would be the talk of the town for weeks, if not years.

He touched her lower lip with his forefinger and watched it intently. It trembled. She looked more vulnerable than he'd seen her in a long time.

"Not at the moment," he said, answering her question. "And you, Noelle? Have you dark secrets?"

"I put a rat snake in my oldest brother's bed when he told my father that I broke the dasher handle on the new churn."

His eyebrows lifted with a smile. "Did you? Aren't you afraid of snakes?"

She shook her head. She studied him. "Are you?" she asked hopefully.

He chuckled. "No."

"Another source of vengeance cut off. You're a city man—shouldn't you be perturbed by creepy, crawly things?"

He caught her by the waist and pulled her against his body lazily, looking down his nose at her. "I'm perturbed by very little," he said. "You've run off my gardener."

"Yes," she said.

"Shall I hire someone else?"

It sounded as if he was offering not to. Her eyes brightened. "Mrs. Hardy's tongue will waggle at both ends if I do it."

"Probably. Do you want to?"

She smiled. "Yes. Will your grandmother mind?"

"I'll speak to her. It's a new age. She'll have to accept many things that are strange to her."

"That's so."

His hands tightened and his eyes narrowed. "I'll permit you to work in the garden—"

"Permit?"

"Permit," he said firmly. "It's my garden."

"Yours? I planted it!" she argued.

"It sits on my land. I say who works in it."

She glowered up at him. The feel of his strong hands on her waist was disconcerting, but she didn't want to let him know it. "Oh, very well."

"As I was saying," he continued, holding her gaze, "I'll permit you to work in the garden until you're with child. Afterward, a man will be employed to take over."

Her eyes became fixed. She didn't breathe. It was the last thing in the world she ever expected him to say.

Incoherent phrases tumbled from her lips. "You think… that I'm a loose woman, that any man will do. How can you want someone like that to be the mother of your children? And you said that you wouldn't sleep with me anyway!"

His hands smoothed up to her rib cage and he looked at her mouth. "I want to sleep with you, Noelle," he whispered softly. "I've always wanted to."

Her hands were cold against his chest, trembling like the rest of her body with nervous excitement. "Oh."

"I've thought of little else since the night I found you in the parlor with my whiskey bottle."

She flushed as vivid memories came back to haunt her.

"Coward," he taunted when she colored. "Don't you like remembering how hungry we were for each other, then and the other night?"

She glowered at him, breathless. "No."

He smiled gently. "You'd better lock your door tonight, my dear," he said, aware of footsteps coming quickly toward the porch behind them. "Because nothing short of a bolt will keep me out. And I'm not even sure that a bolt will."

She swallowed, searching for a reply, when the screen door

opened and slammed and Mrs. Pate, followed by Mrs. Dunn, came outside.

"Noelle, what was all the commotion?" Mrs. Dunn asked. "A man just came to the front door and said that he saw our gardener tearing across the road with a woman brandishing a bottle right behind him. Do you—?" She paused when she saw Jared—and then the whiskey bottle on the ground. She hesitated. Her hand went to her face. "Oh, dear."

"He killed my tomato plants," Noelle said, defending herself. "Look." She pointed at them and winced. "They'd just formed little tomatoes and he hoed them right out of the ground because he was so drunk."

"He left two bushes," Mrs. Pate said, joining them. "So he was drinking again, was he?"

"Excessively," Noelle agreed. "I ran as fast as I could, but I couldn't get close enough to hit him!"

Mrs. Dunn was chuckling. The sound was soft, but quite audible. Noelle looked up.

Mrs. Dunn shook her head. "I see myself in you." She sighed. "I'd forgotten what I was like. Noelle, work in the garden in overalls if you want to," she said surprisingly. "It's a new world. My time is past. This is yours. There's been so much gossip already that some more will not matter—and should not matter. Something so innocent will surely not offend God, even if it offends neighbors. And what, may I ask, does their opinion matter?"

"Now you sound more like the grandmother I remember," Jared commented.

"I feel more like her." She straightened her skirts. "When you finish tending your tomatoes, Noelle, I have a letter that I wish you to write for me. The rheumatism in my hands makes it very difficult to hold a pencil."

"I'll be delighted to help you," she said.

"Unless Jared has other plans?" the older woman added.

Jared stared at Noelle with eyes so wicked that she flushed.

"I must return to the office for a little while," he said. "Noelle and I can talk further when I come home this evening."

"Very well, then. Come, Mrs. Pate, and show me that new crochet pattern I like."

Mrs. Pate shook her head, grinning, as she joined the older woman, leaving the newlyweds alone.

"How discreet of them," he said. "If they could read my mind they'd have been much less anxious to leave."

"It's broad daylight," she said demurely, "and in plain sight of the world."

He sighed. "Yes," he replied wistfully.

"And I have tomatoes to plant, and you a client to defend." She searched his eyes. "Jared, no one has ever tried to shoot you over a case, have they?"

He looked at her amusedly. "A cowboy did, in New Mexico Territory," he said finally. He gestured toward his healed leg. "That's how I got this."

"And…the cowboy who shot you? Was he arrested?" she asked, aghast.

"There was no need." He started to turn away.

"Why?"

He glanced over his shoulder at her, smiling. "Because I shot him, my dear, and shattered his gun arm. He won't be able to pull a gun again for a long time. And even if he can, he'll think twice before he acts."

Her eyes were like saucers. She stared—gaped—at this stranger to whom she was married.

"I did tell you that I had been a Texas Ranger," he reminded her. "I know how to use a gun, Noelle. In fact, I know how to use one all too well."

She stood in her own tracks, watching him, her eyes finding

new things as she traced his face, his eyes, his hair, his hard, thin mouth. "And ride?" she asked.

He nodded.

"And when you were in the cavalry, you…fought?"

He nodded again.

She was barely breathing now. She forced her legs to move and went close to him, looking up. It was a long way. "Andrew was the phony," she whispered. "And you are the genuine article. Is that not so?"

He touched her soft cheek. "Andrew is the youngest son," he said simply. "He longs to be what he can never be. He has no stomach for it."

"But you do." She looked into his eyes and finally she understood. "Jared, you have killed men."

"Yes." He withdrew his hand as bits and pieces of the past flashed horribly into his mind. "Yes, I have."

"And known women."

His jaw clenched. He didn't answer.

"Talk to me," she pleaded, catching him by his coat sleeves. "Tell me."

His chest rose roughly. "You ask for things I can't give you."

"In the very beginning, you said that we would always be honest with each other, Jared."

"The sort of honesty you want would be brutal," he said flatly. "Noelle, I wasn't the man I am now. Do you understand, even a little? I was…" His voice faded away under the look in her soft eyes.

"You don't want to remember, is that the truth?" She moved closer and her eyes never wavered. "Nothing will make any difference to me," she said. "Nothing you've done, nothing you ever do. You've been the best friend I've ever had. Friends don't stop caring because a man has been less than perfect."

"Is that all you require of me, Noelle—friendship?" he

asked quietly, thinking that her anger toward Andrew still had a hollow ring to it. She would probably run to him if he came back with an apology on his lips. He mustn't lose sight of that.

Her eyes fell to his mouth and lingered there. "Isn't friend-ship all you have to give me?" she whispered back, her voice tormented.

Chapter Thirteen

When Jared got back to his office, he forced Noelle from his mind temporarily and went over his case notes. He'd interviewed Brian Clark in the city jail and obtained all the man's movements for the day of the robbery. He had a keen intuition about truth, and it was telling him that the black man was innocent. But Clark himself admitted that he had been in Marlowe's store the day of the robbery and that he was on his way back to the Beale ranch at the time the robbery occurred. He couldn't prove he hadn't robbed Marlowe any more than he could prove that he traveled from town before the robbery occurred, because there was no witness to back up his story. And Marlowe, the victim, was still in a coma.

On the other hand, there was a nasty atmosphere in town about the robbery, more so because old man Marlowe was still in a bad way. And a loudmouthed rabble-rouser had been spreading the story around town that he'd seen Clark come running out of the dry-goods store just after Marlowe was robbed. He was also heard to espouse the cause of necktie justice.

John Garmon, one of the wranglers at Terrance Beale's huge ranch, was also telling everyone who would listen that Clark had said he needed money real bad and would do anything to get it. A brutal man like that, Garmon had added to his small audience, should be lynched. There were murmurs of assent.

Word of that came back to Jared in an unexpected way. He had a visit from Clark's employer, Terrance Beale himself.

The tall, dark-haired man with the scarred face was wearing working clothes. Not one to dress to please anyone but himself, Beale was a hard man who'd lived through rough times and looked it.

The two men measured each other quietly when Beale was ushered into Jared's office.

Jared took off his reading glasses; his piercing blue eyes fixed on the other man's equally pointed dark stare. After a minute, Jared motioned Beale into a chair. The visitor sat down, his leather bat-wing chaps creaking as he crossed his long legs and began to roll a cigarette.

"You're representing my head wrangler on a robbery and assault charge," Beale said after a minute. "He's innocent."

"I know," Jared replied. He sat down, leaning back. "I wouldn't have taken the case if I wasn't certain of that."

Beale chuckled faintly. He paused to finish his cigarette and light it. It fired smoke up to the ceiling while his narrow eyes fixed on the other man. "I didn't know your name in El Paso, but I know you," he said abruptly. "But you don't remember me, do you?"

Jared scowled. Over the years, there had been a lot of cases, a lot of clients.

"No," Beale replied aloud. "I can see that you don't." He fingered the deep scar on his cheek pointedly. "I was living in El Paso, working as a part-time town marshal. One night, three rowdies I'd arrested in a saloon busted out of jail, got tighter than they already were and came looking for me in a dark alley with knives."

Jared's eyes narrowed. He remembered. "You!"

Beale nodded. "You saved my life that night. I've never seen grown men beg for mercy before. It was an enlightening experience." He leaned forward abruptly. "Hell, I never expected to find you in a suit, defending my wrangler. I must confess, it somewhat threw me. You've changed."

"You haven't," Jared said, chuckling. "I can't say you've improved much in looks."

"Well, time does age a man."

"Beale." Jared just shook his head. "I remember you, too, now, but I never would have known you if I hadn't seen you in person. You went under another name on the border."

"I changed it when I married Allison," he said heavily. "I didn't want her to have to worry about men I'd arrested coming after us. I moved here and got a stake." His eyes narrowed. "Wait a minute—you're Andrew Paige's stepbrother."

"That's right," he said tightly. It still irritated him just to hear Andrew's name.

"My daughter, Jennifer, mentioned that Andrew's stepbrother was defending Clark. I heard your name, but I had no idea it was you, of course." He pondered for a minute. "What are Clark's chances?"

"Not good. I'm glad he came to me," Jared replied.

"Yes, on an impulse," the older man said. "I've just been to see him at the city jail. He'd heard about you around town, and knew that you'd practiced criminal law in New York. He figured he'd need the best lawyer he could find." He lifted an eyebrow. "I don't suppose he knows that law isn't all you do well."

"That part of my life is over," Jared said.

"You may think it is," Beale replied. "I had those same ideas, that I could forget what I'd been, what I'd done. You can't, you know. It comes out. It always comes out. Allison had never seen men fight, she knew nothing of violence. Then, one day, a man I'd sent to prison for murder got out on good behavior, just short of his full sentence, and came looking for me." His face hardened. "He killed her. He killed her while I was out on the range, helping the boys brand cattle. He killed her, and then he sat and waited for me to come home and see what he'd done."

Jared's eyes narrowed. "My God."

"She never hurt a soul," he continued, wincing as he remembered. "She was the most gentle woman…" He took a long breath. "Well, he drew on me. I wasn't even armed, but I went for him. I was so damned mad that I didn't even feel the bullet hit me. Before I lost consciousness, I killed him with my bare hands. But it didn't bring her back. Jennifer was twelve," he recalled. "She came in while I was attacking him. It made her a little afraid of me. I think she still is."

"I can understand how you felt."

"You can," he said, "because you've lived through wild times, too. But it's hard for people who haven't to accept."

Jared was thinking of Noelle, and how she might react to the same sort of revelation about him. He tried to imagine his own feelings if someone from his past tried to hurt her. He knew in his heart that he'd do exactly as Beale had done, with no compunctions whatsoever, no regrets. It unsettled him to have to consider that.

"Your stepbrother is a fraud," Beale continued suddenly. "A strutting dandy. But Jennifer is innocent and trusting and she wants him. Is he playing with her?"

"No," Jared replied, although he was only voicing his hopes. He hoped that Andrew really felt something for the girl. Certainly he felt enough not to let himself be pushed into marrying Noelle. Noelle might still love him, but if Andrew stayed away—especially if he found a girl to love—Noelle might forget him. Jared hoped she would, at least.

Beale nodded. "I'm glad. I don't approve of him," he emphasized. "He's too conscious of his background and his money-eyed past. But I can tolerate him, for her sake."

Jared laughed mirthlessly. "I've been tolerating him for my grandmother's," he confessed.

They exchanged smiles.

"There was something said about Andrew leaving your house under a cloud," Beale persisted.

"There was no cloud," Jared said firmly. "He left after I married Noelle Brown, his cousin," he emphasized, stretching the truth a little. "He and Noelle don't get along very well," he added. "An unfortunate result of her getting to know him."

Beale grinned. "Well, maybe the same thing will happen when Jennifer gets a dose of him."

"A good woman might make a man of him," Jared remarked carelessly.

Beale pursed his lips. He didn't reply to that, but took a draw from his cigarette and fixed his dark eyes on the other man. "Another of my wranglers is going to testify for the prosecution," he said out of the blue. "A man named John Garmon. He's from Mississippi and he hates Negroes. He's said things to Clark that I'd have beaten him to his knees for, but Clark just lets it go by him. I understand that Garmon saw Clark going into the dry-goods store just minutes before Marlowe was robbed. He also told some people that Clark had confessed to needing money badly."

"Clark doesn't strike me as a greedy man."

"He isn't," Beale said. "Furthermore, if he needed money, and it would have to be a case of real need, he'd come to me like the honorable man he is and ask for a loan. Which I would extend. And he knew that."

"So why would he resort to beating and robbing a kind old man like Marlowe?" Jared said.

"Exactly."

"This Garmon…how long has he worked for you?"

"Six months," Beale replied. "He hates having to work with Clark. My foreman is retiring, and when I mentioned that I planned to offer the job to Clark instead of Garmon, he heard about it and threw a fit." He leaned forward and put out the cigarette in the big ashtray on Jared's desk. "He gambles," he added, looking straight ahead at Jared. "And from all accounts, it would take a big man to beat Marlowe that badly, even at his age. He's over six foot two and muscular; Garmon's about that size himself. Clark is a smaller build altogether, and his left hand is crippled."

Jared grinned. "You think like I do."

"Once a lawman…" Beale got to his feet. "Clark doesn't have any money except his wages. He doesn't spend much, and he saves enough to send a money order back East to his mother and sister every month. Garmon owes every cent of his wages before he even gets them."

"I'm glad you came in. You've given me something to work with."

"It will help. If all else fails," he added, with a wild glint in his eyes, "you can call Garmon out for me."

Jared lifted an eyebrow. "I don't resort to gunplay to win arguments these days."

"That isn't what they say over in Terrell," the other man replied, tongue in cheek.

"Who's been talking?"

"No need to watch your back with me," Beale replied, moving toward the door. "I heard it from the judge. He plays poker with me every week." He glanced back. "You want to keep an eye on Sims, that city detective. He'll help Garmon if he can. Garmon's spreading lynch talk."

"That's suspicious enough in itself," Jared remarked quietly. "A fair trial is every man's right."

"Well, if you need help, you know where to come. I haven't got arthritis so bad that I can't jerk a gun if I have to. And I can hire other men who can. I don't like necktie justice, either."

"I'll keep that in mind," Jared said.

The lynch talk disturbed him. Jared wanted a speedy trial, but not so swift that he didn't have time to do a proper brief. He already knew that Clark had enemies, and Beale had just given him the man's name, despite the fact that Clark wouldn't. That had been an unexpected break. Now he was going to do some investigating and see what he could dig up about the man.

Toward that end, he cabled an ex-Pinkerton agent he knew in Chicago, Matt Davis, and gave him John Garmon's name, asking him to check it against Pinkerton's files. Matt kept a copy of those he'd worked with during his Pinkerton days, and he wouldn't have to do much investigating if there were cases against the man.

He made his notes, answered two telephone calls from potential clients, dictated answers to letters that had come in the morning mail, and then sat back and thought about Noelle and the sad look in her eyes—and the odd questions she'd asked when they parted at the back porch. "Isn't friendship all you have to give me?" she'd asked. And he still felt the impact of those words hours later.

He toyed with a roll that fit on the Dictaphone machine. He'd tried to spend as little time as possible thinking about his feelings for Noelle. First there had been the differences between them, then her hostility and then Andrew. Now there were no more real barriers, and he found himself wanting her as never before.

His whole body clenched as he remembered the sight of

her pale, freckled breasts in the parlor weeks ago. She might fight him, call him names, even weep on his shoulder. But the instant he touched her, she permitted him to do anything he liked to her body.

He groaned and put the cartridge aside. He'd long ago given up any dreams of a wife and family, and now all he thought about was a child. It was reckless and dangerous. He had a past. This was Texas. He was much more likely to run into old enemies here than in New York, and there had been witnesses to the death of the cowboy the woman Ava had accused of rape and theft in Dodge City so many years ago. It would eventually become impossible to keep the past hidden from Noelle.

He wondered how he could ever tell her about the things he'd done. She never accused or lectured. She simply accepted. But he'd had a full-blown love affair with Ava, and he'd been on the wrong side of the law when he'd killed for her. He'd killed men when he was a Texas Ranger, as well. Noelle knew that. But she didn't know how bad he'd been before he was on the side of the law, even if she knew him as no one else did.

At any rate, he wanted her desperately. And worse, it was more than a physical need to be near her. He'd grown addicted to just the sound of her soft voice and her flares of temper. He chuckled, thinking of her tearing across the neighborhood after Henry. She was unique. How could he ever give her up? If only Andrew would marry Miss Beale and put himself forever out of Noelle's reach. She might still be nursing hopes of getting Andrew back, in spite of what happened. He had to guard his heart until she got over her love for Andrew. Until then, it would be better to keep a distance between them. But just this once—God in heaven, only once—he had to have her. A man must have memories to sustain him.

* * *

He went home after work with all his worries and deep longings lying heavily on his heart. He ate without knowing what he ate, and all the while he stared at Noelle and watched her eyes fence with his, watched her flush at the way he was looking at her. Thank God, she wanted him, he thought. Where desire existed, perhaps love could.

After supper, the talk was of the trial. Noelle glanced at him shyly while he expressed his doubts about the outcome of a straight-out court trial.

"It would depend on finding twelve unbiased jurors who had no prejudices whatsoever—and who would take the word of a Negro against that of several white men," Jared said heavily.

"In other words," Mrs. Dunn added, "a miracle."

He nodded. "I've won cases without hard evidence," he continued. "But in New York City, where a more sophisticated citizenry exists. Out here, it's a different story. A lot of the people here grew up on the frontier. They're hard because they've had to be. They believe what they see, what they know—"

"But the man is innocent," Noelle interrupted.

"Yes," he agreed, smiling at her. "But innocence is no guarantee of a not-guilty verdict. Men have been hanged on less evidence than the prosecution has here. And this cowboy who's spreading lynch talk is the key to the whole case."

"What will you do?" Noelle asked worriedly.

"Whatever I have to," he replied.

Mrs. Dunn put down her embroidery and got to her feet. "Well, I have every confidence in your ability at the bar, my boy," she said warmly. She paused at the doorway. "Sleep well. At my age, I find I tire much sooner than I used to."

"Good night, then," he said, and his words were echoed by a shy Noelle.

It was really no surprise that Mrs. Pate called good night and went home barely two minutes later. Jared and Noelle were left together in the living room. She was still doing embroidery, but he was watching her. The grandfather clock chimed ten. He looked up and so did she, their eyes locking across the room.

He knew then that he would not be able to keep from doing what he ached to do. Her eyes were soft and warm and as hungry as his. It was no use. Just one time, to feed his heart, he assured himself, even as he felt his body clench. "You're tired," he said huskily. "It's been a long day. Why don't you retire early, too?"

She got up, tingling all over, put up her handiwork and paused to look at him with the shy question in her eyes.

He didn't say anything. But he nodded, slowly, and the look in his pale eyes made her heart race.

She turned and went upstairs, undressing hastily down to her skin. She pulled on a thin cotton gown with an embroidered bodice, loosened her hair and put her things away. Her hands trembled as she turned off the light. She wanted to be close to her husband, wanted intimacy with him. But all the years of fear and whispered gossip made her apprehensive. Would it hurt? She loved him. Surely it would not be so bad.

She was lying in her bed with the covers around her waist, apprehensive and excited, her whole body throbbing, when the bedroom door opened and closed.

She heard soft footsteps. A shadowy figure paused beside the bed. Her lips parted as her breathing increased in pace with her heartbeat.

There was a rustling sound, and then the cover was lifted away. The bed shifted under a new weight, and she felt herself turned and pulled to a warm, muscular body that she found, shockingly, completely nude.

Her gasp was audible, like the shudder that went through her as her hands encountered his hair-roughened chest.

"Will it do any good to tell you that there's nothing to be afraid of?" he asked her gently.

"No," she replied in a small voice. His hands contracted, and she stiffened. "Jared, you won't…hurt me?" she whispered.

"Oh, my dear," he said softly. He drew her close and held her, gently, without threat, until she stopped trembling and began to relax.

His hand smoothed her long hair in a silence that grew as the minutes ticked past. He eased onto his back and pulled her with him, so that she rested against his side, with her hand flat on his chest, just above his diaphragm. He was muscular and warm and very hairy. Her hand contracted and shifted, just a little, and it tingled with the unfamiliar feel of him. He made a sound. She paused, and, after a minute, her hand moved again. The sound was deeper, a soft groan.

"Are men…vulnerable when they are touched?" she asked.

"Yes," he said simply.

"Oh."

Her fingers hesitated. She had no experience at all, and while part of her was terrified that she might encounter something shocking, another part was curious and excited.

"Touch me," he invited.

"It sounds as though it hurts you," she protested.

"It hurts in a sweet way," he replied.

She didn't understand, and he laughed.

"Be brave," he coaxed. "Surely there's more than a trace of adventure in your spirited soul?"

"Jared, my idea of adventure is pulling up weeds in the garden," she said demurely. "This is…very mysterious, and a little frightening. You have no clothes on!"

"It's rather difficult to make love fully dressed."

She heard the dry note in his voice. Her hand moved again, and went across his chest to a hard male nipple. She didn't understand the significance of it, so she didn't pause there. His skin was rough with hair, muscular and warm, and she liked the way it rippled when she caressed it. She caught her breath.

"You don't have any idea what this is really about, do you?" he asked through his teeth. "And I thought you were sleeping with my stepbrother!"

"How do you know that I haven't?" she replied angrily.

He put her hand in a place that she hadn't known existed. It paused there only until she realized what it was, and then she cried out and jerked back and sat up.

"*That's* how I know," he said, laughing.

"Jared, you— What are you doing?"

"Shh."

The gown was suddenly on the floor, and she was astride his hips, and what she had touched was against her belly. They were sitting up in the middle of the bed. There was no light coming into the room, but she could feel his chest against her bare breasts and there was an unfamiliar tightness, a swelling, all over her.

She had his shoulders tight in her hands and she was barely breathing at all.

His arms contracted. He held her, without moving, until she got over this newest shock.

"One step at a time, Noelle," he whispered in her ear. And then his cheek slid against hers and she felt his warm, hard mouth cover her own.

For a long time, all he did was kiss her. But inevitably, his tongue went into her mouth in slow, deep thrusts, and his hands touched her in new and exciting ways, in places that she had never imagined a man would touch her.

When he lifted her, she had no idea why until she felt the

probing at her most secret place and felt a hardness that made shocking demands on her innocence.

"Oh, Jared, no!" she cried, her nails biting into his shoulders in fear. "Jared, it hurts!"

"It must, this one time," he whispered grimly, holding her even when she tried to get away. He pulled down on her hips and she felt a burning pain all the way up her spine. "Shh," he whispered, kissing her open mouth as she sobbed. "I wouldn't hurt you for the world unless I had to, my baby. Surely you know that."

Her fingers had moved into the thick hair on his chest and she was sobbing. She was frightened by the pain.

"Noelle, Noelle," he groaned into her tear-wet mouth, while his hands firmed, holding her where it still hurt. "Only a little further, sweetheart," he whispered. "Bear it for me, can't you?"

She felt the tears running down, to be caught by his warm mouth. He was trembling. His hands were fierce on her hips.

"I didn't know that it would hurt so." She wept.

"Forgive me," he groaned. "Forgive me, neither did I. We should have sent you to a doctor first."

"To a…" The comment got through the pain. Her body shivered and she looked through the darkness, trying to see his face. "See a doctor? But why?" she asked through layers of pain.

One hand lifted and went between them, touched her where their bodies were joined, shocking a gasp from her lips. He touched her in a way that made her leap, so that pleasure stabbed into her body and overcame even the pain.

Her nails stabbed into him and she moaned.

"There?" he whispered quickly, and did it again.

"Ja…red!" She cried his name rhythmically, over and over

as he touched her. She moved, shifted, lifted and trembled, and another moan passed her lips. "Oh!"

She was floating. She was free of pain, of anguish; she was free of everything. She felt the mattress at her back. She felt the heated muscles of his body slide tenderly against her from neck to toe, she felt her legs moved apart and her hips lifted. And there was no pain, only a sudden sweet fullness that moved and throbbed and brought her pleasure so overwhelming that she began to sob.

His mouth covered hers, because she was making loud noises in her passion. The arms that held him were possessive, trembling. She heard the slats under the mattress shift, heard his breathing rough and hot at her ear, felt his hands all over her as his powerful body measured itself to hers in a heated, insistent rhythm.

She cried out, the sound muffled by his hard mouth, as red waves carried her beyond what was happening to her taut body. Tension snapped like a pulled thread, and she was falling, shuddering, weeping with a pleasure that only lasted a few sweet, ecstatic seconds. It ended abruptly, and she wept bitterly for its loss, clinging to Jared with all her might to try and bring it back. But he spent himself, too, and went suddenly still, convulsing under her hands before he called her name in a hoarse whisper, was still again and collapsed on her body with his heart beating him half to death.

She felt him over her, against her, inside her. Her hands tested the firm muscles of his back and she struggled to breathe normally again after the most exhausting, explosive pleasure of her life. Her body still trembled rhythmically with the memory of it, as if trying to recapture what it had lost. Her hips moved helplessly, and she felt a tiny hot pain, but even that didn't deter her body from its search.

His hand caught her hip and stilled it. "No," he whispered gently. "You are torn. This will make it worse."

"Torn?" It sounded terrible.

His head lifted. He touched his lips to hers with such tenderness that she felt tears spring to her eyes. "Noelle, have you never been told what happens when a man and a woman come together like this?"

"Who was there to tell me?" she whispered.

He kissed her closed eyelids. "Nature protects a woman's body with a thin membrane called a maidenhead. When a man's body penetrates a virgin's, the membrane tears."

She was so embarrassed that she thanked God it was dark and he couldn't see her face.

"That's why it was painful," he said. "And I apologize to you most humbly for the accusations I made. Your virginity was all too apparent."

"It was supposed to hurt?" she asked.

"I've been told that it has to, sometimes."

Told. Her hands smoothed over the hard, powerful muscles of his shoulders and back. "You do not know?"

He chuckled and his mouth moved slowly to cover her soft breast. "No."

"Then, this was…"

"…my first time with a virgin," he finished for her.

She wanted so badly to ask about the others. She wanted to ask a dozen questions, shameful ones that she could never ask in the light of day. But she hesitated.

"Jared," she began.

He started to pull away, and she cried out. His body stilled at once. He said something under his breath. His hand went to her hip and he eased away from her, bit by bit. "Easy, little one," he whispered soothingly when she clenched and gasped with the pain. "Easy."

When he finally moved away, she felt as if she had been burned. She wept for the pain. He drew her against him and held her gently, nuzzling her face with his.

"I'm sorry," he said softly. "I never wanted to hurt you."

"Oh, but it was worth it," she said fervently, without thinking. "Jared, it was the sweetest thing!"

He let out a long breath. "Was it?"

She lay her cheek against his chest and moved so that she could feel it against just the jut of her breasts. She hesitated, though, when he stiffened. "Shouldn't I do this?" she asked quickly. "You must tell me if I do something I shouldn't. I know so little, Jared."

He drew her back to him. "It excites me to feel your body like this," he told her. "I enjoy the sensation of being aroused, but it's painful when I can't indulge it. You must already know that I can't have you a second time, Noelle. The pain would be unbearable for you."

"I know." She let out a long breath, and another. "Did you... enjoy it? If it hurt me, did it hurt you?"

"A little," he said surprisingly. He laughed at her start of surprise. "That part of me is delicate skin, just as that part of you is."

"Jared!"

He kissed her eyelids closed and stretched, shivering with the aftereffects of so much ecstasy. "I had forgotten how exhausting this is."

She didn't reply. She glowered in the dark.

"Are you jealous?" he whispered, delighted. "Does it make you angry to hear that I've done this before?"

"Yes!" She rolled over and hit his chest. He caught her fist and brought it to his mouth, nipping the knuckles with his teeth lightly.

"I've never done it so perfectly before," he said, his voice deep and slow in the darkness, "or with such tenderness. I've never cared so much that a woman had pleasure from my body."

She sat up, gingerly, because she was very raw. She shivered.

"Have I hurt you badly?" he asked, and he sounded solemn now, stern.

"I'm only sore," she said, flushing when she realized what they were saying to each other. She touched her thigh where it felt wet—and the metallic smell of blood was on her fingers. She grimaced. "Oh, Jared, the sheets… Everyone will know!"

"We're married," he reminded her.

"Yes, but—"

"What a goose you are." He drew her to him and kissed her, touching her breasts with slow, possessive hands. "And what a delight." He released her with a wistful sigh.

She sat up and touched his chest. "After it…heals, will it hurt the next time?"

"No." He couldn't bear to think about a next time. There might not be one for them. He had to put some distance between them. He'd had his one night. If he lost her, it must last him for the rest of his life.

He got up; she heard a rustle as he pulled on his robe.

"You're going away? But…we're married. Can't you stay with me…all night?" she asked hesitantly.

The temptation made him want to cry out, but he didn't dare. He was already besotted with her. He really couldn't risk having her hear the nightmares that plagued him so often in the darkness. When the time was right, if and when she got over Andrew, he would tell her everything and hope for the best. He retrieved her gown from the floor in the dim light and handed it to her. "No. I won't stay."

"But why?" she whispered.

He paused beside the bed, his hands deep in his robe pockets. "Noelle…" he began, wanting so desperately to ask her if she'd been thinking of Andrew while he was loving her.

"Yes?" she asked softly.

He couldn't ask it. It was almost funny that he'd faced down angry men over gun barrels, but he was afraid of words from this woman, who'd come to mean so much to him.

"Nothing," he said abruptly. "Good night."

He went out, closing the door gently behind him. Noelle sat there, puzzled, for a long time before she went to the washstand and gently bathed the raw tissues. The pain was so disturbing that she hardly slept at all, but it was better in the morning.

She went down to breakfast with a lighter step, fascinated by what she'd learned in the darkness about married life. But when she went into the dining room, it was to find the old, familiar Jared sitting at the head of the table. He smiled at her, but without hidden messages, and he was polite, but there was nothing of the lover of the night in his manner. He was like a stranger.

She felt a rush of insecurity. It made her fumble. She was uncomfortable when she sat down, too, and she imagined that everyone saw, everyone knew, even if they weren't looking directly at her.

"Have some eggs, child. I think they came out extra nice this morning," Mrs. Pate said, presenting them on a platter. "After all the exercise you got chasing Mr. Henry yesterday, I expect you need to be built up again!"

She was chuckling as she went out, and Mrs. Dunn made a sound suspiciously like laughter herself.

"He was drinking," Noelle muttered in her own defense. "He chopped down my tomato plants when they had little tomatoes on them. They would have been big enough to eat in two weeks. Now I have only a handful of plants left. He deserved what he got."

"Yes, I know, child," Mrs. Dunn replied. She chuckled. "I can't blame you."

She pursed her lips, remembering what Mrs. Pate had told her about Mrs. Dunn's early faux pas in the community.

Mrs. Dunn must have anticipated that, because her blue eyes, so like her grandson's, twinkled when she looked at Noelle. "I love gardening myself."

She laughed softly. "So you said."

Mrs. Dunn shrugged. "I've been overly sensitive to gossip these past years. I'm learning to live in the new times, but they're difficult for old ones like me."

"You're not so old," Jared said, speaking for the first time. "You still have the spirit I remember from my youth."

"But, alas, not the energy."

Jared was looking at Noelle intently, but when she turned her head, he averted his eyes. He finished his breakfast unhurriedly and wiped his mouth with the linen napkin.

"I have a client to see this morning," he said, looking at his watch.

"You mentioned telegraphing that detective in Chicago," his grandmother remarked. "Is he coming here?"

"I don't expect him to. The investigation I require can be done where he is."

"Couldn't one of the city detectives tell you what you want to know?" his grandmother asked.

"Grandmother, they work for the city, and one of them will be a witness for the prosecution."

"This man in Chicago, can he help you prove the innocence of your client?" Noelle asked.

He looked at her with a new bleakness in his eyes that was at variance with his matter-of-fact tone. "I hope that he can find some evidence to tie the accuser to crimes in the past. I've tried enough criminal cases to have a fair knowledge of a client's guilt or innocence. I'm not infallible, but I think this gentleman is telling the truth. And the fact is, he had no motive that I can find for the theft and beating of Marlowe, not even an argument."

"Then why was he arrested?" she persisted.

He glowered at her. "Because he has enemies and no real alibi."

"I see."

He bent and kissed his grandmother's cheek. Noelle sat, waiting breathlessly, hoping for something similar. But although he glanced in her direction, after the slightest hesitation he nodded politely, then went straight out the door without looking back.

Noelle helped Mrs. Pate carry the dirty dishes and platters into the kitchen, wincing a little with every move.

Mrs. Pate went to the pantry and came back with a small jar of salve. She glanced around to make sure no one could overhear her and handed the tiny vial to a puzzled Noelle.

"For the soreness," she said. "It will help it heal."

Noelle flushed. The sheets—Mrs. Pate would have collected them this morning.

"My dear girl," the older woman said kindly, "all of us have been married. There's no need to be embarrassed. A man's passion and childbirth are part of a woman's lot in life." She patted the girl's hands gently as she passed the salve to her. "It gets much better," she added reassuringly. "When a man gets older, he loses his inclination to spend so much time satisfying his ardor. You can bear it until then."

She turned, smiling to herself, and Noelle stared after her, totally perplexed. Bear it? Would it always be so painful? Jared had said not, but perhaps…

"Mrs. Pate," she asked quietly, joining her at the sink. "Is it…I mean, is there no pleasure to be had from it?"

"For the man," came the reply. "But it's sinful for a woman to feel pleasure, Noelle. The act of creation is for creation.

That is why it's so uncomfortable for a woman. But thankfully, it only takes a minute or two until the man…finishes. And that only once or twice a month—just at first, until his ardor wanes. It won't be so bad always, truly. Hand me those dishes, will you, dear?"

Noelle fetched the rest of the plates from the worktable. She was getting a different picture of married life from the older woman. It appeared that Mrs. Pate's late husband had been not very ardent at all, and very quickly satisfied. Jared had been in no great rush. He'd been incredibly patient. And there had been, after the pain, the most explosive, sinful pleasure. Was it sinful to feel something so glorious in the arms of a much-loved husband? Somehow it seemed false to think so.

Perhaps she would find out when Jared came to her bed again. She blushed at just the thought.

But four days passed, and Jared made no ardent move toward her. The salve had done its work—her body was completely healed. She found no discomfort at all in voiding or having the fabric of her drawers touch the place that had been raw. Surely Jared knew. But he hadn't come one step closer. In fact, he was more remote than he'd been since they'd first met.

The thought occurred to her only later that he might have found her a disappointment in bed and wanted nothing else to do with her in any intimate way. Or perhaps he'd only been curious about her that way. He might have even wanted to make sure she was telling him the truth when she said that Andrew hadn't been her lover. There were many reasons she could formulate to explain his abstinence, his remote courtesy. But the only one that really mattered was that he couldn't be in love with her. A man in love wouldn't have been able to keep his distance. Jared seemed to find her wholly resistible. She was his wife, but now it appeared that she could continue in that capacity only in name. He came no more to her bed.

Chapter Fourteen

The trial was due to start in two days. Noelle saw Jared's brooding, preoccupied face when he came home and knew what had caused it. The story of his client's almost certain guilt was on the front page of the newspaper, along with a quote from the prosecutor about having the case in the bag. There were three eyewitnesses that would swear Clark had been in the dry-goods store just before poor old man Marlowe was beaten and robbed, they saw him run out with a bag just before Marlowe was found. They'd all volunteered to testify for the prosecution, and they had other pertinent information about the wrangler with whom they worked at the Beale ranch, too.

Jared stuck his hands in his pockets and glowered at the paper lying open beside Noelle on the sofa.

"I don't believe you're going to lose," she said matter-of-factly, "even if the prosecutor does."

He laughed pleasantly. "Optimist."

"Everyone speaks of your skill as an attorney," she said simply. "You'd hardly be so well-known if you weren't good at what you do." She was working a complicated embroidery piece. "I'd very much like to come and hear you in court."

He was surprised and pleased at her interest. "Your faith may be misplaced," he said. "Noelle, I know Clark is innocent. Proving it…" He made a gesture with one hand. "That's the rub."

She put down her embroidery and sat looking at him curiously. "What will you do?"

His broad shoulders rose and fell. "Gather evidence until I run out of time, and hope I have enough to convince a jury."

He stuck his hands in his pockets and went to the window to look out. It was misting rain. Supper would be on the table soon, and his grandmother would come downstairs. He was anxious for that. He didn't want to be alone with Noelle too long. His body throbbed from just being in the same room with her. His knowledge of her had kept him restless and sleepless for several nights. He wanted her desperately, but with the trial so close, he really couldn't afford the distraction. Besides, he still wasn't sure about her feelings for Andrew. He couldn't let himself feel so deeply for her when he might yet lose her.

"I hear that Mr. Marlowe is still comatose, too. Do you know who beat him up and left him in such a condition?"

He was thoughtful for a minute. He'd been doing a lot of hard searching in the past three days, a lot of investigating. Everything he'd discovered led back to the man with the loudest voice in this case—the supposed "eyewitness," Garmon. "You know," he replied slowly, "I think I do."

"Can't you go and tell the judge?"

He laughed softly, turning back toward her. "The judge wouldn't take my word for a man's innocence. If Marlowe regains consciousness, I'd have proof. But that may not happen."

"Then you must get proof of another kind."

He studied her with pure pleasure, smiling gently at her trust in him. He stared at her auburn head, bent over her handiwork. She wore the pretty pale blue dress with the lace again, and he thought how it suited her. She was only nineteen, still a child. And yet, in his arms, she had been every dream he'd ever had of a woman. Just the sight of her made him hungry.

She lifted her eyes again, hesitating. There was something she had to tell him, and she didn't want to. He was looking at her as if he liked her, and this was going to be unpleasant.

"What is it?" he asked gently.

She straightened. "There was a letter from Andrew today."

He went very still. Her discomfort made him angry. Andrew, again! "And what did he have to say?"

"I didn't read it." Her voice was stiff, because it was painful for her to remember the embarrassing situation she'd been caught in with Andrew—especially now, when she knew that she loved Jared. "It was addressed to your grandmother. She said he truly regrets what happened, as well as his behavior toward me. He wants us all to forgive him."

"Did he mention anything about Miss Beale?" he asked bluntly, watching her face closely as he mentioned the other woman's name deliberately. "I understand that she was staying in Dallas, too. I hope he hasn't done anything impetuous with her, or Beale will call him out and kill him."

"Mr. Beale? Call him out?" The term was unfamiliar to her.

"Beale was a lawman, among his other vocations in the past," he said grimly. "Like most men who can use a gun well, he has no conscience about killing. And I think that his age is unlikely to slow him down very much," he added, recalling his conversation with Beale in his office. "If Andrew steps out of line with Jennifer, he's going to be in more trouble than he can handle."

"Poor Andrew," she began.

He hated the sympathy in her soft voice for his stepbrother, the look of concern there. So, she still had hopes!

"'Poor Andrew,' indeed," he scoffed. His pale eyes glittered over her. "Have you forgotten so soon how he ran like a yellow dog when he was faced with the prospect of being forced to marry you? In fact, he ran to Miss Beale, didn't he?" he added coldly.

She lifted proud eyes to his. "Yes, he did. But carrying grudges serves no constructive purpose. Anyway, Jared, he's only my brother-in-law now."

He didn't speak. He simply looked at her, certain that there was more, something she hesitated to tell him. He was eaten up with jealousy, now more than ever, and trying desperately not to let it show. But the question was there.

She saw it on his face. "He wants to come home," she said, and smiled.

His blue eyes flashed with rage. "Over my dead body!" he replied.

His vehemence surprised her. "Your grandmother is concerned about him," she persisted. "Why are you so inflexible?" she added.

"Because he's been nothing but a thorn in my side for years. Shall I tell you about your precious Andrew? About the paternity suits, and the threats of reprisal, and the unpaid bills that I've had to settle for him? He's a boy playing at being a man—a liar, and a womanizer, and a braggart."

"I know that, Jared," she replied calmly.

"But where love exists, so does forgiveness," he said on a harsh laugh. He was torn in half with jealousy. She was defending Andrew now, when he'd walked all over her. "Well, I suppose no woman can resist a handsome face and a swagger. Or perhaps women prefer liars because none of them are capable of telling the truth, either. All right. If you want Andrew home so much, then by all means, he can come home."

She stared at him with open surprise, and in his eyes again was the implacability that had puzzled her for so long.

"I—I didn't say that I wanted him here," she faltered.

"Didn't you?" he replied, with a cynical, mocking smile. "Despite the way he treated you, you can't wait to get your arms around him again, can you? What a pity that you couldn't lead him to the altar!"

Her hands rested on the embroidery. "So that's what you think. You don't trust me at all, do you?" she asked evenly. "From the beginning, you kept me at a distance. You never would have married me in the first place if you hadn't felt driven to it, to protect Mrs. Dunn!"

"I'm not a marrying man," he returned coldly. "Although there are some, shall we say, fringe benefits." His eyes went down to her breasts and lingered there.

She threw down the embroidery and got to her feet, red-cheeked with anger. "You cad!"

"What did you expect me to say? As you reminded me, we married to avert a scandal, not for love. And we both know it won't last, Noelle," he added, thinking that if Andrew wanted her enough, she wouldn't hesitate to divorce him.

But Noelle got another sense of his words entirely, and she felt the ground go out from under her. Was he hinting that he wanted a divorce?

Her white face told its own story. He turned away, unable to bear looking at it. Andrew would come back, and she'd be all over him again. Despite the passionate night they'd spent together, she could defend Andrew and plead for his return. And he was so angry he could hardly hold back the words.

But she didn't know what he was feeling, because he was adept at disguising it. He sounded disinterested and indifferent.

"Are you intimating that you want me to leave, Jared?" she asked in quiet desperation.

His heart skipped. He turned on his heels to stare at her, feeling the impact of the words with unexpected pain.

"Leave? When Andrew will be coming home soon?" he taunted. "What a waste that would be? Think of all the nights of passion that you can anticipate with him!"

Her green eyes glittered furiously at him. "I told you, nothing happened beyond what you saw that night."

"So you said," he drawled.

"So you know!" she hissed, coloring at having been forced to make the blatant statement. Her small fists clenched at her sides. She wanted to hit him. She wanted to pound him, to drag that snide expression off his face and make him feel, make him rage, make him lose that exasperating self-control. Even in bed with her, he was cool and deliberate. He never seemed to waver from his stoic self.

"Go ahead," he invited softly. "Hit me."

She shivered with control. "It would be a pleasure," she said angrily. "But I must think of your grandmother. I hear her step on the staircase. She wouldn't understand. She adores you."

"And you don't."

She was breathing audibly in her anger. "I loathe you," she lied. "I regret that I ever came here to live. And I regret marrying you most of all!" she cried, wounded to the heart.

"You don't regret it any more than I do," he shot right back at her. "I would never have married you if my hand hadn't been forced by your precious Andrew."

Well, that was plain enough. She picked up her embroidery

and put it carefully into the carpetbag by the sofa, then turned with all the dignity she could muster and went toward the hall.

Her straight back and uplifted face told their own story. His hands clenched in his pockets. He wanted to call her back, to explain, to apologize. But there was really nothing more that he could say. If she wanted Andrew, there was nothing he could do to prevent her from divorcing him and marrying his stepbrother. He wasn't even sure that she was telling him the truth about the letter. Perhaps Andrew had written not only to his grandmother, but to Noelle, as well. Perhaps, even now, they were making plans for the future. He'd sworn an interest in Miss Beale, but that could have been a red herring. Perhaps he'd realized what a treasure Noelle was and he was coming back to claim her.

When his grandmother came down, she mentioned Andrew's request to come home. Jared agreed to it without a protest, turned and left the house without even stopping to eat. He couldn't bear to sit at the same table with Noelle... knowing that she was wishing he was Andrew.

At the dinner table, his grandmother announced that she'd sent a boy to town with money and a note to telegraph Andrew, inviting him to come back home.

Noelle didn't say a word. She felt nothing. Jared had walked out on her deliberately, turned his back on her. He thought she wanted Andrew. How absurd, when Andrew had betrayed her. She was a wife, but not a wife. She lived with a man who wouldn't come near her. At no time had she felt more of an outsider than she did now. It was just as well that she knew where she stood with Jared, though, she told herself comfortingly. At least she knew that her hopes in that direction could never be realized. Apparently he'd satisfied his curiosity about her and his hunger for her in one night—and wanted nothing more from her. He'd as good as told her that he was going to leave her eventually. It was ironic that she'd fallen so much in love with him.

Andrew arrived the next morning. He was a startlingly different Andrew, though. He neither swaggered nor talked arrogantly. He was in the position of a supplicant now, and he knew it.

He greeted Noelle quietly, and with an apology that he seemed to mean. With Jared he was reserved, and with his grandmother he was respectful and subdued.

Jared kept out of his way. He was so jealous of the man that he couldn't bear to be in the same room with him. But Noelle watched Andrew with quiet interest. It was obvious that he regretted the way he'd treated her. He even said so. He was like a different man, and she wondered at the change in him.

Something else was puzzling, too. Miss Beale had returned to Fort Worth from Dallas, as Andrew had. And Andrew spoke of the woman in a totally different way, as if he was truly infatuated with her. But he made no move to go near her. He seemed to be waiting for something—her father's permission to court the girl, perhaps. She wished that Jared could be home long enough to see that Andrew was courteous and kind but not flirtatious. But Jared spent all of his time at the office, and now he didn't even speak to Noelle unless he had to.

Jared had taken depositions from the two witnesses he'd managed to find who thought they'd seen Clark at the ranch just after the time of the murder. But they both worked for Beale, and one of them was known to drink heavily. Jared had less than he'd ever had at the start of a felony trial. Old man Marlowe was conscious now, but he couldn't tell anyone

who'd robbed him, because he'd been hit from behind before
he saw his assailant. That was the most damning blow of all
to Clark's defense. If the old man had seen the man who'd
struck the blow, it would have cleared Clark automatically.

If Jared couldn't prove Clark innocent, and that looked
likely at the present time, he had to prove someone else guilty.
So he was looking for loopholes, for anything out of the ordi-
nary, and with a keen intuition, he concentrated all his efforts
on Beale's other wrangler, John Garmon.

His Chicago detective hadn't been able to find a thing
about Garmon in his files. Jared had asked Clark for more
information about the man's past, but Clark knew nothing.
He telegraphed police departments in nearby cities in Texas
for any information they had on Garmon, but nothing turned
up. Nothing at all.

It seemed that Garmon had no criminal record. That was
odd, if the man was a compulsive gambler. Over the years,
Jared had dealt with too many compulsive gamblers not to
suspect that Garmon hadn't kept totally out of the way of the
law. And often the methods a man used were like fingerprints.
He smiled to himself and his eyes narrowed in thought. Why
hadn't he considered that sooner?

He had Adrian, his secretary, send a dozen wires to police
departments in surrounding cities, this time asking for news of
any arrests six months ago or longer for suspicion of beating
and robbing storekeepers. The next day, he had two replies,
one from Austin and one from Victoria. Neither of the men
named was Garmon, but there was a description in the Austin
case—the assailant had been a big man with a Southern drawl,
and there had only been one eyewitness, a Negro who refused
to testify against him, so the case was not pursued for lack of
evidence. It wasn't conclusive proof of guilt, but it was enough
to run a bluff if the man was lying—and Jared was certain
that Garmon was.

But the problem was still one of proof. It might be possible to find people from Austin who could identify Garmon and swear that he'd been suspected of robbing a merchant there. But that wouldn't connect him with old man Marlowe's assault and robbery. And to go to Austin and search for those witnesses would take time, something he didn't have.

The best way, the only way, would be to flush Garmon out and make him nervous enough to do something stupid. It was his only chance to save Clark. Garmon had two cronies who would swear that day was night if he told them to. Those were the three "eyewitnesses" for the prosecution; they were all three white, and because of it, they would probably be believed.

What he had to do was use the flimsy circumstantial evidence he'd gathered to convince Garmon that he was onto his game. That would be dangerous, but it seemed the most likely manner in which to proceed. The danger no longer bothered him. He had cared about the future only so long as he had Noelle in his life and in his future. Now that Andrew had returned, he was certain to lose her to the younger man—not because Andrew was a better man, but because Noelle loved him. He had nothing to lose, now. It was like the old, wild days, when not caring gave him the edge. He had it once again, just when he needed it most.

So, having found where Garmon spent his Friday evenings when he came to town, instead of going home to eat a late supper, Jared went looking for him. He found him losing badly at draw poker in one of the saloons in The Acre, Fort Worth's red-light district.

As Garmon threw down his cards and got up, Jared was standing in front of him, blocking his way.

The cowboy was packing. He had a gun in a belt at his hip and his hand went to it, but when he realized who was standing there he laughed and relaxed.

"Well, well. If it ain't the great attorney who's defending Mr. Beale's pet nigg—"

"I'm Clark's lawyer," Jared said, eyeing the other man as two smaller men flanked him, looking as belligerent as Garmon did.

"What are you doing here, lawyer?" Garmon taunted. "Looking for something to drown your sorrows in? Because my buddies and me saw that sorry fellow run out of Marlowe's store like a scalded dog, carrying something in his hand— something like a bag of money. Didn't we, boys?"

"You bet," they chorused, grinning.

"And we're all going to swear to it in court," Garmon added defiantly.

Jared's pale blue eyes narrowed. He looked at Garmon levelly. "What if I told you," he began slowly, "that I have an eyewitness from Austin who's coming down here in a couple of days to discredit your testimony?" he added.

Garmon looked momentarily disconcerted. "What?"

"He can prove that you aren't a trustworthy witness against Clark. He'll testify that you were accused of armed robbery of a storekeeper in Austin, but that you bluffed your way out of it. He'll testify that you were arrested there on suspicion of robbery—and only turned loose for lack of enough evidence to convict."

Garmon lifted his chin. "You can't prove that."

"Can't I?" Jared asked. "You framed Clark."

"And just what makes you think so?" Garmon replied finally, bluffing it through.

"Beale told me your wages are spent before you ever get them. Where did you get the money to get into that game?" he asked, nodding toward the table.

Garmon's hand fell to his gun butt. He whipped the pistol out so fast there were murmurs behind him, leveled it at Jared's belly and smiled. "Why don't I just kill you?" he chided.

"Go ahead," Jared said, looking around at the witnesses.

Garmon's eyes narrowed. The lawyer was unarmed. This wasn't smart. With a considering stare, he spun the pistol back into his holster. He was fast, all right. But not quite fast enough, Jared was thinking.

Garmon postured. "Well, you talk good, fancy pants, but you can't prove nothing. If you're so brave, let's see you take me," he challenged. "You ain't got a gun, but I'll bet somebody'll loan you one, if you ask nice." The smile faded. "Somebody give this dude a gun," he called out, thinking how simple it would be to just shoot the man now. In self-defense, of course.

His two friends moved closer to him, looking as mean as they could.

Jared wasn't intimidated. He'd seen Garmon draw and he knew that he was faster. He could take all three of them, if he had to. But if he killed Garmon here, Clark wasn't going to have a chance. He couldn't overplay his hand. He had to back down, or give the appearance of backing down. He wanted Garmon to stew over the threat all night and come looking for him in the morning in a nervous rage. That was what he expected to happen. But he had to set it up first.

"As you can see—" Jared swept back his coat "—I'm unarmed." He contrived to look nervous. "I wouldn't really know what to do with a pistol," he added deliberately.

The other man relaxed. "How about with a law book?" Garmon demanded, and laughed uproariously at his own joke.

Jared stared into the man's eyes. "When I get my witness on the stand," he said softly, "I'll show you my weapons."

Garmon didn't look quite as confident now. "We'll see," he said.

Jared nodded. "Yes, we will. The trial begins at nine in the morning. I'm sure I'll see you there. Maybe I can even get my witness to come up here tomorrow."

He turned, and, while keeping a careful eye on the crowd out of the corner of his eye, gave the appearance of a man stupid enough to turn his back on this crowd. That convinced Garmon that the man wouldn't fight. But the visit also convinced him that he was going to have to do something quick—or that silver-tongued lawyer would push him into revealing how he got the money to use at the gambling table tonight. He shouldn't have rushed out to spend it. But he'd kindled lynching fever in people over the robbery, and he'd thought something would come of it. But the people in Fort Worth didn't seem to have a mob mentality. He couldn't get people mad enough to act, and old man Marlowe seemed to be recovering, which also took some of the edge off the town's anger.

If Clark had been lynched, Garmon wouldn't have to worry about being caught and put in jail. But now that it hadn't happened, he couldn't risk having that lawyer bring out the robbery arrest in Austin. People would see that Garmon was capable of armed robbery. He'd used another name there—how had Dunn traced him?

He hadn't counted on that lawyer tracing him to another town where he'd robbed a merchant for easy money and got out of town before the trial. Austin wasn't the only place he'd pulled that one. What if Dunn dug deeper? There were no convictions, but he'd been arrested three times. He'd never gone to jail. He'd always slipped by. But what if they caught him? What if he got himself locked up? He couldn't bear the thought of being locked up. It had never occurred to him that he could be caught.

He ordered a drink and stood wolfing it down while he worked on possibilities. Dunn had said he might bring that witness up from Austin tomorrow. He couldn't let that happen.

Nobody would believe him if there was suspicion cast on his past. The black man would get off and he'd probably be the first suspect, since he was supposedly an eyewitness. Somebody might ask why he'd been close enough to see Clark at Marlowe's store.

That lawyer didn't carry a gun, and he obviously didn't know how to shoot one. The best way to handle this thing would be to face him down outside the courtroom tomorrow morning and scare him into giving up Clark's case. Or kill him. That would take care of the Austin witness—if Dunn didn't handle the case, the witness wouldn't be needed. That would keep Garmon's past hidden.

Afterward, if Dunn ran or was killed, Clark would surely never find another attorney brave enough to challenge Garmon's story, and Clark would go to jail for the robbery. Garmon would get away scot-free. He'd get the foreman's job out at Beale's place and have plenty of money to gamble with, and he could settle down here. To his dull brain, it seemed the perfect plan. He was quick enough with his gun, but he wouldn't have to be all that fast. It wouldn't take much to make that prissy lawyer run for his life—if he decided to let him live. He could kill him if he wanted to and call it self-defense.

The more he thought about it, the better it pleased him. Yes, this plan would do the trick.

"Pour me another shot of whiskey," he told the bartender.

"Say, Garmon—that city lawyer as good as accused you of robbing old man Marlowe," one of the patrons remarked.

Garmon whipped out his pistol and leveled it at the man. "You were saying?"

There was a loud clearing of a throat. "Said I'd go shoot me a city lawyer, if I was you, Garmon," the man amended quickly.

Garmon chuckled. He spun the pistol back into his holster.

He liked intimidating people. He'd learned long ago that most men wouldn't argue with a man who could draw as fast as Garmon could. He liked to show off his speed occasionally, just to keep people on their toes. "That's what I thought you said."

Jared stopped by the jail to see Brian Clark, who was looking morose.

"No lynch mobs yet," Clark remarked, with a weary smile. "I've been expecting one."

Jared leaned against the bars. "Garmon can't get enough help," he said dryly. "But I've set the cat among the pigeons. I expect Garmon to come gunning for me in the morning."

Clark stood up. "Mr. Dunn, he's a dangerous man," he said quietly. "I know things about him that I've never told. Don't get yourself killed on my account."

Dunn glanced around. There were no deputies around, no prisoners near enough to hear. "Let me level with you," he said quietly. "I haven't got enough hard evidence to win your case. If it goes to trial, there's a good chance that I'll lose. You have no alibi, no believable eyewitnesses who could vouch for your whereabouts, and it looks like Marlowe won't be able to identify his assailant. Garmon's fanned the fires of hatred around here, and his two cohorts will swear to whatever he tells them. He isn't known here, but his word will be accepted over yours. Your military record and Beale's testimony could help. But not enough." His blue eyes met the man's levelly. "I can't get you off. Not in court."

Clark seemed to shrink. "I see," he said.

"But there's one other way," he continued. "I went to find Garmon tonight. I told him that I could link him with at least one other merchant robbery in Texas, and I've told him I can bring a witness up here from Austin to swear to it in court.

I've spooked him. If he reacts as I expect him to, he'll come looking for me tomorrow before the trial begins."

"You'll get yourself killed," Clark said worriedly.

"Just between the two of us, Mr. Clark, I very much doubt it."

The city detective, Sims, was watching the jail while the jailer had a meal. He put his head around the door and glowered at Jared. "Clear out," he said shortly. "Visiting hours are over."

"I'm not finished," Jared replied evenly.

Sims moved into the room, his hand on his gun belt, his posture threatening. "I said, clear out," he said, with a surly look, sure that the dude wouldn't challenge him. City lawyers didn't bother Sims much.

Jared hesitated, but it was the wrong time to start trouble. He glanced at Clark. "Don't worry," he said. "I know what I'm doing."

He turned and started past Sims, who pursed his lips and looked amused. "Do I make you nervous, lawyer?" Sims drawled, fingering his pistol. "Are you scared of guns?"

Jared lifted an eyebrow. "You have a high opinion of yourself, Sims," he said pleasantly.

"If you mean I'm good with a gun, sure I am," Sims replied. "Know which end of a pistol to point, lawyer?"

Jared laughed to himself. "One of these days," he said very softly, and just for a minute his eyes glittered like blue ice, "you may find out the hard way what I know about pistols."

He walked on out, his hands in his pockets, his mind on tomorrow and what it would bring. Sims, a little less confident than he pretended to be, stared after the man with open curiosity.

Jared went home. Noelle was in the living room with his grandmother, but when he came in and poured himself a whiskey, Mrs. Dunn tactfully left the room on the pretext of going to bed.

Jared sat down across from his wife and stared at her. Beale's words kept coming back to him, about the past catching up with men when they least expected it. He hadn't wanted a confrontation, but the only way he was going to save Clark from the gallows was to deliberately provoke one. It went against everything he believed in, against his respect for the law, but he'd backed himself into a corner.

"Where's Andrew?" he asked coldly.

She didn't look up from her handiwork, and although her heart was racing, she seemed as calm as a summer day. "He went out this evening," she replied, and she didn't tell him that Andrew had gone, finally, to call on Miss Beale.

"And he didn't take you with him?" he asked coldly.

She did look up then. Jared looked preoccupied, even as he mocked her. There was something there, something beneath the sarcasm. He was worried.

"What's wrong?" she asked quietly. "Can't you tell me?"

Her perception startled him. He'd forgotten how far she could see into his soul at times. It had to be a rare thing. He only wished that he could start over with her. But it was much too late. Tomorrow he would more than likely have to face down a gunman who would try to kill him. He could beat Garmon to the draw, but being fast didn't guarantee the outcome. A man had to be levelheaded, calm, deadly accurate. Most of all, he couldn't allow his mind to wander. He couldn't have distractions, or Garmon would have the edge.

"It's the trial, isn't it?" she persisted.

He leaned back with a long sigh. "Yes."

He remembered vividly the way he'd spoken to her at their last meeting, the harsh remarks he'd made about Andrew, his bitter accusations. He felt bad about that. If she genuinely loved the other man, her happiness should come first with him. He should care about her feelings. At least, he thought, he could leave her a kind memory of him to offset the coldness he'd shown to her days before.

"I've been unkind to you," he said abruptly, startling her into looking up. "I've been judgmental and inflexible, and I haven't considered your feelings at all. I'm sorry."

She knew that he rarely apologized. That made the apology all the more poignant. Her hands stilled. "Oh, Jared. I know how much you have on your mind," she said gently. "Perhaps I can even understand how you feel about Andrew coming back here." Her eyes fell. "And as you said, you were landed with me; we didn't marry for love. I had no right to expect anything from you."

His eyes closed. He felt a stab of pain right through him. "Do you think anyone could have forced me to marry you if I hadn't wanted to?" he asked shortly.

Her thin eyebrows arched. "Well…you—you do love your grandmother," she said, faltering.

"Indeed I do," he said quickly. "But the situation could have been salvaged some other way. I married you because I wanted to, Noelle," he added quietly, admitting it at last. "I wanted to, very much. And I lied when I said I regretted it. I don't. I'm only sorry that I had so little to give you."

She frowned. "You sound as if you're saying goodbye." She laughed nervously.

"Perhaps I am, in a way," he told her. He searched her flushed face hungrily, although none of that hunger showed. "You came closer than I've ever let anyone else get to me," he said huskily. "Perhaps, in time, we might have…" He took a long breath and took another sip of his whiskey. "Well, it's no good talking about what might have been. I want you to be happy, Noelle. We both know by now that we can't have a future together."

Her hands grasped the embroidery and crumpled it while

she stared at him. "You seem very certain of it," she managed in a choked tone.

"I am." For as long as she loved Andrew, what happiness could they have? He stared down at his boots. They were dusty, and it did little good to polish them. He missed her tormented expression. "When the trial is over, I'll see about getting your freedom for you."

She couldn't even breathe. "You mean…a divorce?" she whispered.

"It would seem to be the only way. But who knows?" he asked on a cold laugh. "Maybe you'll get it without court intervention." If Garmon's aim was true, he was thinking. He glanced up at her. "I'm sure you're glad to have Andrew back."

She was still reeling over his talk of giving her her freedom. "Yes. He was very grateful that you let him come home," she said absently, recalling his delight when Miss Beale had sent word to him that he was invited to supper at the Beale home this evening. "His heart is here, now."

Jared stiffened. "Yes. I know it is."

She didn't see the flash of jealousy in his cold eyes, because he lowered them at once.

He sipped his whiskey, thinking how pretty she looked in her lacy dress. He remembered much too well how she looked without her lacy dress. He'd been too damned cautious, refusing to share his life with her, protecting himself from betrayal.

Now he knew with perfect certainty that she wasn't like Ava, that she'd never lie to him. And he knew that if she'd been able to love him, as she loved Andrew, she'd never think of walking out on him, either, even if she knew exactly what he was, what he'd been. But Andrew was back, and she loved him. He had to let her go, so that she could have the one man she loved.

"The trial begins tomorrow, doesn't it?" she asked.

He frowned. "Yes."

"Have you found your proof?"

"I've found suspicion. I don't have enough proof to save Clark."

"Oh, Jared," she said gently, lifting her eyes to his. "I'm very sorry."

"Don't be. I expect the situation to resolve itself quite soon," he said, thinking about the morning to come and Garmon with his mocking grin.

"How?"

He finished his whiskey and got to his feet. He didn't limp at all now. He looked elegant and fit and vital. He walked to where Noelle sat and leaned over her with a hand on the back of the chair. His blue eyes stared right into hers.

"Don't come into town for the trial in the morning," he said abruptly.

"Why not?" she asked unsteadily, because he was very close.

He searched her eyes slowly. "I can't tell you. You'll have to take my word for it. If you go out, make certain you're with Andrew. He'll protect you."

She'd never seen Jared like this, and she was worried. Her brows drew together. "Jared, they won't try to lynch Mr. Clark, will they?" she asked.

"Right now, that's the least of my worries."

Her green eyes searched his blue ones and her heart raced. As she watched, he bent toward her, hesitating just as his lips hovered over hers. Now that Andrew was back, she might not want this with him. But he did, so desperately, want her mouth one last time!

"Noelle," he whispered unsteadily.

She looked at his lips, so close to hers. "Oh, come here…" She pulled his head down and kissed him as hungrily as he

kissed her. Did she sense that he might not see her again after
the morning? Was she offering him comfort? He didn't know,
didn't care. His mouth devoured hers until his body forced him
to pull away as the sharp edge of desire made him rigid. Her
arms clung when he raised his head, and he groaned as she
pulled him back. Once more, he thought, as he crushed her
warm mouth under his lips. He lifted her clear off the chair
and enveloped her completely against him, so hungry that he
couldn't restrain his ardor.

She felt her knees give way, and was grateful for the
strength of his hard arms around her as the kiss went on and
on and on.

It hurt him to let her go. He eased her away, breath by
breath, his hands firm on her arms as he disengaged them
from around his neck. His blue eyes were glittering with
banked-down desire and he shuddered with the force of it as
he pushed her away. He saw her tremble from his fingertips,
saw her huge, misty green eyes watching him, unblinking, as
he fought for control.

How could she kiss him like that when she loved Andrew?
he wondered furiously. How could she permit him to touch
her at all?

"You have…never kissed me like that before," she managed
in a choked whisper.

"Perhaps I should have, that day in the kitchen," he replied
huskily, searching her flushed face with quick, soft eyes.

She put a hand to her swollen lips. "That day… Why did
you throw my hand off, as if I'd contaminated you?" she
asked.

He took a steadying breath. "Because I wanted you suddenly, to the point of madness. I didn't want you to see, to
know how vulnerable I was to your touch, Noelle." He managed a strained smile. "I could hardly tell you that before we
were married. I had to let you think I was repulsed."

She looked at him with new eyes, with hope, with wonder. "You keep too many secrets," she whispered.

He nodded. His eyes searched hers slowly. "You are the most beautiful thing in my life," he said harshly. "The world would have been diminished without you in it."

She moved closer, but he backed away with a cold laugh.

"No," he said abruptly, holding up a hand. "No. I've said too much already."

She didn't understand at all. Her eyes pleaded with him. "Something is wrong," she said suddenly. "I know it. Jared, please, tell me!"

But he couldn't. He moved away from her quickly, to stare out the window with his hands in his pockets until he could get his breath back.

She watched him. She could still taste the whiskey on his hard mouth, the desperation in his kiss.

"What's wrong?" she asked again.

He took a deep breath, turned and looked at her until she flushed, memorizing every soft, sweet line of her beloved face. He looked tormented for an instant. But then, quickly, he composed himself. After a minute he turned away. "Nothing. I have some last-minute things to do before I retire. Sleep well."

He started out of the room. "Jared?"

He paused with his hand on the door, one eyebrow raised.

She sensed how hungry he was for her. She could feel the whip of it, and her body burned with the memories of the last time, with her own need of him. But she hesitated. It was such a forward thing to say to a man, even a husband—especially one who'd just said flatly that he was going to divorce her. But he was worried about the trial, and she could give him the ease of her body, if nothing else. And perhaps, if she could make him want her enough, he might change his mind about freeing her.

"If you wanted to, you could...we could..." She blushed, embarrassed by what she was offering him.

"Would you really make that sort of sacrifice for me?" he asked softly, fighting the temptation to accept it. But he couldn't. She was Andrew's. He took a deep breath and mockery flared in his eyes. "Are you sorry for me, Noelle?" he taunted.

She glared at him, now furious. "I'm not in the least sorry for you! And I don't want to sleep with you, anyway!"

His eyebrows arched. "Was it really so bad?" he taunted.

She gasped.

He laughed mirthlessly. His eyes narrowed as he looked at her. "It was almost sacred," he said roughly. "I'll never touch another woman as long as I live. The memory will be enough for me, long after you're gone."

She didn't understand what he was saying. Her lips parted. "Jared, you never came to my bed again," she said softly, mindful of anyone who might be outside the door and hear her.

"I didn't dare," he replied, his eyes blazing with feeling. "My God, do you think I didn't want to?" He took a quick breath. "Noelle, we have to play the cards we're dealt. Your future doesn't lie with me. What you gave me was more than I ever expected." His eyes were somber, solemn now. "Try to remember that, won't you? You're very young, my dear. You'll be happier with someone...closer to your own age." He meant Andrew, but he couldn't get the name out of his mouth. He stared at her puzzled face with exquisite pain. He loved her. "I guess, one way or another, you'll know it all tomorrow."

She frowned. "I don't understand."

"Believe me, you will." His eyes narrowed, even now his

one thought was to protect her from any harm. "Remember what I said. Stay out of town in the morning."

He went through the doorway abruptly. Her mind raced ahead to the next day. And one thing she was certainly going to do was go into town for the trial. There was some danger, she knew it. And if her husband was in danger, she was going to be right where he was, whether he approved or not, even if he did want to divorce her! If only she could understand why he kissed her like a man desperately in love and the next instant talked of setting her free to marry a younger man. Why, who was he thinking of? Surely he knew that Andrew wanted to marry Jennifer Beale. Or did he?

Chapter Fifteen

Jared was taciturn and stoic the next morning; he left the house just after breakfast. He'd barely eaten anything, and he was unusually tense. No one knew that he'd been up most of the night, deliberating over what he was going to do this morning. There had been one long, terrible conflict between his need to save Clark and his respect for the letter of the law. He'd broken the rules before and never regretted it. But this time, he had less choice than ever before. If he didn't bend the law a little, an innocent man would go to the gallows.

Noelle's ardor had also kept him sleepless. Apparently she was as helpless as he was in their mutual attraction for each other. The difference was that she loved Andrew. That might be just as well, given the possibility that Jared could die today.

He alone knew the enormity of what lay ahead. He was tense, but he didn't speak. When he was ready to leave, he kissed Mrs. Dunn. He even shook hands with Andrew. But for Noelle, there was nothing except one long, achingly intense look that seemed to actually hurt him. He didn't dare touch her—because he didn't want his feelings for her to be obvious to everyone in the household. The memory of her sweet kisses the night before would have to carry him through whatever lay ahead.

He left the house, resplendent and elegant. His last sight of Noelle was with Andrew right by her side, very close. As he looked, Andrew smiled down at her and she smiled back. Well, what had he expected? He knew why Andrew had wanted to come home. He'd come to his senses about Noelle and they seemed to be back on their old footing. How could he blame Andrew? She was one hell of a woman. He put on his hat and went out the gate. And he didn't look back.

Noelle watched him leave with a sense of foreboding that made her knees weak. She knew something was wrong.

"He looked odd," she mentioned to the others.

"It's this trial," Andrew said carelessly, and he smiled gently at her. "All the controversy. Why in heaven's name he had to take the case is beyond me. Everyone's talking about it, even in Dallas."

"But the man is innocent, Andrew," Noelle said curtly.

He shrugged. "What difference does it make?"

"Well, it should make a difference," Mrs. Dunn broke in. "You watch your tongue in my house, young man."

"Yes, ma'am," he murmured sheepishly.

"I'm going to town," Noelle announced sharply.

"So am I," Mrs. Dunn seconded.

Andrew hesitated. "I'm expected for lunch at the Beale house. Mr. Beale seems to be coming around about my suit for Miss Beale's hand—" he noticed their angry looks "—but I have time enough to go with you both to town this morning. I'll just get my hat."

* * *

Jared went to his office without looking back. He didn't wear a gun. It was still in his trunk, along with the other memorabilia of his past. Having had the night to think over his next move, he hoped that there would be no serious gunplay. Garmon would surely come to town to try and scare him off the case. But if it came to that, Jared could wound him. He didn't have to kill the man.

There was also the city ordinance against carrying concealed weapons, and it was enforced. If Garmon came to town packing a gun, he'd be arrested.

But if all went well, Jared could get the man on the witness stand, and, if he worked Garmon over properly, he could force a confession from him. He might salvage this case against all the odds. He had done it once before, to his credit. But somehow, in the back of his mind, he knew that it wasn't going to be that easy. Garmon was that sort of man who liked to show off. And he thought Dunn was a fancy dude who didn't know a gun from a stick. Jared himself had set the stage. It was unlikely that Garmon was going to back down—he had too much to lose. Right now, Jared had nothing to lose except his client's life. He couldn't afford to back down, whatever the personal cost. At least Noelle was safely at home and wouldn't see whatever violence transpired. Garmon might even have second thoughts and make a run for it, before he was unmasked. But Jared didn't think he was going to let the chance of intimidating the city lawyer go by.

And he didn't. Jared's premonition about Garmon came true. Just ten minutes before he was due to leave his office to go to the courtroom, a loud voice called to him from the street in front of his office. "Dunn! Jared Dunn, come on out here! I want to talk to you!"

Jared heard the loud voice and stepped out the front door.

Sure enough, there stood John Garmon with a gun strapped low across his hips, waiting with an ear-to-ear grin. He had his two cronies with him, and several people who had come to town for the trial stopped to watch from the sidewalks.

Jared whipped off his reading glasses and walked out into the edge of the dusty street to stare at the man. "I hear you, Garmon. What do you want?"

"You're defending a filthy robbing black boy, Dunn!" Garmon raged, noticing that a small crowd of onlookers was beginning to gather. Good. Witnesses could serve his purpose very well. "He beat old man Marlowe to his knees and stole all his money, and you're going in that court to get him off by telling lies about me!" He turned to the crowd, playing to it like a professional actor, his arms wide to embrace it. "He's going to try to accuse me of doing the robbing, folks, to save that ignorant slave in the jail. He's from up North, where they like those black boys, you see. He's going to try to convince you that I hurt that poor old man and took his money myself. You see, a lawyer has to have somebody to blame it on!"

Jared listened with interest. So that was the way Garmon was going to play it—attack before you were attacked and get the first word in. It was good strategy. But it wasn't going to work.

"You robbed Marlowe, Garmon," Jared replied. "You've done exactly the same thing before, in two other towns that I know of. In Austin, there was an eyewitness."

Garmon whirled to face him, furious at the accusation. He couldn't afford not to challenge it, because it was true. "You're a liar. You're a filthy, yellow liar. Come out here, you Yankee coward, and let's see if you can tell the truth when you're forced to. If you've got a gun, get it, or I'll kill you where you stand!"

The challenge sent a murmur through the crowd that had gathered, and it included three people on the sidewalk barely half a block away. Noelle peered anxiously through the gap in the crowd to see her husband standing in the street with a huge man wearing a holstered pistol. And now, all at once, Noelle understood Jared's insistence that she stay home. He'd expected this!

Oh, for heaven's sake! That's why he was acting so strangely last night, she said to herself.

The man, Garmon, was yelling insults. Jared moved farther into the street.

"He can't do this," Noelle said desperately. "He can't be thinking of facing that man! He'll be shot down… Andrew," Noelle cried, grasping his coat sleeve. "Andrew, get up there and do something. Stop them. You were a soldier, you know how to stop trouble."

"Noelle, that cowboy has a gun!" Andrew gasped. "Are you crazy?"

"He'll kill Jared!" Noelle burst out, her wide eyes filled with terror. "Why won't you do something?" she raged when Andrew refused to move. She sighed furiously. "I must stop him!"

But as she started forward, Mrs. Dunn caught her arm. "No," she said firmly. "Don't shame Jared."

"Shame him? That man says he's going to kill him."

"Be still, child," Mrs. Dunn said, because she knew very well that Jared would take care of the situation, that he knew exactly what to do. She didn't dare let Noelle interfere, because she had a fairly good idea of how Jared felt about his wife. He couldn't afford any distractions right now. "It will be all right, Noelle. I promise you, it will. Wait."

Noelle couldn't fight that firm old hand. Oh, God, how would she live if Jared were killed? He had been a lawman once, but that was long ago. Surely he didn't have a gun with him?

Unaware that his relatives were close and watching, Jared

slowly pulled back his jacket on both sides. "I'm not armed," he told Garmon, playing the role he'd given himself.

"Then get a gun," Garmon demanded. His swarthy face was smug, haughty. He knew the lawyer couldn't beat him with a pistol. If he ran, that would solve part of the problem. If he didn't run, it would be legal murder, with witnesses. He might be arrested for breaking the firearm ordinance, but it would appear to be a fair fight. Except that Jared Dunn would lie dead at the end of it. But Garmon was sure now that Dunn didn't have the guts to strap on a pistol and face him like a man.

Sims, the city detective, saw the perfect opportunity to show off his own prowess with a gun. He grinned as he stepped out into the street, his hand wavering over his own low-slung gun butt. "That's enough, Garmon," he said, loud enough for everyone to hear, confident that he could easily outdraw the other man. "Put the gun down now, and—"

"Thank God!" Noelle began, watching.

At the same time she spoke, a loud pop interrupted her. She hadn't even seen Garmon's hand move, but his pistol suddenly sang once and Sim's leg collapsed. Sims squeezed off a shot as he went down, and the bullet thudded into the dust in the street as another loud pop echoed in the street. Pungent smoke rose from the barrels of both his pistol and Garmon's. There were gasps from the crowd. Noelle put a hand to her throat as the reality of the violence brought the taste of the danger Jared was in into her mouth.

Sims didn't feel the stinging pain for several seconds. He found himself sitting in the dust like a child, bleeding, dumbfounded, while everyone stared at him.

Garmon, bristling with confidence now, spun the smoking pistol into his holster and turned back to Jared, crouching slightly. "You're next," he said hotly. "Get a pistol or I'll shoot you where you stand, Dunn. Unless you want to run, that is," he invited.

Noelle held her breath while she waited for Jared's reply, and he took his time giving it. Don't, she was praying. Don't, Jared!

"All right, Garmon. It's your call," Jared replied finally. He moved slowly toward Sims. His eyes never left Garmon. He wasn't looking intimidated, and he should, Garmon thought curiously.

Jared bent, carelessly unbuckling Sims's holster. He whipped it off and picked up the pistol. "Does it shoot true?" he asked Sims, and all the while he was still looking at Garmon, with eyes as cold as blue death.

"Yes," Sims said, groaning.

Noelle, watching, gasped. "Oh, my God! He's putting on that gun belt!"

Mrs. Dunn held on to her even more firmly. "Courage, child," she said.

"But—"

"Courage," the older woman repeated. "He knows exactly what he's doing."

Sims reached up and caught Jared's arm as he fastened the gun belt. "Man, don't do it. It's suicide." Sims gasped. "Did you see him draw? My God, he beat me!"

"As slow as you are, no damned wonder," Jared said in a clipped voice as he jerked away from Sims's hand and buckled the gun belt low around his lean hips. He tied the long strings around his powerful thigh, checked the pistol, and shifted the holster until the tip of the gun was slanted just slightly forward and the butt of the Colt .45 was within smooth, easy reach. "Hold these." He tossed his round-rimmed reading glasses onto Sims's chest and shucked his jacket off, tossing that into Sims's hands, as well.

Then he moved beyond Sims, toward Garmon, every step

calculated, straight. His eyes never blinked, never wavered. People nearby moved back. Noelle clung to Mrs. Dunn, watching with horror. She wanted to scream. When Sims had gone down, her stomach had begun to churn. Sims was very quick, but that burly man had moved without even appearing to. Jared would have no chance. What was he doing? Where were the city police? Why didn't they come?

"You sure you know which end of that gun to point, lawyer?" Garmon taunted loudly.

Jared stopped a few yards from him. He smiled coolly. "Oh, I think I can figure it out." His hand dropped slowly to his side and hung there, waiting. His posture altered just slightly, just enough to make a couple of old-timers in the crowd go tense. But Garmon didn't seem to see the significance of that, or the way Jared's blue eyes stared straight at him, unblinking. He nodded slowly toward Garmon, who was barely ten feet from him. "Fill your hand, Garmon."

Garmon was surprised at the man's grit. But anyone could wear a gun. He shot his hand down to his gun butt with grinning confidence. But as fast as he was, before he had the pistol halfway out of the holster, his gun hand shattered under Jared's first shot. The pistol fell from Garmon's hand with a thud as it hit the dust. A second after it landed, one bullet hit it, then another, spinning it out of Garmon's reach. Garmon stared at Jared Dunn dumbly, with a dropped jaw, holding his bleeding hand and struggling through waves of pain and shock to understand what had just happened to him.

Noelle, like the rest of the spectators, gasped when she realized what had happened. Her tame lawyer husband had just outdrawn a gunman. Moreover, he'd placed a shot right through the man's hand instead of his guts. The skill required for both actions wasn't lost on her, or on anyone close to her.

Jared held his pistol leveled at his waist, dark smoke rising from the barrel, and he started walking, straight toward Garmon. His steely blue eyes were as cold as winter skies, and death was in them—it was in every step he took.

The walk as well as his expression were familiar to men who had lived in wild country. The lawyer was no city dude. He kept coming, and Garmon felt panic against all reason as he advanced with that cool, even stride that looked as if it would prevail against the very fires of hell.

"No!" Garmon burst out as Jared reached him. He gritted his teeth against the pain and fell to his knees. "No, man. It'll be cold-blooded murder!" he pleaded. "Look, there are witnesses," he added, his eyes casting desperately around him in hopes that they might save him.

But still Jared kept coming. He sent a bullet into the dirt between Garmon's splayed knees; the other man jumped violently.

"You robbed Marlowe and framed Clark for it." Jared stopped right in front of him with the pistol aimed from the waist, right at Garmon's belly. His voice was calm, deep, relentless. It held cold authority, as lethal a weapon as the one in his hand. "Tell them."

"I never did—"

Jared cocked the pistol. The eyes that met Garmon's were as cold as the steel of the metal. They were a killer's eyes, and Garmon had realized it almost too late. The man wouldn't hesitate to pull the trigger. It was right there, in those pale, glittering icy blue eyes.

"All right, I did it," he said, loud enough for bystanders to hear. "I did it! I wanted that foreman's job and Beale was going to give it to that old black man. I needed some money, anyway, so I took it from Marlowe and blamed Clark for it. What the hell did Beale want to offer him that job for? *I* should have got that job. No filthy black boy's going to order me around at my own job!" He caught his breath, because Jared still hadn't lowered the pistol barrel. "All right, I confessed. I told you the truth. Now, you—you put that thing down!"

Jared smiled cruelly. "What's the matter, Garmon?" he taunted softly. "Are you only brave with men you can bully with that gun?"

He looked straight into Garmon's eyes, furious at the man's lie. Clark could have died for it. The gun was still leveled at Garmon's guts. Jared hesitated for an instant. Then he pulled the trigger.

Garmon cried out sharply and flinched, anticipating the shock of a bullet. But there was only the click of an empty chamber. He shivered in reaction, the pain in his shattered hand forgotten in the stark terror of the moment. His heartbeat was shaking his shirt.

Jared laughed coldly as he slowly pulled bullets from the gun belt around his lean hips and slid five bullets back into the empty chambers with steady, deft hands. "Only a greenhorn fills all six chambers, or had you forgotten that the hammer always rests on an empty one? Sims fired once, I fired four shots. The last chamber was empty. I didn't have a bullet left." He gazed at the man on the ground with utter contempt. "You wouldn't have lasted a week on the border," he added harshly.

Still watching the man, he clicked the loaded cylinder in place and spun the pistol back into the holster with a flourish that wasn't lost on anyone watching. A young police officer who had been standing nearby quickly arrested Garmon and pulled him to his feet, to take him away, with a respectful glance toward Jared. It was obvious to the bystanders that he had no plans to disarm that lawyer.

Noelle thought she might faint. She was dizzy, and she leaned on Andrew for support. He was trembling, too, and when she looked up at him, his face was stark white. Beside her, Mrs. Dunn was stoic, whispering a prayerful thanks.

Jared slipped off the gun belt and tossed it on the ground beside Sims, retrieving his jacket and the glasses. Sims was closer than the spectators, close enough to see Jared Dunn's ice-blue eyes and feel the residue of violence that was still in him. He was fresh out of swaggering bravado. He shivered.

"Are you nervous about pistols, Sims?" Jared drawled sarcastically when he saw the downed man's apprehensive expression. "Why? You're a *real* gunman, aren't you?"

He stood up and walked slowly away. Sims didn't move at once, not for several long seconds. Jared was several yards away before he remembered that he'd been shot and his leg was bleeding.

Mrs. Dunn went toward her grandson, with Noelle and Andrew right behind her, but Noelle noticed that she hesitated visibly to touch him or even go very close. "Jared, are you all right?" Mrs. Dunn asked nervously.

He was trying to deal with the aftermath of the violence, the tension. He could barely get his breath—and he knew that tremors were running through his powerful body. All around him, people were backing away. His eyes were still terrible. He hadn't killed anyone, though. He hadn't killed. But he would have...

Noelle alone wasn't afraid. She went very close. Her eyes sought Jared's bravely; she laid a gloved hand delicately over his heart where the jacket hung open. "Jared," she said softly. "Are you all right?"

He looked down at her without recognition for a few seconds. Then his features hardened and he seemed to go rigid.

Her hand pressed closer. "It's over," she whispered. "It's over now."

He took a long, heavy breath and let it out. His clouded eyes began to clear, like crystal. They searched hers, narrowing. "I told you to stay the hell at home!" he bit off, furiously.

She understood without being told that he was still in the grip of the violence. "I know you did," she replied.

Andrew had her by the hand now and he was obviously nervous about his stepbrother, too. "You, uh...you shot him," he faltered. His face was stark white under his blond hair. His voice shook.

Jared hadn't missed the way he was holding Noelle's hand. He was more jealous than he'd ever been in his life, but he couldn't say a word. Noelle had made her choice. It wasn't Andrew's fault that she loved him. People couldn't love to order. "Take Noelle and my grandmother home," he said evenly.

Andrew swallowed. "Yes, of course. I'll do that immediately." His eyes went from Jared to Sims, who was being helped up by two bystanders, and then to the retreating figure of Garmon in the uniformed policeman's grasp. "They were both very, very fast," Andrew remarked.

"Fast is no good unless you're accurate with it," Jared said. His glittering pale blue eyes met Andrew's and he laughed coldly. "I've killed men who were a hell of a lot faster with a pistol than Garmon. He was damned lucky I didn't kill him."

"You didn't learn that in New York," Andrew persisted. It was a question.

"No. I didn't." Jared's chin lifted. "Before I went East to study law, I was a gunman in Kansas, and then I was a Texas Ranger down on the border," Jared replied, enjoying Andrew's discomfiture. "A man never forgets how to kill. But you wouldn't know, would you? The only thing you ever killed during the war was time, sitting behind your damned desk in the Philippines!"

Andrew had to swallow down a retort. Jared wasn't quite controlled even now, and the sight of his stoic stepbrother out of control made him very nervous. He was suddenly a stranger, and those unblinking ice-blue eyes frightened Andrew.

"I'll get the women to safety," he said in a whisper.

"Yes, you do that," Jared snapped.

Andrew took Mrs. Dunn's arm and then Noelle's, but Noelle pulled away from him and walked back to Jared.

He stared at her with the same cold, unseeing eyes. "Go home," he said shortly. "There's nothing for you here."

"I'll go in a minute," she promised, because she knew what he was telling her—that he didn't care for her. She nodded toward the crowd and stepped a little closer, so that only he could hear her. "You've frightened them," she whispered. "You have to stop looking so ferocious, or some of the women may faint," she added, trying to lighten that terrible somberness about his lean face.

He looked around him, and then he realized what she was doing. Her action seemed to bring the spectators back to their senses. People stopped looking at Jared as if he were a museum exhibit and they began moving normally about their business again. The apprehension was still there, but it was tempered with compassion as the pretty young woman clung to her husband with such fierce loyalty.

Her soft hand calmed him a little, but the wildness was still in him. He wanted to knock Andrew to his knees.

Even as he entertained the thought, Noelle's soft, gloved hand contracted on his arm. "Are you coming home with us now?" she asked, because her courage was just about to fade away and leave her shaking. She hadn't felt well at all this week, and she was a bit nauseated even now. It would be a shame to spoil her courageous image by fainting at his feet. Jared had come so close to death. She didn't know how she'd kept from screaming.

"I can't leave yet," he told her. He searched her eyes. "I'm going to get the prosecutor and go over to see the judge. Garmon will have to stand trial, but I don't think the judge will want to hold Clark. Too many witnesses heard Garmon confess."

Jared's narrow eyes looked into Noelle's. He hadn't expected her reaction to what she'd seen.

"You aren't afraid of me," he said curiously.

"That's right."

"Garmon was," he replied. "So were Sims and Andrew—even my grandmother."

"I know."

He looked down at her over his wire-rimmed reading glasses. He didn't ask why, but his eyes did.

She sighed heavily. Her gloved hand reached up toward his face and she touched his lean cheek lightly. "You may find me irritating, and I may annoy you greatly, but I've never been afraid of you," she said simply. "I was very proud, Jared. You made him tell the truth. And you never backed down an inch." Her eyes were full of wonder, of pride.

His were confused. That didn't explain why she wasn't repulsed by what she had seen, by knowing the truth about him.

"Didn't you hear what I told Andrew?" he asked quietly. "I was a gunman, Noelle. I killed men. For a while, I was even wanted by the law."

"Then how did you become a Texas Ranger?"

"I helped them capture a worse man than I was, and found myself wearing a badge on the border," he said. His chest rose and fell harshly. "Noelle, there was a woman. I killed for her. I killed an innocent man, because she accused him."

Her eyes didn't waver. She didn't flinch. She knew about the woman, or a little about her. It was amazing that she'd had to find out about her husband on the streets of Fort Worth. This was what he'd meant last night, that he hadn't told her the truth about his past. But why should he have? He didn't love her.

She'd been living in a fool's paradise, hoping for his heart, for his ardor at least. But he'd refused her bed last night, and he'd even said flatly that they had no future together. Now, in the aftermath of the shooting, it seemed very much as though he'd been telling her last night that he didn't want her anymore, at all. That was why he'd apologized and acted as if he was saying goodbye. He *had* been saying goodbye.

"Did you hear me?" he demanded.

She nodded. She was more miserable than she'd ever been. He didn't love her. He didn't want her.

"Then say something!" he growled.

"What would you have me say, Jared?" she asked quietly. She managed a wan smile. "I knew your life had been a violent one when you told me you'd been a lawman, and in the military. Today was unexpected," she added tautly, "but it changes nothing. It changes nothing at all," she said wearily.

"I know that, far too well," he replied, with a cold glance toward Andrew. He moved away from her. "I have to see the judge," he added curtly.

She sighed as she searched Jared's hard, cold eyes. "I wish…" she whispered huskily, her face contorted with sadness.

"You wish what?" he demanded.

"Noelle," Andrew interrupted suddenly, hesitating a few yards away with Mrs. Dunn's arm in his hand, "do come on." He was going to be late for his discussion with Mr. Beale; his whole future depended on it.

She glanced toward him, frowned and then looked back at Jared. "I'll be right there, Andrew," she said.

Jared smiled without humor. "By all means, go with him," he told her, bristling with bad temper as he stared past her at his posturing, strutting stepbrother. Even through his anger, it amused him that Andrew didn't come one step closer, still intimidated by him. "There's really nothing more for us to say to each other," he added coolly, searching her face. "Now, go home."

"That's a very good idea, Jared," she returned, wounded to the bone. "I really think I should do exactly that."

She turned on her heel and went to Andrew, eagerly taking the arm he offered. Jared didn't try to stop her. He watched her go, seething with jealousy and uncertainty. Damn Andrew!

Unaware that Jared had totally misread her new relationship with Andrew, Noelle walked back down the street with a firm step. It was just as well that he didn't question where home was; she was on her way to her uncle in Galveston, but he wouldn't find that out just yet. Ironically, Fort Worth now held many more terrors for her than Galveston and the past.

Chapter Sixteen

Andrew no sooner got the women home than he grabbed his hat and gloves and prepared to leave for Miss Beale's house.

He barely stopped to say goodbye, doffing his derby hat. For a minute he was the old, dashing Andrew of whom Noelle had once been so fond, his lips smiling under his blond mustache.

"I'm sorry to rush, but this is very important to me," he told Noelle. "I hope to hear that Mr. Beale has given his consent for me to court Jennifer." He looked briefly shamefaced. "I've been a cad to you, Noelle," he added gently. "And I'm truly sorry. But things have gone well for you, haven't they? I mean, Jared is wealthy, you'll always be provided for…"

"Yes, of course," she said, without much enthusiasm. "I'm very happy for you, too, Andrew," Noelle said, and meant it.

"I had no idea that Jared—" He stopped. "He isn't what he appears to be, is he? I never knew him at all."

"None of us did," Noelle replied sadly.

"You aren't afraid of him?" he asked, and he looked worried.

She smiled. "No, Andrew. I've never been afraid of him. He's been kind to me."

"Kinder than I've been," he agreed. "It would serve me right if Miss Beale loathed me. But she feels just as I do. Her father was reluctant before this trial came up, but it seems that his regard for my stepbrother has turned the tide in my favor. I must be careful to keep in his good graces."

"I wish you well," she told him.

"And I wish you well. We'll truly be relatives now," he said, with a gentle smile.

"So we will," she said dully, and all the while she was hearing Jared's deep voice talking about giving her back her freedom.

He held out a lean hand. "Shall we be friends, if you can forgive me? I've seen myself as I truly am. I only hope that I can change enough to make Jennifer proud to be my wife."

She took the hand. "You aren't a bad man, Andrew. But stop pretending to be what you aren't."

"Advice which you could give equally to my stepbrother," he murmured dryly. "Although after today, I think his secret will be well and truly notorious."

Her face closed up. "Jared will hear no advice from me," she said. "Hurry, Andrew, or you'll be late."

"Yes, I must." He waved and went down the street toward the livery stable.

Noelle smiled blankly at Mrs. Dunn as she closed the front door.

"Noelle?"

She turned. The older woman was still standing in the doorway of the living room. Mrs. Dunn was subdued and she looked faintly worried. "I hope you realize that Jared was driven to it—to what happened in town," she said quietly. "He isn't a killer. He only wounded the man. He could have done so much worse twenty years ago."

"I know. I don't blame him. I understand why he did it. He saved Mr. Clark's life."

"That's a load off my mind, that you aren't repelled by him now," the older woman said heavily. "He's a hard man to know. He keeps what he feels to himself. But I think that he would fall apart without you."

"The iron man?" She scoffed. "Hardly. He needs no one."

"How can you think that?" Mrs. Dunn asked gently. "Noelle, you have no idea how Jared has changed since he came back home and found you here. He laughs, he smiles, he spends time with us… Why, the Jared who used to visit was so quiet that we hardly knew he was in the house. And such a somber, taciturn man he was. He never smiled. He had nothing to do with women. Well, with decent women," she amended uncomfortably, because she'd heard stories.

"Jared married me because Andrew and I were found together in a compromising situation," Noelle said curtly. "He made certain that I knew it. He may find me desirable, but there's nothing more to it than that. He told me last night that our marriage was only a temporary condition, and that we had no future together. I'm certain that he means to divorce me." She lifted her skirts and started up the steps. "I've decided that I'm going back to my uncle," she said. "Jared can do what he likes. He's an attorney, after all. If he wants a divorce, then he knows how to have our marriage set aside. He won't need anything more from me except my signature on some document when the time comes."

Mrs. Dunn was horrified. "Noelle, you must be mistaken!"

"There's no mistake. He doesn't love me, and he doesn't want me." The words hurt her. She kept walking.

It only took her an hour to pack everything she owned in the world. She left her pretty new things hanging in the chifforobe—because she didn't want anything that Jared's money had bought—as she prepared to leave for the second time. Jared had forced her to make such a decision once before, when she and Andrew had been caught together. Perhaps this time she would get farther, because she did have a little money now. She could stay with her uncle until she could find a job as a housekeeper or a nursemaid in Galveston. The memories would be there, but she could cope now. Her marriage had made her strong. She was no longer the naive young girl who had come to Fort Worth to live.

She looked around the room she'd inhabited and stared at the bed with narrow, pained eyes. Her first and only experience of intimacy had been in that bed, with a man whose motive was only to make sure of her and legalize their marriage. He had never wanted to repeat the experience. In fact, it seemed that he now only wanted to forget it.

She put on her hat and wrapped her cloak around her, because the sunshine of the morning had given way to heavy clouds. It was now misting rain. She picked up her small valise and her string purse and started down the staircase for the last time.

Jared had been to see the judge, along with the prosecutor and the tall, young city policeman who'd arrested Garmon and overheard his confession. The circuit judge, a longtime acquaintance of Jared's, dismissed the case against Clark and ordered Garmon charged with assault and robbery. His arraignment hearing was set, and Jared felt certain he would be bound over for a preliminary hearing.

The judge stared at Jared with pursed lips. "And what's

this I hear about you pulling a gun on Mr. Garmon right in the town square?"

The young police officer stepped forward. "Sir, Mr. Dunn had no choice in the matter," he said firmly. "Mr. Garmon had already shot Mr. Sims—and he was crazy enough to shoot anybody else who moved. Mr. Dunn did the citizens of Fort Worth a service."

"I'm not questioning that, young man," the judge said. "I'm questioning the possession of a firearm in the city limits."

"It was Mr. Sims's firearm, your honor," the young man persisted courageously. "He loaned it to Mr. Dunn." He straightened and lifted his chin. "Mr. Dunn was acting in the stead of a city law-enforcement officer. You may consider him deputized for the duration of the incident. I'll swear to that, sir."

Jared smiled indulgently at the unexpected gesture from the young man, who looked embarrassed.

"Very well," the judge said. He smiled, too. "You aren't old enough to remember wild times in Kansas, young man, but I am. I know Mr. Dunn quite well. I was only tormenting him, for old time's sake, and he knows it."

Jared chuckled. "Nevertheless, Officer…?"

"Ryan, sir."

"Well, Officer Ryan. Thank you for your intervention, and your support. I won't forget you."

He offered his hand, and the young man shook it. "You're very welcome, sir," he replied, grinning. He nodded to Jared and the judge and strode quickly out the door, the smile still on his face as he walked toward the corner.

Jared escorted Brian Clark from his jail cell to the stable, where he hired the black man a good horse and handed him back his possessions, which had been turned over by the police.

Clark shook hands with the attorney. "I can't even pay you," he said miserably.

"Mr. Clark, you were innocent," he said. "It's a sad fact of life that generally only the rich go free, innocent or guilty. But in this case, justice was done. It did me good to work on your behalf. I don't begrudge you my fee." He didn't add that Beale had offered to pay it, but he had refused. Some things were more rewarding than money.

Clark seemed to understand. He nodded. "I'll do something, someday, to make you glad that you gained my freedom for me."

Jared smiled. "See that you do. A man of your intellect is wasted doing odd jobs on a ranch, sir. A good education would benefit you."

Clark considered that. "I think it might, indeed," he said thoughtfully. "Thank you for the loan of the horse, as well. I'll send it back to you once I'm at Beale's ranch. He's a good man to work for."

"He's a good man, period," Jared said, with genuine feeling. "I only wish I'd had enough evidence to clear you, without having to resort to somewhat dubious methods to get at the truth," he added, with a smile.

"I think that your 'dubious methods' will be the talk of Fort Worth for many years to come," Clark said, chuckling. "I thank you for taking such a risk on my behalf."

"Some risks are worth the end result." He shook hands with the man and watched him mount up.

As he trotted off down the street, dust flew up from the horse's hooves and splatters of rain started to slam into it. Clouds had come up suddenly. Just as well, Jared thought, for Noelle's tomato plants. She was having to water them every day because it had been so dry.

Noelle. He sighed. He wondered if even now, she and cursed Andrew were planning their future. He'd saved Clark's life, but he couldn't save his own marriage. He was losing the thing that meant more to him than the whole world. He turned and walked back toward his office. He'd clear out the rest of the day's work, he decided, before he went home. After all, there was no rush.

Little did he know that Noelle was already sitting in the train depot with her bag and a ticket to Galveston in her gloved hand.

She stared quietly into space, drawn and pale from the ending of her brief marriage. She had nothing to look forward to except years without Jared. He'd probably be relieved to see the last of her.

She recalled her first days with him, when he was interested in her, when he'd taught her to dance and all the social graces. He'd prepared her as a suitable escort for Andrew, and then he'd been forced to marry her. That was when they stopped being friends. He hadn't wanted her, but he'd taken her to bed just the same. Now she wondered why. Perhaps he'd just wanted a woman. But it had been everything to her, to lie in the arms of the man she loved most in all the world. But how often had Jared told her that there was nothing of love in him? Presumably that woman he'd killed for in Kansas so many years before had been his one true love. He hadn't room for another woman in his heart. So it was just as well that Noelle was leaving.

Two other people came into the depot carrying bags. One was an elderly man, the other much younger, his grandson, perhaps. The older man sat down near Noelle and tipped his hat respectfully while the younger one went to the ticket agent at the counter.

"Two tickets for St. Louis, please, one way," the boy said, producing his billfold.

"Yes, sir. Bit of excitement in town today, we heard," the

ticket agent murmured while he worked. "They said some cowboy drew on the wrong man."

"Never saw anything like it," the young man said, unaware of Noelle's rapt interest. "The fellow's hand barely moved and the cowboy went down. You could see how surprised he was, like he didn't expect anybody in a fancy suit could ever best him with a gun." He shook his head. "They say that lawyer was a gunman in Kansas. Granddad knew him," he added, smiling proudly at the old man.

"Happens I did," the old man agreed. "But it weren't in Kansas. I knew him in El Paso, when he was a Texas Ranger. Stood off a lynch mob down there, saved a feller's life. Nobody messed with Captain Dunn, no sir!"

"Captain?" Noelle burst out.

"Why, yes, ma'am," came the reply. "He was one bad hombre before he joined the Rangers, they said," he added, nodding. "He helped track down a murderer and saved one of the Ranger company that was chasing him. They got him a pardon and signed him on, on the spot. He spent a long time out there, around El Paso. Nobody messed with Captain Dunn," he repeated. He noticed Noelle's wide-eyed stare. "Sorry, ma'am. Guess all this isn't fit talk around a lady." He smiled apologetically.

She smiled back, but her eyes were troubled. Now total strangers were telling her things about Jared, about her own husband, that she didn't know. If she hadn't already had the ticket, she would have gone back to Jared's office and thrown something at him for keeping so many secrets from her. It was just as well that she was leaving. She really had married a stranger.

Jared finished the last of his paperwork and was just getting ready to leave the office when his secretary poked his head in the door.

"Telephone, sir," he announced.

Jared nodded absentmindedly and picked up the receiver. He was expecting a call from the clerk at the court. "Dunn," he said into the mouthpiece.

"Jared?"

It was his grandmother's voice. "Yes," he said quickly. "Grandmother, what is it?"

"Noelle's gone, son."

He stared at the desk, looking at the swirling patterns in the oak with eyes that barely registered it. "Gone?"

"To Galveston," she said sadly. "I did try to talk to her, but she wouldn't listen. She just said that she was leaving… She didn't even take any of her new things, Jared. They're all hanging in the chifforobe."

"Did Andrew go with her?" he asked stiffly.

Mrs. Dunn coughed. "Andrew?"

"Yes," he muttered. The connection was terrible; he could hardly hear her. "Are they going away together?"

"Jared, Andrew has gone to Miss Beale's house. He hopes to obtain Mr. Beale's permission to marry Jennifer. Noelle and I are very happy for him. We hoped you would be, too."

"What?"

Mrs. Dunn held the phone a little away from her ear. How close he sounded! "Andrew hopes to marry Miss Beale," she repeated. "Didn't you know?"

"No, I didn't know. How could I…?" He paused. "You say Noelle's gone to Galveston? When?"

"She left an hour ago," she said sadly.

He held on to his temper by a thread. "Why didn't you call sooner, Grandmother?"

"There was no point, dear," she said. "She wouldn't have talked to you. She'd made up her mind, you see. She said it was for the best. And maybe she was right, Jared," she added firmly. "You've been very unkind to her lately. She said that you'd told her you didn't have a future together. She thought you meant that you wanted a divorce. She said that you'd be glad to be rid of her, because you didn't care about her."

He had been unkind to her, that was true. He didn't like having that pointed out to him. But he hadn't meant that he wanted a divorce. He'd thought *she'd* wanted one, so that she could marry Andrew. But if Andrew was marrying Miss Beale... And Noelle was leaving because she thought Jared didn't care about her...

His heart lifted like a bird freed of a rope. "Which train did she catch?" he asked quickly.

"I don't know. I haven't seen the schedules."

"I'll be home soon," he said, and hung up. Noelle had left him. She'd said she was going home, and he'd assumed she meant his house. She'd meant her uncle's house. She'd left him. She'd thought he wanted a divorce.

He laughed out loud. He'd given her up so that she could marry Andrew, and she thought *he* didn't want *her!* He'd only given her up because he loved her and he wanted her to be happy! Didn't she know, for God's sake?

He got up from the desk, shouldered into his jacket and grabbed his hat. "Close up and go home," he told his secretary on his way out the door.

It was only a short walk to the train depot. He bypassed the streetcar, his hat and turned-up collar protecting him against the misting rain. He opened the door of the depot and walked into the waiting room, his pale eyes scanning it. It was full now, but Noelle stood out. She was the only unescorted woman in the room, sitting quietly beside an old man and a younger one on the long, smooth oak bench, with her small valise at her feet. She looked totally out of sorts.

He stuck his hands in his pockets and stopped just in front of her. The old man, who recognized him, started to speak.

But before he could, Noelle recognized her husband and took a sharp breath.

"So it's you," she said. "Have you come to wave me off?"

His chin lifted. He looked down his nose at her. The reading glasses were off, and his eyes were very blue. "No. I've come to take you back home, where you belong."

"Home?" she queried. "Ha! It isn't a home. It's your house, and I certainly don't belong there!"

His eyebrows jerked. "This is hardly the place for a private discussion," he remarked, indicating the amount of attention they were attracting.

Noelle glared at him. "You keep saying that! Well, why isn't it?" she demanded. "Everyone in town seems to know more about you than I do!"

He had the grace to admit that this was so. "I haven't been truthful with you," he agreed quietly.

"No, you haven't. I thought you were a sophisticated New York lawyer. I had no idea that you could handle a sidearm so well, or that you'd been a captain in the Texas Rangers…until today. Everything I know about you I learned by accident or from other people."

"I didn't know how to tell you all of it," he said quietly.

"Obviously. A wife should know a little something about her own husband—and not have to find out about him from total strangers!" she raged.

The old man beside her was gaping now. So were several other people.

"If you'd come home with me," he said, "we could discuss this."

"I've nothing to discuss with you," she told him. "I'm going back to Galveston. You can divorce me whenever you like."

"I'm not going to divorce you," he snapped.

"No? That was what you said last night!"

"I thought you wanted a divorce," he said flatly.

"And I do," she said angrily. "There's nothing I want more! You've kept secrets from me and ignored and avoided me and insulted me... Why should I wish to stay with such a man?"

He smiled wistfully. "I have no idea," he said.

She clutched her small bag. Her green eyes glittered up at him angrily. "Why do you want me to stay?"

His eyebrows lifted. "Did I say that I did?" he drawled.

She averted her face. He hadn't said so. She hoped the train would hurry up and come. She wanted to get away. He was embarrassing her in front of all these strangers.

He stared down at her with frustration. He couldn't get her to come back. He didn't know how. He glared around at the interested onlookers, wishing them miles away.

"At least wait until tomorrow to go," he said. "My grandmother celebrates her seventy-fifth birthday tomorrow. She was heartbroken that you'd gone."

She looked up. "Her birthday? She said nothing to me."

She'd said nothing to Jared, either, since it wasn't her birthday. But Noelle didn't know that. And if he could get her back to the house, under any pretense, perhaps he could persuade her out of this journey.

"She didn't want to impede you," he said.

She glared at him. She didn't want to go back. On the other hand, Mrs. Dunn had been kind to her. It seemed shabby to go away just before the woman's birthday, without even a good wish. She wasn't going to admit that she wanted to stay, or that it pleased her very much that Jared wanted her to go home with him, even if only for his grandmother's birthday.

"I suppose one more day wouldn't matter," she began.

"Good." He picked up her bag and caught her arm to help her up. He nodded politely toward the gaping people in the depot and led Noelle out the door.

They walked half a block in silence, although she noticed

that he refused to let go of her elbow. He seemed to think she might escape.

"That man who was sitting next to me told me you were a captain in the Rangers," she remarked.

He nodded.

She waited, but nothing else was forthcoming. She stopped dead, forcing him to. Her green eyes were still full of exasperation and anger. "And?" she prompted.

His hand tightened on the grip of the valise as he looked at her face and knew a relentless hunger for her. She was asking for more than an answer. She was asking for total honesty. He didn't know if he could give her that.

Her thin shoulders fell. "Let me leave, Jared," she said quietly. "I already have my ticket. This is useless. Hopeless."

She reached for the valise, but he wouldn't let go.

His jaw tautened. "No."

She let out a furious breath. "What's the point of my staying?" she demanded. "It will be just as it was before. You reminded me only the other day that you only married me because of the scandal. I'm sparing you a loveless marriage. So why won't you let me go?"

His chest expanded for a long moment and he stared at her rigidly. His teeth clenched. He couldn't get the words out.

"Is it the blemish on your reputation that concerns you?" she demanded. "Will it affect your practice if I leave you? Is that it?"

He didn't speak, or move.

She threw up both hands. "Jared!"

The hand that had been holding her elbow let go of it and came up, so slowly, to touch her flushed cheek. He traced it softly, his brows drawn while he searched her wide, green eyes.

"I was a killer before I was a lawman," he said huskily. "I was an outlaw. I ran with bad men. It was only a quirk of fate that landed me in the Rangers, and even there, I killed. What you see now is only the facade of respectability. Under it, I'm…still what I was, Noelle. I haven't really changed at all. The past doesn't die. There are always people who'll remember." He remembered painfully what Beale had said about the tragedy of his wife. "As you saw today, I haven't truly escaped what I was. I couldn't bear to have you hurt because of something I did years ago."

She had no idea what he meant. She didn't speak, or move, for a minute, while his words rang in her numb mind.

"You think that I'm afraid because I know about your past?" she said slowly as she realized what he was saying. "Is that why you spoke of a divorce?"

"I offered you a divorce so that you could marry Andrew," he said flatly.

She gasped. Her eyebrows rose. "Thank you very much! And when did I say that I wanted a mealymouthed coward for a husband?"

His shoulders shifted and he glared at her. "You never told me that he came back because of Miss Beale. I thought he came back because he realized what a mistake he'd made by letting you go."

"He didn't exactly let me go," she reminded him. "He ran like a scalded cat."

He stared down at her with no expression on his face. "He seemed to be all that I wasn't," he replied. "You never knew me, until today. At the beginning, you were infatuated with Andrew, who was young and dashing and cultured—all the things I never was. I lived like a desperado, Noelle. I was a bad man. I ran with wicked people. I don't even know who my father was! And it seemed that you felt nothing but pity for me." He smiled faintly. "You were forever fussing about my leg, or trying to open doors for me. Even last night, you offered yourself to me because you sensed somehow that I needed comforting. You pitied me."

She let out the breath she'd been holding. She was astonished. He had no idea what she felt for him. "Pitied you? You thought that I...pitied you? You idiot!" she burst out, suddenly enraged that he should mistake her feelings for him so badly. "Oh, you idiot!" She hit him. She hit him again, barely registering the shocked look on his face when she jerked off his hat and threw it on the sidewalk and stomped on it several times. "Of all the incredible, unbelievable, totally irrelevant reasons to want to throw a woman out of your life. You idiot!"

He backed into a post and stood there, staring at her, shocked.

"I never really cared for Andrew at all!" she raged, grabbing her valise from his numb hand. "I was mildly infatuated with him, until you came home and growled at me the minute I opened the front door. I was attracted to you the minute I saw you, and I spent weeks and weeks trying to understand why I was so happy with you and so miserable with Andrew. I could have died when Andrew made it look as if we were lovers. You married me, and I hoped— But you wanted nothing to do with me except that once, and never again. You said we only married to spare your grandmother a scandal. You said we had no future together." Tears filled her eyes, so that she couldn't see the joyous expression that suddenly claimed his face. "And I loved you so much, Jared, so much! Even when I thought you were an old, bookwormish milksop of a cripple, I loved you to distraction," she whispered brokenly. "Do you think I care how bad you were twenty years ago, or what you did? I wouldn't have traded you for a dozen Andrews, and today I was so proud of you that I could have cheered. How could you be so blind as to think your past would drive me away? Nothing could change the way I feel about you. Nothing!"

The radiance on his face was blinding. "My God, Noelle," he breathed.

"But you don't want me, Jared," she continued miserably. "You don't love me, and you never will. I'm not going to go on like this, eating my heart out day after day while you ignore me. I'm not going to stay here another day. In fact, I'm leaving right now!"

She whirled and started back down the street toward the depot in a fine fury, while behind her, a lean face broke into a glorious smile. He left the hat where it lay, and, with eyes so wicked they would have made her blush, he started after her, laughing softly to himself.

Chapter Seventeen

Noelle could barely see the sidewalk ahead for the tears, and she'd never been so miserable. But just as she reached the corner, she felt herself suddenly caught. Her valise was taken from her hands and left sitting on the sidewalk. She was turned and lifted completely off the ground in a pair of steely warm arms and cradled against a broad chest.

"Oh, no, you don't," Jared said, meeting her shocked, tear-filled eyes.

He started walking back the way they'd come.

"My valise," she said weakly.

"Someone will return it. If they don't, it won't be any terrible tragedy."

"Mrs. Dunn, you've dropped your bag," an amused loud voice called after them.

"Keep it for her," Jared called over his shoulder.

"Yes, sir!"

"Where are you taking me now?" she mumbled angrily,

wiping away tears. "And just look at the damage you're doing your leg! You have no business putting so much weight on it, just as it's healing so nicely."

"Nag, nag, nag," he murmured, without looking down at her. Her concern delighted him. "You shrew."

"You blackguard," she countered. "Put me down."

"When we get home," he promised.

"Jared!"

He did look down then, and the way he looked at her made her blush. His pale blue eyes searched hers until her heart ran wild. She subsided without an argument, curving into his body as naturally as if she were made to fit it, her arms around his neck, her heart throbbing as she pressed close and clung.

He actually shivered. His arms tightened as he walked, and she thought she heard him groan as he shifted her even closer.

"I won't live with a stranger who shares no part of himself with me," she whispered miserably.

"Hush," he whispered back, his voice tender at her ear.

She buried her soft face in his throat. "It would be kinder to let me leave," she said.

"Kinder for whom? I'd sooner cut off my arm than lose you," he said roughly.

She started. He sounded angry, but there was something under it, something she'd never heard in his deep voice.

"Lost for words?" he taunted. "You were vocal enough earlier. And we're here."

He walked up the short path to the house, up the steps. Mrs. Pate saw them coming and opened the door, grinning from ear to ear.

"Coffee, sir?" she offered.

"Oh, no," Jared said, glaring at the burden in his arms. "Not just yet."

"Your grandmother is lying down."

"Leave her there. We wouldn't want the loud voices to upset her, would we, my dear?" Jared asked, with a mocking smile, as he carried a worried Noelle toward the living room. "Close the door behind us, if you would, Mrs. Pate."

"Of course, Mr. Jared."

Noelle was getting more confused by the minute. The door closed with a snap, and Jared walked toward the long, velvet-covered sofa. All at once, he dumped Noelle on it and bent over her with eyes that threatened violence of one sort or another.

She lay there, waiting, uneasy, looking up at him with wide, uncertain eyes.

"You little termagant," he said huskily. "I should thrash you, I really should."

She swallowed, marshaling all the arguments she could find, only to discover seconds later that they were unnecessary. He bent and his mouth fitted itself slowly, tenderly, to hers. She stiffened only for a few seconds before her lips melted under his and her arms reached up to enfold him.

She felt his chest pressing against hers, his mouth insistent on her parted lips, the rough sigh of his breath as he kissed her hungrily, without restraint. It was like no way he'd kissed her before, even when they were most intimate, even last night.

His hands framed her soft face and he pressed brief, biting kisses on her mouth, kisses that grew rougher by the minute, until he kindled her body to passion.

He groaned again harshly, and she found herself lying on the rug with Jared's lean, powerful body totally against hers, his mouth invasive and insistent. His hands were in her hair now, tearing out pins, loosening the glory of her auburn hair so that he could ripple it through his hands.

"Leave me, would you?" he growled at her breasts. "Try it. You won't get as far as the front door next time."

She was breathless. She tried to speak, but his mouth

covered hers again and she gave it up. She had no mind left to think with, anyway. Her hands tangled in the thick hair at his nape and she smiled under his lips as his body shifted hungrily onto hers.

He felt a slight movement and lifted away only enough to catch his breath. His eyes were blazing with desire. "I'm not going to stop," he said huskily. His hands reached under her to lift her skirts. "Now, laugh!"

She gasped. "But…we can't!"

There was the metallic sound of a buckle hitting the floor and laughter in the mouth that was pressing her head back onto the floor.

He imprisoned her mouth at the same instant his body invaded hers. She gasped and cried out, but when he moved again, her hips lifted up to invite him, welcome him. She moaned, shivering, as the quick, hard rhythm shattered every memory she had of that one intimacy. There was no pain—she noticed that at once—but the pleasure…

She sobbed under his mouth as it came, washing over her in huge, crushing layers, each more intense than the one before. She thought that her body would be torn apart by it. And still his hands gripped her, jerked her hips into his. He laughed like a predator, deep in his throat, feeling her tension snap even as his built to flash point. He was still laughing when he shot off into the sun and his body convulsed helplessly in a maelstrom of heat and glory.

She lay in his arms, shivering helplessly, clinging to him while the sun spilled into the room through the lacy curtains and made rose patterns on her fluttering bodice. Her nails were biting into his arms through his jacket and her body felt hot and throbbing.

While she trembled, he quietly rearranged disheveled clothing and did up fastenings. All the while, he held her close, brushing tender kisses against her hot cheeks, her closed eyes, her swollen lips.

When her eyes opened, he didn't look in the least repentant for what amounted to a brazen act of sordid dimensions. She gaped at him.

"I'm a brute," he prompted. "Go ahead." He smiled. "I'm sure you can think of several other adjectives."

She looked down at the rumpled folds of her dress and the wrinkles in his once immaculate white shirt where her hands had gripped him so fiercely as passion bit into her body. She flushed scarlet.

"Have I robbed you of speech?" He bent and brushed his lips softly over hers. He laughed huskily and rolled her over onto her back. He leaned over her, and his eyes were blazing with feelings he couldn't express in words.

She was devoid of speech, all right. But a blind woman could see what his eyes were telling her. There was no more subterfuge, no pretense. Everything he felt for her was there, vulnerable.

She reached up and touched his mouth with her fingertips. "I love you," she whispered.

"Yes." The smile faded as he searched her eyes. He pushed back her damp, disheveled hair. "I would have let you go, even to Andrew, if that had been what you really wanted."

"It wasn't. I don't want to leave you," she said. "I don't love Andrew, and your past doesn't make the least bit of difference to me."

He drew in a long, slow breath. His fingers lazily traced her straight nose and her lips. "It did to me," he replied. "At first, I didn't know if you could live with it. Sometimes I have nightmares. That's why I wouldn't stay with you, the night we were intimate—or last night. I very much wanted to, you know."

"I had nightmares, too, after the flood," she said gently. "If we sleep together, we can comfort each other."

He chuckled. "Imagine that."

She stretched and grimaced at the strain her muscles had taken. She looked at him and then around them and blushed again.

"Yes, I know—it was shameful, on the floor in broad daylight. But I couldn't wait long enough to get you upstairs," he whispered mischievously.

This dynamic, impulsive, mischievous and unconventional man was so foreign that she could hardly believe he was her husband. He fascinated her.

He traced her swollen lips. "I lost control," he said softly. "It's been a very long time since that happened."

"Yes, well…I suppose…" She searched his eyes and felt breathless. "I loved it," she whispered, and then hid her face against him.

He laughed, rippling with delight. His arms held her close and he sighed with amazing contentment. "It tortured me, to feel such a need for you and think that you wanted Andrew. And then today, on the street, I expected you to shrink from me after the fight." His arms tightened hungrily. "But you came to me, right to me. You were completely without fear."

"As so many others were not," she said seriously, remembering. "They were afraid of you." She sighed. "I was only afraid that the man would kill you."

"Perhaps you're forgetting that I would have killed Garmon if he'd reached for his gun again, and also without conscience," he said, as if it worried him.

She drew away from him and sat up on the rug, looking down at him with calm, loving eyes. "Can't you really see the difference between yourself and a man like that?" She touched his face gently. "You were the only thing standing between Mr. Clark and death. You weren't concerned about a big fee or making a name for yourself. You were concerned only about saving an innocent man. I could hardly say that you were without conscience, Jared."

He let out a long breath. The pale eyes that met hers were old and sad. He drew her soft hand to his lips. "Yet, I was," he replied. "When I was a young man, living in Dodge City, I became involved with Ava, one of the saloon girls. She…" He stopped, grimacing. "I think you can imagine the relationship we had. I was very young, impressionable, and I fancied myself in love for the first time. She came to me with bruises and cuts and told me that she'd been raped and robbed. Without questioning her accusation, I went for the cowboy, called him out and killed him. Only later, I found out that she'd lied. He'd done nothing except spurn her attentions. She used me to get even with him." The pain of the confession was in his face. "I started drinking. Alcohol got a terrible hold on me, and I lost all reason. I got into one fight after another and eventually fell in with a gang of outlaws. A Texas Ranger sobered me up, dragged me back into the decent world and got me to turn state's evidence. I went with him to rout them, and most of them were killed. One got away, but he was caught and sent to federal prison for his crimes, where he died. I became a Texas Ranger and worked on the border, out of El Paso."

"You said you were in the cavalry," she prompted, fascinated by what he was confiding in her. She knew instinctively that even Mrs. Dunn was not so privileged.

He smiled. "A brief stint. I was in for two years and I served with the outfit that fought Geronimo in '85 and '86," he said quietly. "But I grew tired of rules and regulations, so I mustered out and went back to the Rangers. Soon after that my mother, who had married Andrew's father some years before, took ill and begged me to come home to her. She thought I was still living the wild life. She begged me to go East and read law, and to ease her last hours, I gave my word.

I could hardly break such a solemn vow, and Ranger life was not much different from being a desperado in those days," he added with a smile.

"When the Spanish-American War broke out, I reenlisted," he continued, "but I only served in Cuba, briefly, taking leave from my law practice in New York."

"That man at the depot said you were a captain in the Rangers," she added. "You must have been very good at your job to achieve such a high rank."

He nodded. "I had nothing to live for and nothing to lose," he reminded her. "I had an innocent cowboy's death on my conscience and a woman's betrayal. I suppose in a way I courted death. It made me fearless."

"Is that how you felt today, Jared?" she asked gently. "As if you had nothing to lose?"

He lowered his eyes to her mouth. "Yes," he said honestly. He looked back up and grimaced at her expression. "Noelle, I thought that you loved Andrew. I'd convinced myself that he came back for you. Without you, I had nothing to lose, nothing at all. Or so I thought." He searched her eyes with wonder. "I didn't know that you loved me. I never dreamed that you could."

She managed a faint smile. "You still seem to have trouble believing it."

"You're a gentlewoman," he replied solemnly. "You've never known violence of the sort you saw today. But I lived with that kind of violence most of my life. Even in a court of law. I told you about the fight in Terrell, New Mexico Territory, over a court case, Noelle," he added. "I told you that I shot the man, but I didn't tell you that it was in a gunfight."

Her breath caught. She stared at him with returning horror. He could have been killed!

He caught her hand and pressed it hard against his chest. "There have been other incidents over the years," he said.

"Not many. We live in an increasingly civilized world. But there are still wild places and men who grew up settling their arguments with hot lead. Until all the old-timers are gone, there'll always be the threat of violence out here in the West. You saw how Garmon behaved today. I've known dozens like him—men who are basically bullies and think they're still living twenty years in the past, when they could live by no rules at all."

She bit her lower lip hard. "I'm no coward, you know that," she said. "But if I lost you now, I'd die, Jared."

He sat up and pulled her against him hungrily, wrapping her tight in his arms. He looked down at her possessively. "As I would, without you," he said huskily, and meant every word. "I'll take no more cases out of state. And I swear to you, there'll be no more gunplay."

She nuzzled her face into his throat, clinging. "You never give your word lightly," she whispered.

"No."

Her soft lips touched his throat. "Will it be very hard for you, having a wife and a family?"

He chuckled. "No. I don't think…" His powerful body stilled. He touched her hair hesitantly. "A…family?"

She nodded.

He seemed not to breathe for a minute. His hand pressed her face closer. "Are you with child?" he whispered.

She smiled into his throat. "I don't know. It's much too soon to tell, after only a few days. But it's very possible. I can't face breakfast and I've been sick two mornings. And I don't think it's from anything I've eaten." She laughed shyly. "Mrs. Pate noticed and said that some women become sick from the very day they conceive."

His heart was hammering. There might be a child. A child. His eyes closed and he shuddered with the most incredible pleasure at the thought of it. His arms contracted protectively.

"It's too soon to tell for sure," she added. "But…oh, I hope, Jared. I hope!"

He caught his breath. "My darling!" he whispered breathlessly.

There was hardly any need to ask if he was pleased. She closed her eyes and lay quietly against him, smiling. There was so much to look forward to now. And just when she had counted it all lost.

A little later, he kissed her soft eyelids. "What a blissful end to a day that started in such anguish," he whispered. "Come. Let's go and tell the others that you're staying."

He helped her to her feet. He picked up her scattered hairpins and handed them to her with a rueful smile.

She laughed. Once, it would have embarrassed her to have been seen in such a disheveled condition. "We're married," she whispered wickedly, "and we've only just made up after a frightful argument. They won't be surprised."

He pursed his lips. "Not if we keep the whole truth from them," he said, smiling.

She laughed. The love in her eyes almost blinded him. He took her hand and they went out the door together.

No one was surprised. Noelle was such a part of the family already that the shock had been her announcement that she was going back to Galveston. Supper was a gay and happy meal, a celebration. And every time Jared looked at her, he loved her. The older women glanced from one to the other with covert amusement. They were so obvious about the way they felt that no one could mistake it. Besides, Noelle had lost her breakfast. Christening clothes would have to be sewn and appropriate furniture purchased. What a lot they had to look forward to!

* * *

Noelle slipped away from the kitchen after the meal long enough to go into the garden while there was still light. Minutes later, with her apron clutched in both hands, she ran back into the house, her eyes glowing.

"Look!" she announced to the family.

In her apron were four tiny pinkish-colored tomatoes of perfect shape and form.

Jared only smiled. His pale eyes went quietly to her waistline and he was thinking of another sort of fruit. It was no longer a trial to think of himself as a family man. In fact, it was an event that he would welcome.

Noelle read that thought in his face. She laughed, the tomatoes forgotten. She could see the future in his eyes, and it was bright and beautiful.

Months later, Christmas morning came with a sprinkling of snow, while a blossoming Noelle lay in Jared's arms and savored their warmth. Andrew and his lovely Miss Beale had been married a week ago, and Terrance Beale was a frequent guest of Jared's now that the two families were merging. Noelle liked the older man, seeing in him a man very much like her own beloved husband.

"Happy birthday," Jared whispered, interrupting her thoughts, and produced a small package from the drawer of the bedside table. He placed it in her hands and lay back to watch her open it.

Inside was a tiny angel, made of pure gold. She caught her breath at its beauty.

"That is you," he said teasingly, but the look in his pale eyes wasn't humorous—it was rapt and full of love. "It's what you are to me, what you always will be. My own angel."

She cried easily of late, due to her condition. But these tears were of joy, because she had never dreamed of so much happiness. She bent, her long hair falling around her shoulders, and kissed him reverently.

"I'll keep it for our son," she whispered, smiling. "We shall start a family tradition. Perhaps one day, he may give it to a woman whom he loves."

His lean fingers traced her soft skin with wonder. It was still hard to believe himself so blessed. "I've never said the words to you, yet you know how I feel, don't you?"

She smiled warmly. "Every time you look at me, every time you touch me, I know," she said. "Some emotions are so strong that they require no words."

His eyes searched hers. "Mine are stronger than I ever imagined they might be," he said. "You've closed the old doors. You've taken away the nightmares and made each day full of joy." He took her soft hand, the one that wasn't clasping the angel to her breast, and pressed it to his mouth. "I love you more than my life," he whispered. "I'll love you until I die, Noelle."

Her heart jumped into her throat. She drew his head to her breasts and held him there, pressing soft kisses against his dark, wavy hair. There were a hundred replies she could have made, but her heart was too full to speak them. She nuzzled her face against his until she found his mouth, and her answer was in her warm, loving kiss. She felt him smile, and as the snow shower fell more noticeably outside, she held Christmas and the future in her heart.

* * * * *

THE
Essential
COLLECTION

by Diana Palmer

YES! Please send me *The Essential Collection* by Diana Palmer. This collection will begin with 3 FREE BOOKS and 2 FREE GIFTS in my very first shipment—and more valuable free gifts will follow! My books will arrive in 8 monthly shipments until I have the entire 51-book *Essential Collection* by Diana Palmer. I will receive 2 free books in each shipment and I will pay just $4.49 U.S./$5.39 CDN for each of the other 4 books in each shipment, plus $2.99 for shipping and handling.* If I decide to keep the entire collection, I'll only have paid for 32 books because 19 books are free. I understand that accepting the 3 free books and gifts places me under no obligation to buy anything. I can always return a shipment and cancel at any time. My free books and gifts are mine to keep no matter what I decide.

279 HDK 9860   479 HDK 9860

Name	(PLEASE PRINT)	
Address		Apt. #
City	State/Prov.	Zip/Postal Code

Signature (if under 18, a parent or guardian must sign)

Mail to the **Reader Service**:
IN U.S.A.: P.O. Box 1867, Buffalo, NY 14240-1867
IN CANADA: P.O. Box 609, Fort Erie, Ontario L2A 5X3

* Terms and prices subject to change without notice. Prices do not include applicable taxes. Sales tax applicable in N.Y. Canadian residents will be charged applicable taxes. This offer is limited to one order per household. All orders subject to credit approval. Credit or debit balances in a customer's account(s) may be offset by any other outstanding balance owed by or to the customer. Please allow 4–6 weeks for delivery. Offer available while quantities last. Offer not available to Quebec residents.

Your Privacy—The Reader Service is committed to protecting your privacy. Our Privacy Policy is available online at www.ReaderService.com or upon request from the Reader Service.

We make a portion of our mailing list available to reputable third parties that offer products we believe may interest you. If you prefer that we not exchange your name with third parties, or if you wish to clarify or modify your communication preferences, please visit us at www.ReaderService.com/consumerschoice or write to us at Reader Service Preference Service, P.O. Box 9062, Buffalo, NY 14269. Include your complete name and address.